STRIPPING DOWN TO SCARS

TALES OF THE ROUGAROU BOOK 2

JULIE MCGALLIARD

Edited by Shannon Page
Cover Art and Design by C.S. Inman
and Julie McGalliard

Library of Congress Control Number:2019915635

ISBN:978-1-951598-03-7

For Pat & Fred McGalliard,
my parents and earliest fan club

1

A DEAD MAN IN AN EMPTY HOUSE

The dead man lies stretched on a bare wooden floor, surrounded by empty bottles and cigarette butts. His right hand rests on his abdomen, against a tight black T-shirt. Blondish hair, brown eyes, smooth tan, no freckles. He looks strangely peaceful. There's no sign of blood or violence, but the fog of a party, booze and smoke and sweat, hangs in the air around him.

"Abby! What are you doing here? Did you do this?"

Behind me, Vivienne steps into the house, bringing a swirl of outside air. This is the French Quarter in August: a sweltering stew of spices, garbage, flowers, horse droppings, vomit, perfume, coffee, sugar, diesel, mud. And alcohol, of course. Always alcohol.

My heart races. No, I didn't do this. I can't possibly have done this. I would remember, wouldn't I? Even if the wolf killed him?

I lean forward and inhale deeply of the dead man. The fresh stink gets me coughing. I don't pick up any trace of myself, but there is something familiar here, some elusive quality that reminds me of something I can't place. It's—it's—

"Abby, look at me, did you *do* this?" Vivienne grabs my arm and spins me around to force eye contact.

For a second we stare at each other, eyes locked. Hers flash amber, and I know mine flash green. She wants to out-stare me, but can't, and flings her gaze at the bare wall, shoulders tightening in frustration.

"Tell me the truth, Abby."

"I didn't do it, Viv. I was just walking home and found him like this."

"Huh." She grunts, folds her arms, stares at me without meeting my eyes. Vivienne is pretty much exactly what I would picture if I heard the words "werewolf lawyer." She's tall and fierce and beautiful from the top of her tightly coiled auburn hair to the soles of her designer shoes. Sometimes I like her. She reminds me of my older sister Chastity. But every time we meet, we argue about something. "So. You smelled a dead body and just had to break in to take a look?"

"The door was unlocked. I think they're remodeling."

She glances around the room, flares her nostrils, nods. "There's some damp rot here. Did you call the cops?" She circles around to the other side of the dead man, heels loud in the empty room. She kneels, stretches out her hand to hold it a few inches above his nose and mouth. After a few moments of that she opens her sleek leather briefcase, pulls out a glove, sheaths her hand, places blue fingers on his neck. Checking for a pulse, I guess, although both of us can easily smell that he's dead. In this heat, it doesn't take long for a body to start decaying.

"I didn't call anybody."

"Good." She nods. "Don't." With her gloved hand she presses down his tongue, peers intently into his mouth. "Choked on his own vomit, looks like." She snaps off the glove, pulls it inside out, stuffs it back into her briefcase. "You're right, you didn't do it. But if you do need to report a body in the future, whether you're responsible or not, call me, not the NOLA PD. You have my number, don't you?"

I nod. I do have her number in my phone, saved as "annoying werewolf auntie" which would probably get me in trouble if she ever saw it. "Why should I call you? So you can cover up my crimes?"

"You think you're being sarcastic, but the answer is yes. If you end up killing someone, we do have to clean things up afterward."

My stomach churns in dread. The wolf has killed, once. It's not an experience I want to repeat. "I'm not planning to kill anyone."

"Of course not. The deaths happen when you don't plan." She lifts her gaze from the dead man and catches my eyes, her expression cold and serious. "If the thought of killing someone bothers you, little one, come out and stay with your own people in Bayou Galene. Nothing to worry about there. Only Varger for miles around."

"Varger" is what my werewolf relatives call themselves. Vivienne is the legal representative and adopted daughter of my biological grandfather Claude Verreaux, and she's spent the last three weeks ambushing me at unexpected moments to try to convince me to go out and live with him. It's every bit as creepy as it sounds.

"Have you ever killed anyone?" I ask.

"None of your business." She taps something into her phone, looks at me. "I've already notified my police contact. You should go. You don't want to contaminate a possible crime scene."

"You think he was murdered?" I crouch down, careful not to touch anything. I stare into the man's loose, empty face.

"I told you I thought he choked on his own vomit, how would that be murder?"

"You were the one who said it might be a crime scene."

"Every dead human body must be treated as a potential crime scene."

I stand up again. That elusive scent keeps tugging at my awareness, like a memory that won't come clear.

"Abby, look at me," Viv says, and I do. Right into her eyes, where, once again, we flash at each other and she glances away. "Fine. I can't out-dominance you. But I know what I'm talking about, so you should listen to me anyway. As long as you stay here in town, you will find dead bodies just like this one. You'll discover crimes and atrocities as they are being committed. You'll sniff out fear and terror and violence and conflict of every kind. But unless you're acting directly to protect yourself or one of your own, you have to let that go. Don't investigate the dead bodies. Don't interfere with the muggings or the rapes. Ignore the drug deals and the domestic violence and the drunk drivers and the suicides. Do not get yourself involved."

"Why not?"

"Because you are not the cops, and your wolf is brand new. You haven't even begun to master her power. I help the police sometimes myself, but I trained for years to do this. You're just a pup. You could easily take actions, thinking to help, that make things worse."

I grimace at her, unhappy because I'm worried she might be right. About some of it, anyway. The part where I'm brand new and don't know what I'm doing. Resentment makes me want to needle her. "Fine. I know I'm not Batman. But I'm still not running off to join your werewolf swamp cult."

Viv glares at me. "We're not a cult. We're a people. Your family."

"That doesn't mean you're not a cult. New Harmony was also my family, did you forget?"

She works her mouth as if she'd like to spit something out of it, then takes a deep breath and tries again. "You need to meet with Pere Claude, your grandfather. You'll see he's no Father Wisdom.

And you have other family, half siblings, eager to welcome and teach you. Your wolf gives you many gifts, but without training, she just causes trouble. You know this. You created that man George as an infected wolf and then you had to kill him."

My heart thumps. Not me. It was the wolf who killed him.

She presses her advantage, stepping forward, emphasizing her height over mine. "You don't want to keep doing that, do you, little one? Creating infected wolves and then having to kill them?"

"It only happened the first time the wolf came. It's not going to happen again."

"Hmm." She folds her arms, looking skeptical. "You know so little about yourself, about the wolf, how do you know it's not going to happen again?"

Good question. Actually.

She sees that I think it's a good question.

She smirks, ready for victory.

But I feel a rush of resentment, raise my head in defiance. "Fine. If it's really so important for me to be trained, you can train me here in town."

Frustrated, she growls slightly. "You're as pigheaded as your father."

"My father? He was stubborn?" She's told me exactly three things about my biological father Leon: that he's dead, that he left behind a handful of illegitimate children, and that I look like him. Something about the subject of my father upsets her, but she won't go into details. The first time we met, she lied, telling me she didn't know him well, when they were adopted siblings. And she wonders why I don't trust her.

She tightens her lips. "If you agree to meet with Pere Claude, you can ask him to tell you about his son."

"That's it, huh? 'Do what we want and we'll give you information'?"

She shrugs and seems about to say something else, but the

sound of approaching sirens distracts us both. She says, "You should leave before the police get here."

I nod. I have no desire to talk to the cops. As I push against the green shutter doors, and she calls out, "The full moon is just two days away, little one. You have to decide soon what you're going to do. The moon doesn't wait for you to make up your mind."

The doors burst open, dumping me out onto the street where the sun is bright and the air is moist and hot. I pause to inhale and get my bearings. I notice the place where I can still, barely, make out the spray-painted cross mark left by FEMA so many years ago. I guess the building hasn't been painted since then.

Wait. There's a smell. Something —

I inhale again. That's it. That thing that's been nagging at the edges of my awareness, I know what it is now.

In a trash can near the house, there's a discarded piece of clothing worn recently by a woman who I'm pretty sure is my half sister.

2

DENNIS

The clothing turns out to be a bra, lacy and purple. I pull it out of the garbage and bring it up to my nose, hope nobody is watching.

It's pungent with booze and sweat, but I think her wolf hasn't appeared yet. Her sweat is missing that distinctive peppery snap. I stuff the bra into my sweatshirt pocket and sniff around until I pick up her trail again.

New Orleans in August is good for scent-tracking. Heat bakes memories off the sidewalk, while syrupy humidity holds everything suspended in mid-air. I close my eyes to allow my sense of smell to dominate, and my sister's trail becomes ribbons of soft turquoise twisting in the air.

A few blocks away, the ribbons sharpen. A more recent trail, leading into a bar. I follow it inside, hoping nobody asks for my ID.

The interior is cool and quiet. My sister perches on a bar stool, talking to a big man, but leaning away from him as if she doesn't like him much.

I listen to their conversation for a moment, trying to figure out if it's okay to interrupt. My sister is dressed nicely, in a pretty dress and pastel makeup. Did she just come from church? Or is she on a date? Her voice drips southern molasses as she talks.

"Dennis, no, hon, it's not like that at all." She places a soothing hand on his arm.

"I know what I saw." His voice is low, accented, maybe eastern European? He broods over his beer for a moment, then turns abruptly toward her, his posture so aggressive that I have an impulse to put myself in between them. "But, you lied to me before."

She laughs, a tinkling high-pitched cascade of bells. "Aw, sugar, please. You've never told the truth once in your whole life. It's what I like most about you."

His posture remains sullen, but he grins, almost reluctantly, and drains his glass. "Is true when I say, more vodka."

While Dennis tries to catch the eye of the bartender, I walk up on my sister's other side.

"Hi, excuse me—"

She whips around at the sound of my voice, blinks, then smiles brightly. "Why, hello there sweetie, what can I do for you?"

"I, uh, I just wondered—I thought you looked familiar—is your father Leon Verreaux?"

Wow, that was awkward. But she nods in response. "Why yes, he is, why do you ask?"

I inhale, about to start explaining, but the bartender interrupts me with a glare. "Kid, this is a bar, what are you doing in here?"

Uh-oh, busted. I feel a rush of shame that makes me defiant. "I'm not a kid." But I'm also not twenty-one.

"You got some ID to prove that?"

"Sorry, I don't have anything proving I exist at all." I deliver this with sarcasm and flounce out to the street. It's shockingly hot and bright after the cool darkness of the bar. I take off my sweatshirt, tie it around my waist.

Now what? I know that woman in there is my sister, but I didn't even catch her name. What do I do, just hang around outside until she leaves? That's almost as creepy as what Viv keeps doing to me. But what else can I do?

At a convenience store I buy a cold bottle of water and the August issue of *Teen Mode* magazine. An interview with me is supposed to come out in the September issue, and I'm not entirely sure what to expect. I've read a few of their online articles, but never looked at a print copy before. Maybe I made a huge mistake talking to them.

I find a shaded stoop and park myself on a step. The act of sitting on rough bricks reminds me that I'm still wearing church clothes: white sandals and a pale green dress that Steph and her mom picked out. I smooth the dress over my knees, feeling half naked, as if I'm wearing tissue paper.

My phone buzzes and I pull it out of the sweatshirt pocket. It's Steph.

> Abby, where did you go?

She's been texting for almost an hour, and I didn't notice. Guilt nags at me as I write back.

> Sorry, just got your text now. Walking around the neighborhood, nothing special

> Are you ok?

> Now that I'm not in church

> Haha

> Glad you're ok see you soon

I close my eyes. For a second I'm back in that church pew, listening to the priest intone the words of a prayer.

Our father in heaven, bless us this day…

Father, heaven, bless: all these words used to be so familiar to me. At New Harmony I heard them every day. But I haven't been inside a church for months now, and this morning every word stabbed into my gut with a painful physical intensity, as if I were literally being assaulted by the words. Phantom claws scrabbled at the back of my head as if trying to break my head open. It was intolerable. I wanted to scream; run; vomit; hit something.

It's a spiritual attack, a demon.

No, I don't believe in demons anymore.

Steph noticed me huddled and shaking, whispered, "Are you okay?" I shook my head, and scurried out of the church as quietly as possible.

Now that I think about it, the last time I was in a church was before the wolf came. In the rougarou legends from Steph's Cajun grandma, we aren't able to go into a church.

It can't possibly be that.

Can it?

I flip through the pages of *Teen Mode*, inhaling the chemical pop of glossy paper and printing ink. The magazine has all the celebrity fashion photographs and "how to wear nail polish" articles of a lifestyle magazine, but it also has articles about safe sex and how to run for political office. It seems like I made the right choice, not that it was entirely my choice.

A couple of weeks ago, just after the New Harmony cult meltdown made a big splash in the news, I happened to catch my stepmother Meekness and older brother Justice on a religious talk show. She was calling herself Mercy and he was calling himself Justin, and they were calling Father Wisdom by his given name, John Wise, the name his books were published under.

They were in the middle of a story about John Wise

attempting an exorcism, and I listened in disgusted fascination for a few moments until I realized they were talking about *me*. They were describing him trying to drive out my "beast" as if it was a benign religious experience involving nothing but prayer and "spiritual warfare," rather than a brutal punishment in which I was beaten so severely that I could have died.

Sputtering rage, I contacted every magazine I could find, telling them my name, that I was a New Harmony survivor, that I was willing to give an exclusive interview with the real story.

Most of them ignored me. But Janelle Barker from *Teen Mode* gave me a call. We met in New Orleans and spent an afternoon walking around the city while her photographer took pictures. We talked on the day of the new moon, so I was feeling depressed, and despair made me reckless. Who cares if everybody can see my scars? If everybody knows every last little thing about me?

But now I'm starting to worry about what's going to happen when the new issue comes out. What if I said something revealing? I know I didn't come right out and say "oh, by the way, I'm a werewolf" but maybe I said something almost that bad.

I rise to my feet and start pacing around. Now that I think about it, there's something else to worry about: I told Janelle Barker that I was eighteen. Or, rather, I signed a piece of paper to that effect, asserting that I was my own guardian, giving my own consent for the interview. She didn't fight me on it. But when Steph and I go down to the courthouse to get me a real ID, she's probably going to say I'm sixteen. Is anybody going to compare my signature in the *Teen Mode* archives to the archives of the state of Louisiana? Could I get in trouble for that? Could Janelle Barker? I liked her, I don't want to get her in trouble.

Vague worries keep me occupied until my sister and Dennis finally leave the bar. They seem to be arguing.

"Don't care," he says. "You won't get away from this."

"I told them how it's gonna be," she says. She spots me and

waves. "Hey there, sugar. You were that girl who wanted to talk about Leon, weren't you?"

"Shit, ignore little punk." Dennis takes her arm and forces her attention his way. He's stressed out and giddy, his sweat tainted with a sickly yellow-purple stink in addition to the sour reek of half-processed alcohol. Maybe a stimulant? His body is definitely jacked up on something, heart racing and temperature high.

My body responds, wolf snapping to attention.

"You. Always yanking chain." Dennis presses my sister against a brick wall, makes a cage for her with his beefy, pumped-up arms. Maybe that drug I'm smelling is steroids? "Say it now. With me or no?"

"Please." Her voice is small and frightened, but I don't smell spiky yellow terror in her sweat. Maybe she's playing more frightened than she really is?

"Please what?" He leans into her face, intimate, as if for a kiss, but his face is red and angry.

"Please go away. Please leave me alone." Her eyes find mine, get wide and pleading.

"Hey, you heard that, leave her alone," I step closer to them, stand as tall as I can. Which is about five nothing, last I checked. Nobody finds that intimidating.

The man turns his head to regard me, making a point of how far down he has to look to see my face. "Get away now, punk child. Not your business."

The wolf bristles at this challenge to our authority. Not our business? He doesn't get to say what's our business. "She said to leave her alone." I try to catch his eyes with mine, but his gaze darts around randomly and I can't hold him with my stare.

He peels himself away from the wall and turns his body toward me. Released from the cage of his arms, my sister moves to the other end of the block, but doesn't go any further. She has her phone out. Maybe calling the cops, or at least, getting ready to? I think about what Viv told me. If you end up killing some-body, call me, not the cops.

But I'm not going to kill this guy.

Of course not.

My heart races, body tensing. I'm scared about what's going to happen, but excited too. Is he really going to start this fight? Is he going to hurt me? Am I going to hurt him?

"Bitch. I told you get gone, now."

"Leave my sister alone and I will."

"Sister? You say?" He frowns, glancing from her to me. His lip curls into a scornful smile. "You. Must come from ugly side of family." He takes out a knife, releases the blade with a metallic swish. He takes a step toward me. "Too ugly for rape, so——"

I close off his neck, never let him finish the thought. By the neck I press him up against the brick wall, my arms extended to their full length so that I can hold him a few inches off the ground. His weight drags his chin against my fingers. He chokes, sputtering, scrabbling. He drops the knife. I kick it away.

I let go. He falls to the sidewalk, gasping for a moment before gathering himself into a crouch, flicking out a second knife. He glares up at me with dark eyes that flash pure, gleeful rage. "Oh, you." He laughs. "You pay for that."

I kick him in the knee, the groin, the other knee. He collapses, but continues to hold the knife pointed at me. I grab it by the blade, cutting my hand. Blood gushes for a moment, then the wound heals.

I hit him in the jaw, a punch borrowed from action movies that feels awkward in real life. Still, he reels, and another punch sends him falling backwards, all the way to the sidewalk.

Now that he's prone I hit him a few more times for good measure. He pisses himself.

My sister comes up behind me. "Miss? Miss, come on, we have to go. Come with me, now. Please. You don't want to kill him, do you? He's not worth it. Come on, now. We have to go."

The words "kill him" snap me fully back into myself.

Was I really going to kill him? I look down at his dark, puffy face, bruises already swallowing up his eyes and nose. He looks bad. But he's breathing. He's fine, isn't he?

"Come on." She tugs my arm. "We need to go. This way."

I allow her to lead me away. I don't know where we're going.

3

OPAL

"Here's your sweater now, sugar." My sister hands me the sweatshirt that was tied around my waist. I don't remember losing it. "I'm Opal. And you are?"

"Abby." Chilled by fading adrenaline, I put the sweatshirt back on. My phone is still there in my pocket, thank goodness.

"And you think we're sisters?"

"I know we are."

"Well that's just fantastic, isn't it? Here we are at my car, why don't you let me give you a ride home so we can talk a bit?"

I climb inside. Her car is full of fast food discards and coffee cups, and smells of her very strongly. She pulls out into traffic, then glances at me with a smile. "So, Miss Abby, you're a wolf?"

"I—what?"

She laughs. "No need to be coy, hon. Leon raised me to know what we are. And, I see a little thing like you beating so hard on a big man like Dennis, I know where you get that kind of power."

"Dennis? Oh no, he was a friend of yours, wasn't he? Do we need to take him to the hospital? Oh, I'm so sorry, I screwed it all up, I wasn't thinking—"

She wrinkles her nose as if she smells something unpleasant.

"Friend? No, I would not say friend. Associate. And he thinks he can intimidate me." Her eyes glitter. "He *thought* he could intimidate me, anyway. I'm wolfless, sugar, there's no way I could stand up to him the way you did."

"I know, your wolf hasn't appeared yet."

"No. I'm twenty-six. My wolf never is gonna show up. Some of us are born that way, I guess. All the genes for it, but then she never comes."

"I'm sorry, I didn't know." I'm not sure what I'm apologizing for, but she smiles in response.

"It's all right. I'm used to it. You were raised out in the wild, though, weren't you? No idea what was coming?"

"That's right." I don't mention being raised in a cult. That seems like a bit much to go into right now. "You weren't, though? You were raised by Leon?"

"Not raised, exactly. But he did show up on occasion. I haven't seen him in years, though. I came out to New Orleans looking for him, but you're the first connection I've made."

"Leon is dead." It sounds harsh coming out of my mouth like that, so I try to soften the blow. "I mean, that's what I've been told. By his family."

She wrinkles up her nose. "The Varger, I know. He did tell me about them." We're stopped at a traffic light and she glances my way. "Say, Miss Abby, do you want me to take you home? Or do you want to keep on driving around and talking?"

"Talking, if that's okay. But why talk in the car? Why don't we go to a coffee shop or something?"

"We're deep in Varger territory right now, sugar, and unless we want them to know every last thing about our business, we'll stay right here in the car."

It makes sense, now that I think about it. I've tried to scent-track a car and it didn't really work. I run fast, but not faster than a car. I have keen hearing, but not keen enough to hear what somebody in a car is saying to another person in that car.

"Wow, I never thought of it before. Cars are like werewolf kryptonite."

She barks out a surprised laugh."I guess you could say that, couldn't you? Werewolf kryptonite. You're so funny, hon. I never heard that one before."

She stops talking for a moment to navigate more complex traffic, and I put my hands in my sweatshirt pockets again. Right, the bra. I pull it out. "This belongs to you, doesn't it?"

She glances at it and snickers. "Oh, that. My goodness. It got soaked through with this horrible sticky drink and I just couldn't stand wearing it anymore. Is that how you found me? Picked up my trail from that?"

"There was a dead man. In a house next to where this bra was."

"A dead man?" She widens her eyes. "Who was it?"

"Not somebody I know. A tall man. White, very tanned, blondish hair. There had been a party, I think. The house was empty, no furniture or anything. I think it's been empty for a while."

She frowns thoughtfully. "How was he dressed?"

"Jeans and T-shirt. Nothing special."

"Was the T-shirt black and gold?" I nod. "Was it for the Delta Lambda Delta fraternity?"

"No, I didn't see any words on it. Just symbols."

"Well, it would have been the Greek letters. Pyramid, open triangle, pyramid?"

"Oh. right. Maybe?"

"Probably Andreas." She sighs, shaking her head. "Damn it. When I left that party, he was drunk as a skunk but he was still breathing. How did he die?"

"Choked on his own vomit, I think."

"Well, damn. I'm sorry you had to find him like that. I guess with that wolfy nose of yours, you're gonna find all the dirty rotten secrets this town tries to hide, huh?"

"I guess so." I look out the window, realize I can't see land in any direction, just pelicans and snowy egrets flying overhead. "You said he didn't raise you, but did you know Leon well?"

"Well enough. You know, I happen to have something in the car with me now that you might like to see. Be a doll and lean over the back seat, would you? There's a metal container back there. Bring it up here and open it."

I unhook my seatbelt and turn around, rifle through empty food packages, old newspapers, discarded clothing, until I find a latched aluminum box, buried under an assortment of plastic bags. Opal clearly spends a lot of time in her car.

I place the box in my lap, undo the latches. Air whooshes out, perfumed heavily with the smell of tanned leather, ink, aged paper, and more subtly with a person smell, one I don't know at all, and yet instantly I do.

"This belonged to Leon." I remove the lid all the way and stare at the stained brown leather of a medium-sized notebook, about the size of a trade paperback book.

"It did. He gave it to me when I turned twelve. That was when he told me all about the wolf. Everything he thought was coming my way."

I remove the notebook from its box. The leather cover is soft, worn by finger grease and water spots, smelling of coffee and red wine. I run my fingers over the surface, where the stamped letters LEV can still be made out. "What does the E stand for?"

"Evangeline, I think. That was his mother's name. He used it as an initial. Leon E. Verreaux."

"His mother." I exhale, suddenly so full of excitement I can barely sit still. He had a mother. I have a grandmother. "Is she alive?"

"Sorry, sugar, I'm afraid not. Grandma died when Leon was only a teenager. Killed by hunters. Terrible thing. Kinda broke him, if you want to know the truth. Some of the story is in there." She nods at the book.

"Do you mind if I read through it?"

"That's why I gave it to you. It's a precious thing to me, but I've read it many times already. Memorized it, you could say. But if you were raised on the outside, and you have a wolf now, you have more need of it than I do."

"So it has information about being a wolf? Like, tips and tricks?"

She chuckles. "I guess you could say that. But it's a good way to get to know Leon, if you're curious about him."

Of course I'm curious. I'm practically dying of curiosity. But I try to stay cool. "Would you say he was a good person?"

"Would I? I don't know. How do you know if somebody's a good person?"

"Well, you know. A good person does good things and doesn't do bad things."

She gives me a wry grin. "Oh, now, sweetie, you're young, but I know you know better than that. Everybody does good things sometimes and bad things other times. Are you a good person? Do you always do good things? Beating up on Dennis, now, was that a good thing? Maybe not. But you did it to protect me. So maybe yes. You see?"

My heart pounds. "I guess you're right. I'm not a good person myself, so who am I to judge?"

"Oh, come on now, you know that's not what I meant. I think you probably are a good person, to be honest. I don't think the bad people care one way or the other. But Leon, now, he's a bit of an interesting case." She shrugs. "I thought he was good, but I don't know if you would agree. He seemed good to me because my stepfather was so very bad."

"Bad how?"

"He was a very domineering kind of man." She makes a disgusted face. "My mama started going back to church when I was about twelve years old, and it was one of those patriarchy-style churches. Very fundamentalist. Girls have to wear dresses and keep their hair long? It was called, let me see, the American Renewal Fellowship."

"I can't believe it, that's one of the outsider churches we used to go to! American Renewal Fellowship!"

She peers at me curiously. "Outsider churches?"

"Most of the time we were home-churched, but sometimes my father would be a guest preacher at these other churches and we called them outsider churches, to distinguish them from false churches, like Catholics or Episcopalians."

"Oh, my. So it sounds like you will know some of what I've been through. My mama found herself a man, older, wealthy enough she could marry him and stop working, play the house-wife. I guess that's what she wanted, everything all traditional.

"But I didn't want that. And I wasn't young enough to take it all for granted, you know? So when they started grooming me to be some man's submissive little helpmeet, I was old enough to fight back."

"What did you do?"

"For one thing, I wouldn't let him spank me. When he tried, I'd run away. Then one time he tried and he kind of had me trapped so I couldn't run. He managed to spank me that time, and I hit him back. So there we were, fighting, an all-out brawl, and he hit me in the face. It left a bruise. I almost got him in trouble for that. But he told the child protection people it was an accident and my mama backed him up. They're scared of the religious folk, you know? I guess the church has a lot of power. So then I went to Leon."

"And what did Leon do?"

"Leon gave him the stare." She glances at me with a sly smile. "Do you know what that is?"

"I'm not sure. Do you mean that thing where we look into somebody's eyes, then our eyes flash, and then the other person gets kinda blank for a moment?"

"That would be it, yes. So you've got the stare yourself? Lucky you. Leon, now, he was an expert at it. When he came to see me on my fifteenth birthday, he told Roland Matthews, that's my stepfather, he told him 'Leave Opal alone' with so much force that it stuck for months. And by the time the effect wore off, he was in the habit of leaving me alone. He was still an asshole, but he didn't try to spank me anymore."

"So that's what Leon did for you. He got your fundamentalist stepfather to back off."

"That's right." Her mood darkens. "But he never told me what to do if the wolf didn't come. That's why I headed out here to look for him, when I hadn't seen him for a few years." She puts on a forced-looking smile. "But that's all old news. Miss Abby, you go ahead and look through that diary, now, I can tell you're chomping at the bit to see it."

I flip through the notebook, breathing in the ghosts of times past, echoes of coffee shops, taverns, meals. Sweat, and even a little blood. The dust of the swamp, the dust of the city, caught in these pages, exhaling like a breath, as if the book itself is alive.

My father's handwriting, in a dozen colors of ink and at least three pens, surprises me with its fineness and precision. Somehow, everything I knew about him prepared me for bold, wild penmanship that I would struggle to read. Instead his script is almost as legible as the words in a normal printed book.

My eye catches on the words "I have to find a way to leave" and I flip back to the beginning of the section, dated with the month and day but not the year: January sixth. I read:

Sixth day of training. Bitterly cold. Told them I'd do it myself, used the agnara to make a cross wound to the gut and the wolf came as usual. Spent the rest of the day in a foul mood, drained of everything but despair. Felt like a black moon. Don't know how long I can keep up this pace. May scale back to twice a week, in spite of Pere's objections. He wants me trained as quickly as possible. But each day has been more brutal than the last.

He is too involved in his own ambitions for me, wanting me to

follow his path, never questioning. Why do we do this to
ourselves? Why do we live this way? My own father, who
claims to love me, torturing me on a daily basis.

He says it will make me a better man. A stronger Wolf.
But I just feel broken.

I swallow, over a lump in my throat. Broken. He felt broken
by his father.

I glance at Opal. "Do you know what he's talking about
here? Some kind of training through torture? A thing called the
agnara?"

"I don't, I'm sorry. But his father's people, they have traditions that go back hundreds of years, and some of them are
definitely what you'd call Medieval."

"That's what Viv wants to do to me, isn't it?" I sink down in
the seat, panic and despair washing over me. "That's the thing
she won't tell me about. It's going to be torture, just like New
Harmony."

"Viv?" Opal gives me a questioning look.

"Vivienne. One of his father's people. His lawyer, actually.
She is officially the lawyer for Claude Verreaux."

"His lawyer? Well, now." She gives me a quirky smile. "You
don't really trust the Varger, do you?" I shake my head. "Good.
You should not trust them. They have their own agenda."

My phone buzzes again. It's Steph.

You're not here yet?

On my way

"I'm sorry, I have to go home."
"Sure thing. Where am I taking you?"
"Bywater."
"We'll turn around once we're on the other side of the
causeway. Let's exchange phone numbers, shall we? The full

moon is coming soon. Are you gonna need any help dealing with that?"

"I've got a plan."

"Well, if you do need anything, any help at all, you just call me, okay? Anytime, sister. Just call."

4

SURPRISE

Opal drops me off a couple of blocks away from Steph's family home, since my cover story is that I was out for a walk. It shouldn't be a big deal that I was on a drive with my sister instead, but I've started to hate explaining myself to Steph's family.

Well, Steph's mom, mostly. She seems to think that whenever I'm out on my own I'm getting up to some kind of stereotypical teenage shenanigans: sex, drugs, rock and roll, smoking, drinking, drag racing, unsavory characters, disorderly conduct. I guess that's what Steph would have been doing when she was my age. But most of those kinds of trouble require friends, and until meeting Opal just now, I didn't have any friends in town. Who would I be getting in trouble with?

Walking destroys the already wobbly heel on one of the delicate little church sandals I'm still wearing. Not combat-ready, I guess. Now I start to wonder what kind of damage I did to the floaty tissue dress.

I examine myself for blood, scrapes, bruises. I heal quickly enough that the big cut on my hand is already closed, but it did spray blood everywhere, which lingers as brown splotches on my clothes and skin and probably hair. With no mirror I try to rub my face clean. Shoot. I should have asked Opal to help me with this, but I didn't think of it until just now.

I take off the shoes and hope I can slip into the house, get to a shower before anybody notices me.

No such luck. Steph and baby Terry are out on the front porch, listening to her father play guitar softly. Her father has a can of cheap beer. Steph has an iced tea with lemon.

"Hi honey," Steph says. "Are you feeling better?"

I nod and plop onto the porch swing. "I think I just needed some fresh air."

"You got a book?"

"What? Oh, right. I went to that little used bookstore in the Quarter that I like? You know the one. "

Terry makes hand-grabby motions at me. I take him into my lap and we swing back and forth. Steph's dad plays a tune to match our movement, singing low. *I went down to Saint James infirmary…*

Steph says, "Can you be ready to go to the airport in twenty minutes?"

"I guess. Why are we going to the airport?"

"We're going out to pick up my brother, remember?"

"Oh, right, I forgot. Do I have to go?"

"You'll want to come along," she says firmly.

"Fine." I hug Terry and hand him over to Steph's dad. "But I need a shower before I go anywhere."

"Just be quick."

Terry bangs his little hands on the guitar strings and laughs at the sound.

"Natural-born musician for sure," Steph's dad says, with approval.

I head inside and Steph's mom ambushes me, smelling of anger and donuts.

"You walked out of the service, Abby," she says.

I stare at her for a moment, not sure why she's telling me this. "I did do that, yeah."

She folds her arms, raises her head, gives me a suspicious glare. "Steph said not to worry about you."

"She knows I can take care of myself."

"Did you go out to meet someone? A boy?"

I'm so startled by this accusation that I laugh out loud. There's only one boy I'd want to meet that way, and he's all the way back in Seattle.

Her frown deepens. "Don't laugh, Abby, tell me the truth. Did you go out to meet a boy?"

"Mrs. Marchande, I don't know anybody in town, who would I meet?"

"Well, I don't know about that. I don't know what you do when you're gone all day, out gallivanting around."

"Gallivanting? Is that what I do?"

She fumes harder. "Gallivanting is exactly what you do, missy! Wandering all over town by yourself!"

"Wait, I thought you were worried that I was meeting a boy? Now you're worried that I'm by myself?" I'm genuinely confused.

"It isn't safe out there!" she snaps.

"Okay, but, is that why you're mad? You're worried that I'm putting myself in some kind of danger?"

"It's one thing that you've got no concern for yourself. You're sixteen, I guess all you kids think you're kings of the world at that age. But do you know what it would do to Steph if you got yourself in trouble? If you got yourself hurt?"

I close my eyes for a moment. Yes, I know. But anything bad enough to hurt me isn't something Steph, or Steph's family, could possibly protect me from. "Mrs. Marchande, I know you're worried, but give your daughter a little credit. If she trusts me, maybe you should too."

She bristles. If she had a wolf she would growl. But she gives up, with a huge sigh of frustration. "You're such a tomboy, I can't believe you got that dress all tore up already. That's one trial Steph never put me through. Now, go get washed up."

Huh. She just ordered me to do what I was planning to do anyway. So now, when I do it, she can feel victorious, and I can feel resentful.

I try to ignore that feeling and just do what I was planning. I climb a narrow spiraling staircase into the hot, humid, me-smelling air of the loft. It's got a low, slanting ceiling, a private bathroom, a bunch of clothes Steph and Morgan abandoned during high school, and no air conditioning. This is where Steph and Morgan slept while they were growing up, in "rooms" parti-tioned off by curtains. But lately Steph and Terry have been sleeping in what used to be her parents' bedroom, while her parents sleep in the bedroom they built in what used to be the carriage house. When Morgan gets here, he's going to sleep on an air mattress in the living room.

The private shower is nice, if cramped. I wash blood out of my hair and rinse off scabs that formed on injuries I didn't notice getting. That's what adrenaline will do for you, I guess. But it's the wolf too. Before the wolf, I could endure a beating, but as the adrenaline wore off, I would start to ache from every bruise and cut. My injuries today are already healed up. Nothing to feel.

I rub soapy fingers over the ridge of scars on my right shoul-der. I remember the whipping that gave them to me, scarring not because the cuts were worse than usual, but because they got infected. I was thirteen, so it wasn't all that long ago, even if it seems like another life. There were a few days where my fever was so high that I was thrashing and delirious and everybody thought I might die. Father Wisdom was nicer to me than he'd ever been, and I think it's only because he was hoping I would die. But I didn't. I just came through scarred.

The chastisements weren't intended to leave scars, of course. It would have been wicked to mark the body on purpose, like Steph's many tattoos. But somehow, if you didn't intend it, but it happened anyway, that was God's will and that was fine.

Just like it would have been wicked for Wisdom to decide to

beat my little sister Ash to death. But if he beat her, and then she died? God's will. Not murder at all.

My body tenses up, ready to fight an enemy I know is dead.

Out of the shower, I put on a dress made from two T-shirts that I got while hitch-hiking across the country last month. Only last month? It already seems like forever ago. The dress turned out pretty well, I think. I took the time to tailor it a bit, center the skull logos (one from a band that gave me a ride in their van, one from a pirate-themed store that was going out of business) and turned the sleeves on the lower shirt into pockets. I'm still grateful to Louanne Kaffa, the Seattle police officer who first showed me that you could stretch out the neck on a large T-shirt and wear it as a skirt. That's the kind of trick that comes in handy when you find yourself naked in public and have to make an outfit in a hurry.

Steph waits at the bottom of the spiral staircase with an impatient air. "My app is saying the traffic out to the freeway is terrible, we'd best get going."

I nod, and follow her to the car. It's Sunday, but the traffic is rush-hour heavy as we pull onto the freeway. Louis Armstrong Airport is way out in Kenner and not actually New Orleans at all. The view from my side of the car quickly becomes very suburban, full of square single-story development, houses and strip malls and fast food chains. The ugliness of this part of town makes me think longingly of Seattle, where even the dreariest neighborhoods usually have plenty of tall trees.

I lean my head against the window and zone out.

"...Church?" Steph says.

I didn't notice myself falling asleep, but I have the sensation of startling awake. "I'm sorry?"

"I was asking about church. Were you physically not well or just stressed out?"

"Uh..." I wasn't expecting the question. "Stressed out, I guess. Sick and stressed out feel kind of the same at first, but I felt okay as soon as I was out of the building."

She nods. "That's what I thought. Church is going to trigger your PTSD, I bet, so unless you really want to go, you should probably keep away. I'll tell mama she should stop pestering you about it."

Steph is sure I have post-traumatic stress disorder from my time in the cult. I don't think she's wrong, exactly, but she wants to send me to counselors and doctors and so on, and I don't want to do that. I'm pretty sure they can't help, when there's one very important thing about myself that I can't possibly tell them. And if they tried medication? I have no idea how normal medications work on me. Mostly, when I've tried things like aspirin, they do nothing. But what if something intended as an antidepressant or a sedative actually made me extra-violent? That's not a risk I want to take.

"So, what did you do once you were out of church? See any new parts of town?"

I think about telling her everything that happened, but there's too much and I can't figure out what to say. I found a dead body and my werewolf relatives bugged me again and I met a new sister and I beat a guy within an inch of his life and I found out that my real father left behind a diary with eerie parallels to my own experience. "I don't know. Nothing I want to get into right now."

Her eyes twinkle. "I know, you don't have friends in town, do you?"

"That's right." But why is she twinkling? Like she's got a surprise lined up?

"I get it. But things will be better when Morgan gets here, you'll see."

"Maybe. But I'd rather go back to Seattle. Aren't we still planning to do that?"

She looks away and her mood darkens. "That was the original plan, yes."

"But it's not the plan now?"

"I'm not sure, sweetie. There's a lot to talk about."

My gut lurches. Bad news is coming. I can feel it.

THE AIRPORT IS DAMP AND SMELLS LIKE STALE CIGARS. WITH Steph I stand in the baggage claim area, watching in numb fascination as bag after bag emerges through a row of black plastic flaps, which make a fwap-fwap noise. The bags ride around in a long oval loop, then disappear behind flaps on the other side. The whole thing seems weirdly menacing, to have your bag appear, only to disappear again. What if it never comes back? Where does the unseen portion of the loop go?

"Abby, we're over here." Steph beckons, and I leave off my hypnotized staring at the carousel to begin hypnotized staring at the line of people trickling into the baggage area. "I bet that guy's from Seattle." She points to a man in a blue and bright green Seahawks T-shirt. "Why do you suppose he came here on this flight?"

"Um. To see music and get drunk?"

"Good call." She laughs. "What about her?" She points out a woman with beauty-pageant makeup and elaborately coiffed hair, moving in a toxic cloud of perfume.

"I think she's here... to see music and get drunk."

Steph sighs. "You're grouchy today."

"Come on, Steph. You know I'm right."

"And you know you're grouchy."

I guess, but I don't feel grouchy at the moment. I feel revved-up, impatient, like I want to get started on something that's long overdue. Nothing like the soul-sucking despair that hits me at the new moon, when I would describe myself as grouchy.

The black moon. Wait. Leon said something about the black moon in his diary. Is my new-moon despair what he was talking about? That would be something else we have in common.

Morgan is here. I notice the familiar friendly person smell

long before I can see him. I run up the stairs to arrival level, and we hug. Sometimes I'm not sure if he likes me, but he hugs back with enthusiasm.

Steph joins us. "Did you check luggage?" she asks.

"Of course. I came prepared to stay a couple of months at least."

"A couple of months?" My stomach lurches. "Why so long?"

He frowns at Steph. "Didn't you tell her?"

Steph turns defensive. "I wasn't sure. Is it real? I didn't want to tell her if it isn't real."

"It's real. I didn't tell you until it was real."

"Is what real?" I interrupt. None of this sounds good.

Steph sighs. "Uh. Okay. There's a developer in Seattle who might be interested in the house."

"Is interested in the house." Morgan corrects her. "Is in fact interested in the house."

"A developer? But does that mean they'll tear it down?" All of a sudden I'm in a panic. "You'd let them tear it down?"

Morgan shrugs. "We like that house, but it's no precious historical artifact. Just an ordinary Craftsman bungalow. Seattle has hundreds. Thousands."

"But—" My world is suddenly slipping away. "But you can't. We're supposed to go back. I'm supposed to go to school. Isn't that what we're doing? Going back to Seattle and I'm going to Saint Sebastian? I'll be a junior!"

Steph sighs, ruffles my hair. "Sweetie, we don't know. Even if we sell the house we might go back to Seattle. Or somewhere else. Nothing is for sure yet. A lot has happened in the last few months. We all have a lot to deal with."

"If we sell the house for as much money as I think we can get, we can blow off everything and go on a world cruise for a year." Morgan grins. I guess that's what he wants to do.

"All of us. Including me?"

"Well of course, honey," Steph says.

"Not of course. You know I'm not really family."

Steph hugs me. "Don't be ridiculous, Abby. You're part of my family now."

People are still streaming off the plane, and I catch another whiff of familiar person, this one a complete shock: Deena, my friend from Saint Sebastian, her scent laced with cheap hairspray and stale tobacco smoke. And her friend, Edison, the gorgeous college boy who a couple of months ago sort of maybe seemed a little bit like he wanted to think about the possibility of dating me.

"Steph, did you know my Seattle friends are here? Wait, of course you did. You invited them."

She laughs, nervously. "Surprise! When Morgan told me about the house sale, I thought, well, I promised you we were going back to Seattle before the start of the school year, and once I didn't know if I could keep that promise, I thought I could at least bring your school friends out here to see you." Her smile turns fragile, uncertain. "That was good, right?"

I give her a hug. "Yeah, that was good." I don't add: and also uncomfortably close to the full moon. During the full moon at the end of July, she sat up with me all night while I resisted the urge to change. She acted like she believed me about the wolf, but ever since then, I've suspected that she might have been humoring me. Maybe it was a mistake not to show her the wolf, but I didn't want to take that risk. I didn't trust the wolf then, and I still don't.

Without seeming to make any conscious choice, I'm running to greet my friends in a warm, enthusiastic hug.

"Deena! Edison! Welcome to New Orleans!" I feel myself grinning with naked enthusiasm, like a dog getting super excited because those people she likes are here, wanting to jump all over them and slobber in joy. At least, as a human, I manage to keep my tongue in my mouth.

"Oh my God, Abby, I love the hair." Deena rubs her hand over her own hair, which is short except for a wavy mass of bangs dyed in Mardi Gras colors of green and purple. "I've been thinking about going really short with mine, what do you think?"

"It would look great. But you always look great." Deena is extremely hip, with a terrific, quirky fashion sense.

But now I'm self-conscious about what I look like. My head was completely shaved about four weeks ago, when I went back to New Harmony for the last time, and it's currently a little more than an inch long, barely long enough to get messy. I don't want to think of myself as a vain person, but standing in front of Edison right now, I realize I'm a little vain about my hair. It's naturally a bright, vivid red, with deep auburn shadows and golden highlights, and it gets wavy when longer. What if the only thing Edison liked about me was my pretty hair?

But he's smiling at me, shy through dark bangs. "Hey, Abby. It's good to see you."

"You too," This is a huge understatement, because it's way better than good to see Edison. Kind of makes my whole day, in fact. Picture a beautiful actor who would play the sweet, earnest superhero back when he was in college, and that's Edison. He's in a band. He plays on the University of Washington football team. And he smells good. He doesn't go in for hair gel or colognes. He smells like—I don't know, like a boy, I guess, but somehow better than most boys smell. Spicy, like I want to lick him.

Damn it. I should not be having thoughts like that in an airport.

He breaks the spell when he turns toward a clump of three young men who just caught up with us. He gestures toward each one in turn. "These are my friends Reed Nelson, Brad Taylor, and Ward Parker. They're still mad at me for not joining their frat, so I'm making it up to them with a trip to New Orleans."

"Just call them the bros, that's what I do," Deena says. "They all answer to 'bro.'"

I study them, trying to remember which name goes with which guy, but I've already forgotten. I'm pretty sure I've never met them before, although they could have been at the Howl, the big full-moon party in the woods where I first realized I was a werewolf. They look like a lot of the guys I saw there: tall, clean-cut, good-looking in a generic, square-jawed fashion. They differ from each other in small ways, but if I tried to draw them, they would all come out more or less the same. They stand the same, dress the same, even smell the same, thanks to a shared passion for the same harsh cologne.

Their maroon T-shirts seem to commemorate a sport called Beer Pong played on behalf of the fraternal organization of Psi Phi Theta (trident, circle with a line through it, circle with a line through it going the other way). There are little differences. One of them has a shirt that identifies him as BEER PONG PLAYER and another has a shirt that promises BEER PONG GETS YOUR BALLS WET.

Edison is wearing a maroon T-shirt in a similar design that identifies him as GUEST BEER PONG CHAMPION.

I lead them back downstairs to baggage claim. Edison and Deena greet Steph and Morgan, then introduce the bros.

Steph regards them warily. "Deena, I know I invited you and Edison to stay with us, but the loft doesn't have room for this many people."

"That's okay, Ms. Marchande," Deena says. "Once the bros were coming too, we got a suite in the French Quarter. You don't have to worry about a thing. In fact, Reed rented a car, so you don't even have to drive us from the airport."

"Oh. Okay." Steph frowns, obviously dismayed, but not sure if there's really a problem. "So I guess you're all set then?"

"We're all set," Deena declares cheerfully.

"When I thought it was just you and Edison, I planned to take you out to CharliQ's for dinner," Steph says.

"We can meet you there after we get checked into the hotel." Deena types into her phone, holds up a map. "Is this the place?" Steph nods. "Cool, it's right at the end of Chartres, it looks easy to find."

"Charters," I say. "I know it's spelled Char-tres, but the people here say Charters."

She laughs. "See, that is fantastic. I love knowing that." She turns to the bros. "You dudes all have checked luggage, right?" They nod. She smiles at me. "The bros like to travel with these giant suitcases you could hide a body in." She mock-frowns at them. "Wait a minute, you dudes don't actually have bodies in your suitcases, do you?" They laugh. "Anyway, you don't have to wait for us."

Steph nods. "I guess we'll see you at the restaurant."

Morgan and I follow her back to the car. I'm happy but worried. How am I going to manage my friends, plus their friends, plus the full moon?

"Surprise," I mutter to myself.

5

THE MEAT DIED HAPPY AND WENT TO A BETTER PLACE

It seems to take forever to drive back to Bywater, through sluggish traffic. Steph parks the car next to a decayed fence badly in need of a coat of paint. We emerge from the air-conditioned car back into the heavy New Orleans summer. A small dog on the other side of the fence starts barking madly. Territorial. He smells me and doesn't like it.

"Those are poisonous," Morgan points at a bush hanging out over the fence, heavy with white, trumpet-shaped flowers tipped in lavender along their spiraling ruffled edges. They emanate a syrupy-sweet odor. "Devil's trumpet. You wouldn't believe how many common landscape plants are toxic."

"Now that I have Terry, I'm very well aware of that," Steph says. "Babies really like to put things in their mouths."

Morgan stops to inhale deeply, not of the flowers. "Mm, CharliQ's still smells amazing. Best smoked meat you can get anywhere, for any price."

I inhale too, try to deny that it smells good. I'm still trying to live as a vegetarian when in human form, although sometimes I'm not sure what the point is. I already know the wolf is a carnivore, a predator. Maybe it's a gesture of defiance: the wolf is not the boss of me. But also, I have a lot of conflicted and weird feelings that come up when I think about eating meat.

Father Wisdom preached that when Jesus came again to establish the Millennial Kingdom, everybody would be a vegetarian. No humans would eat meat anymore. Even animals wouldn't eat each other. The lion would lie down with the lamb, and so forth. So, to prepare ourselves for that kingdom, we also were vegetarians.

We did keep sheep for milk and wool, chickens for eggs, and dogs for guarding, but we didn't eat their flesh. I was often assigned animal care as if it were punishment. It was a hard and dirty job, but I loved it. I loved our animals, and they seemed to love me, showing a raw physical affection that contrasted with Wisdom's harsh punishments. I loved them, so how could I possibly want to eat them? It meant something to me, when Wisdom took us to a slaughterhouse or a butcher shop to demonstrate what meat really was: not a neatly sliced pink morsel wrapped in sanitized plastic, but carnage, raw and bloody, bought through death and pain. A butcher is, indeed, a *butcher*. A slaughterhouse engages in *slaughter*.

Without the soul, what are we, Abnegation?

Meat, sir. Nothing but meat.

And now I don't know. The wolf kills and eats, and there doesn't seem to be anything I can do about that. But I'm not starving right now, so I don't have to do things her way.

Morgan leads us to CharliQ's, a two-story building of exposed bricks partly covered with plaster. It sits right on the corner of Chartres and Poland, where Chartres terminates in a giant concrete navy building, long-abandoned. The rougarou do come here a lot, judging by the overlaid scent traces, but so far we've managed to avoid awkward run-ins.

We enter through the convenience store-slash-deli and Isobelle Quemper, Izzy, catches my eye and smiles. "Hey, Abby. Smoked tofu po-boy?" Then she notices Morgan and Steph. "Oh, more Marchandes! You all want a table outside?"

Morgan nods. "People are joining us later, so if we could get one of the big round ones?"

"I think we can manage that. Be with you in a minute." She disappears for a moment, comes back, gestures, and leads us out through a side door, into a small brick courtyard, through that into a bigger courtyard full of barrel-shaped smokers and casual furniture.

Morgan looks around with a slight frown. "Why is it so crowded with post-Katrina hipsters around here?"

Izzy grins. "We're just popular. And Grandma Charli got herself another TV spot."

"Television?" Morgan groans. "Shoot. I forgot about all that."

"Be nice, Morgan. Those hipsters and TV spots are paying for my college." She gestures at a round wrought iron table. "Sit right here." She plucks a yellow pencil out of her hair, where she always has three or four of them stuck into her bun of long, fine dreadlocks. Her eyeglass frames are the same shade of yellow, flattering against her warmly dark skin. She pulls a pad of paper out of the pocket of her black apron, which is printed with scarlet letters that say CHARLIQ'S CREOLE BBQ: THE MEAT DIED HAPPY AND WENT TO A BETTER PLACE. She hovers the pencil over the pad of paper. "You want a beer, Morgan?" He nods. "Steph, do you want the green or the black iced tea?"

"Green?" She raises her eyebrows. "How long have you been doing that?"

"Not long. We try to keep Grandma Charli from reading trendy restaurant magazines, but you know how she is." She winks. "It's good though. She doesn't serve anything here unless she'd eat or drink it her very own self."

"Then I guess I'll try the green."

"What about you, Abby? You want a beer, iced tea, a Coke?"

"She's too young for beer," Morgan jumps in.

I grimace at him. Just like with Steph's mom, I wasn't planning to order the beer, but having him tell me not to makes me
feel defiant. "Iced tea, I guess. Green."

Izzy disappears briefly and comes back with a plastic cup of
beer, and two white foam cups full of tea. "Do you want to hear
about the specials or are you ready to order?"

"The duck etouffee if you've got it," Morgan says.

"Sorry, we're out of the duck. Everybody's ordering duck
today. We've got squab and pheasant jambalaya, though. "

"Squab? I don't eat pigeon." Morgan scowls at the menu.
"How about the Creole rabbit?"

"Rabbit, okay." She makes a mark on the paper.

"What's wrong with eating pigeon? If you're going to eat a
bird anyway?" I feel strangely irritated by his reaction. Maybe
I'm just defensive. I imagine at some point my wolf is going to
eat a pigeon, or possibly already has.

"Pigeons are basically flying rats."

"Not our pigeons." Isobelle folds her arms and gives him a
look of mock sternness. "We don't just go on down to Bourbon
Street and pick up some random bird out of the gutter. You do
know that, right?"

"I know. I'm sorry, I just have a squick factor about
pigeons."

"Hey, you make fun of me for having a squick factor about
meat in general. Hypocrite."

"Abby, please." Steph frowns at me, then smiles at Izzy.
"Pulled pork salad, please."

"What about you, Abby? We have a vegetarian special today,
coconut curry rice and lentils. I think you'll like it."

"Is that Indian food? I like Indian food. Our neighbor is
teaching me to cook it." Our neighbor on Capitol Hill, the one
who lives with his husband right next door to the house we're
never going back to. Our neighbor who was always really nice to
me even though the first time I saw him with his husband I
called them sodomites because that's what Father Wisdom

taught me to call gay men, and maybe I'll never even see them again, and I feel gut-punched by that. That was my neighborhood. They were my neighbors. I felt at home there.

I guess this feeling is what they call being homesick, isn't it?

"I don't know that I'd call it Indian food, exactly. Grandma Charli gets a little experimental with the vegetarian options. It's not really a part of traditional New Orleans Creole cooking, so she tries to have fun."

"I acknowledge that Charlotte Quemper is a culinary genius," Morgan says. "How is she doing, by the way?"

"Her health is good. My mom and Uncle Roderic handle a lot of the day-to-day operation, but they still send her out to talk to the camera crews."

"All recovered from that Frere Jack's business?"

Izzy laughs. "We'll have those yellow T-shirts forever, but yes, the bottom line looks good. I'm hoping to find a way to still do the books when I'm in school. Grammy's a food genius, but a business needs math to stay profitable."

"Did you decide where you're going to go to school?" Steph asks. "You were thinking about going for the big guns at one point, right? MIT or something like that?"

Izzy sighs. "Yeah, maybe, if the scholarships had been better. But I couldn't make the cost-benefit work out. So right now I'm planning to go to the University of Washington in Seattle. Small world, right?"

"Seattle?" I feel a hard squeeze of envy. "You're going to the U-Dub?"

"That's the plan. You guys have been living out there, right? Is it really like they say?"

"That depends on what they say," Morgan says.

"Does it really rain all the time?"

"Just half the year."

"Mostly it's cloudy," I say. "It doesn't rain like it does here, where it pours and pours and the streets flood. Usually the rain is more of a sprinkle. You can walk around in it, no big deal. It's nice." My throat tightens, as if I'm about to cry. So we're not going back to Seattle, is that really such a tragedy? Seattle was the first place I ever felt at home, but couldn't I feel at home here, too, in time?

"Is Capitol Hill still the gay district?"

"Yes it is."

"It's also the district for million-dollar condos for programmers who work downtown," Morgan says. "Which is what's going to happen to our family home, apparently. It's getting turned into condos."

"Oh. You're selling the house?" Izzy can't conceal her disappointment as he nods. "Okay. Thanks for letting me know." She leaves the table.

Deena appears in the courtyard, smelling of fresh cigarette smoke, smiling hugely as she pulls up an empty chair and sits down. "Hey, have you guys seen the house that made an exact metal replica of their FEMA cross from Katrina and mounted it as a sculpture right above the spray paint? This town is awesome."

Steph smiles. "Glad you like it."

"Where's Edison?" I ask.

"Eh, the bros had some frat-related thing out near Tulane they wanted to go to and he went along."

"But Edison's not even in the frat, why did he go?"

"I don't know, they made it sound fun I guess. But I have a strict 'no frat parties' rule. I've seen too many movies and TV shows where you get sacrificed to dark gods that way." She looks around the courtyard, snaps a few pictures with her phone. "Does everything in New Orleans look like this? All the bricks and the wrought iron and the patina of genteel decay?"

"In the historic districts, sure," Steph says.

"What kind of trees are those? The enormous ones with the big gnarly trunks?"

"Live oaks," Morgan says.

Deena laughs. "As opposed to dead ones?"

"It's because they stay green in the winter."

Izzy shows up at our table, smiling at Deena. "Hey, new girl, can I get you something? I'm Isobelle, Izzy if you're nice." She pulls out one of her yellow hair pencils and a pad of paper.

"I'm Deena, pretty much under any circumstances. Although in junior high I did try to get people to call me Deen, as in James Dean? But that didn't stick."

"Izzy, Deena lives on Capitol Hill," I tell her. Then, to Deena, "Izzy is going to U-Dub in the fall."

"Well, that makes two of us," Deena says. "Maybe we can hang out there. I'll show you around Seattle."

"What? I didn't realize you graduated already." If Deena's not going back to Saint Sebastian either, maybe I'm not missing out as much as I feared.

Deena grins. "Yup. I'm eighteen and college-bound. This trip is my graduation and birthday present combined, which is pretty much how I managed to swing the money from my parents."

"Well, it's nice to meet you, Deen." Izzy takes Deena's hand for a shake that lingers just a little longer than average. They make eye contact, then blush and look away.

Wait, did I read that right?

"Are you originally from Seattle?" Izzy asks.

"I am. Born and raised on Capitol Hill. Are you originally from New Orleans?"

She nods. Her eyes never leave Deena's face. "Born and raised. Your first time here?"

"It is. I really like it so far." Deena smiles. Izzy smiles. Deena smiles wider. "I was thinking about ordering the oyster po-boy, is that good?"

"It's the best. If you like oysters."

"Oh, I love oysters. Oysters are my absolute favorite."

I don't think either of them intended to deliver that exchange as sexual innuendo, but once the words are out, both of them blush like crazy, go up in body temperature, dilate their pupils, and the smell of their sweat changes.

They are super into each other.

I feel a weird sense of pride, as if I'm personally responsible for this bit of matchmaking. I didn't know Deena was gay, but then, I never asked.

But right away my happiness is undermined by a nervous feeling as terrible words begin to mutter in my head, deep down in the poisoned swamp where Father Wisdom spent sixteen years pouring his toxic hatred into my brain. Wicked, sinful, demons, fornicators, sodomites, burning with unnatural lusts. The back of my head tingles unpleasantly just like it did in church, as if something evil is clawing at it, trying to get in.

I rub the back of my neck, try to make the feeling go away. I smile at Deena, at Izzy. I love my friends. I want them to be happy. My father is dead and rotting and his words should rot there with him.

"Do you want something to drink?" Izzy asks.

"You have to be twenty-one to drink in this town, right?"

"Officially, yes."

Big, sparkly grin. "What about unofficially?"

"I'll bring you an iced tea, how about that?" She winks.

"Sure. Sure." Deena watches intently as Izzy walks off, a dreamy look on her face, then snaps out of it. "Right. The trip. Abby. We're all in town until Thursday."

Right through the full moon. I figured as much.

"Do you have plans?" Steph asks.

"Well, I have a bunch of walking tours that I want to do. Ghost tours, murder tours, cemetery tours. And a swamp tour, have you ever done one of those? I want to see an alligator. And swamps of course. I love swamps."

"Sounds like you're covered," Steph says, with a small laugh. "My dad can get you tickets to Preservation Hall, if you're interested in seeing music. They have all-ages shows."

"Terrific. I was a bit worried that all the best venues would be twenty-one and over, like they are in Seattle. Reed is the only bro who's twenty-one."

"If you're interested in music, I can talk to my dad about the shows this week and figure out which ones are all ages."

Morgan says, "Whatever you do, don't go on any walking tour where the guide is dressed like a vampire."

Deena laughs. "Oh, but there was a time when that would have been exactly the tour I wanted to go on. In fact, I think if the rest of my Saint Sebastian posse was here, we'd all go on one for old time's sake. I know the vampire stuff is all fake. But they've also got this Cajun swamp monster I want to look out for, the rougarou?"

Steph and I exchange looks. "Interesting," Steph says.

"That's kind of like a werewolf, right?" I say, suppressing a slightly maniacal grin.

"Kind of a Wolf Man, kind of a Sasquatch, kind of a mystical figure. Just a really interesting bit of folklore."

"Yep. Very interesting." I can't suppress the giggles anymore and they come out as an awkward snort.

"You think I'm silly."

"No, that's not it. That's not why I'm laughing. It really is interesting. I'm serious. Go on."

"Okay. Did you know the blue dog, the famous one by the Cajun painter Rodrigue? That's a rougarou. I guess it's based on the stories he heard growing up. But the really interesting thing, to me, is the way in the earliest paintings the blue dog is more of a spooky, eerie figure, like a ghost dog. But eventually he becomes this friendly pop creature who hangs out with the Blues Brothers and everything. I'm not sure what to make of that, but I think it might be the artist coming to terms with his own death."

"Huh." Steph looks thoughtful for a moment. "Wow, okay. I guess I never would have seen it like that."

"Sorry." Deena laughs. "I don't mean to be morbid and creepy. It just comes naturally."

Steph says, "If you like the blue dog, you should check out the Rodrigue gallery on Royal Street. There's also a giant blue dog in the sculpture garden at City Park."

"Hey, thanks," Deena says. "You really know this town, don't you?"

Steph smiles, a little shyly. "Yeah. I like Seattle, but New Orleans is my home."

I sip my tea, covering up an unexpected emotional pang. New Orleans is her home, but I feel like Seattle is mine. Someday maybe that's going to drive us apart.

Izzy returns, to deliver iced tea that smells strongly of alcohol. "Here you go. Iced tea." She winks. A pencil and the pad come out again, and she writes a phone number and hands it off. "Give me a call if you're interested in having somebody take you around. Show you some things that aren't on the usual tourist beat."

"Thank you, that's so great." Another long, lingering look, another full-body blush for both of them, then Izzy takes off again. I glance at Steph and Morgan. Are they really missing this as completely as it seems? Should I say something?

No, I shouldn't say anything.

Izzy comes back to our table with a dish that I don't think any of us ordered. "Little lagniappe for y'all. Pork medallions with fig and goat cheese. And one fig stuffed with goat cheese and Marcona almond for Miss Abby." She sets down the platter.

"Did you make these?" Deena asks, holding up one of the pork medallions with a look of wonder. "They smell amazing."

"Well, I didn't come up with the recipe, that was Grammy. But I did assemble the ingredients, yes. I am a fully qualified ingredient-assembler."

Deena eats half of the pork medallion, chewing slowly. "My God, I think that's the best thing I ever had in my mouth."

"Just wait until your oysters get here," Izzy says.

Once again, I don't think either of them started out intending innuendo, but both of them blush.

By the end of the meal, we've gotten so many drinks and lagniappes that nobody can finish their entree. So we leave with leftovers in aluminum foil, worked into animal shapes by Izzy herself. It's hard to miss that she took extra time fashioning Deena's into a pretty fair representation of a snowy egret. Steph and I both have simple swans, while Morgan gets a pigeon and a wink.

As we step out onto the street, Deena checks her phone. "Ha! The frat thing was a bust. I knew it. Abby, you want to go back to the Royal Sonesta for cocktails?"

"Sure," I say.

"Cocktails?" Morgan looks appalled. "Abby isn't old enough for cocktails."

"Morgan," Steph says, with a sigh. "Abby is old enough to have cocktails in a hotel room with her friends. Her friends who I invited to come here."

"Abby," Morgan tries appealing to me. "You've never even had a drink before, do you really think you can handle cocktails?"

"I'll look after her, Mr. Marchande," Deena says. "Don't worry. I know all about pacing yourself and drinking water and standing up sometimes. I've coached a lot of people through their first cocktail party."

"Uh-huh." He's skeptical. "Don't think I didn't notice your iced tea was doctored."

My annoyance rises high enough that I snap. "Morgan. You're not my dad, okay? What the hell do you think you're trying to protect me from?"

He bristles in response, not backing down, turning to face me. "Drunk people make stupid decisions. Inexperienced drunk people make stupider decisions than that. Teenagers make stupider decisions than anybody. So a teenager drunk for the first time just might make the stupidest decision there's ever been. That's what I'm trying to protect you from. Not just stupid, but deadly stupid. Pay-for-it-the-rest-of-your-life stupid. Drowning-in-the-river stupid, STD stupid, pregnancy stupid."

We make eye contact. I feel a familiar surge of intensity, and know my eyes flash green. "Morgan. I can take care of myself."

He blinks, confused, relaxing slightly. "I know that. But—" he shakes his head, giving up, but not happy about it. "Well, I guess you'll do what you want whether I say it's okay or not."

Steph folds her arms, irritated. "And it's not your call anyway, *little* brother. I'm the one serving as Abby's guardian, and I find it offensive that you think you need to step in and play the strict parent in defiance of my own judgment."

Deena takes a deep breath and exhales hard, obviously uncomfortable. "So, how about those Saints, huh? Sportsball! Whooo!"

Steph, still annoyed, smiles tightly at me and Deena. "I'll give you two a ride back to the Quarter if you like." She glares at Morgan. "You can walk home."

"Saves me a Lyft," Deena says, cheerfully.

6

KREWE DE LOUPE

"I love this town. You can walk right out of your fancy-pants hotel lobby, and right into Red Hot Honeys for a Jaegermeister shot and a pole dance." Deena points from the elaborate front of the historic hotel to the neon signs on the other side of Bourbon Street. "Where else can you do that?"

"Nowhere I know of, that's for sure." Steph shakes her head with a smile.

"I like Seattle, but compared to New Orleans it seems kind of, you know, boring."

"Steph, did you coach her to do this? Talk up the attractions of New Orleans for the whole visit so I'll be glad we're staying here?"

"That depends. Is it working?"

"Not yet."

"Maybe after cocktails," Deena says.

Steph turns serious for a moment. "I don't expect you to account for your every move tonight, Abby. But there are two things I do expect you to do. Be back at the house by sunrise if not before. And keep your phone with you. Call me the instant you think something's getting out of hand, or if you need me for any reason. Don't worry about what I'm going to think. Don't worry about my mama, or my brother. Just call or text me if you need to. Okay? And whatever you do, don't let anybody drive drunk." She hands me a wad of twenty-dollar bills, at least a hundred dollars. Wow. "Take a taxi or something, or call me, but do not let drunk driving happen. Steal keys if you have to, I'm deadly serious about this."

I nod. "I will sit on people if necessary. Thank you, Steph." We hug, and then I'm out on the street.

Deena and I pass through a supremely elegant lobby of marble and chandeliers, up a grand staircase, into a suite that was hit by a hurricane made of cologne, T-shirts, and whiskey. As we enter, the bros frantically toss chaos from the sitting room into the bedroom and shut the bedroom door.

"Do you girls want a Manhattan?" One of the bros holds up a silver cocktail shaker. I hesitate for a moment, then nod and accept a martini glass full of mostly bourbon, with a super-sweet cherry. I'll sip it slowly. Morgan was being a bit ridiculous, but I also don't want to get drunk and out of control. Then again, I don't want to be bored all evening because I'm just sitting around watching other people get drunk. And, just like every other drug, I have no idea how alcohol is going to affect me.

I clink glasses with Deena and start sipping. The bourbon has a sharp, sweet flavor that travels straight up my nose. But I think I like it. I study the bros, trying to remember which name goes with which big chunk of guy. Cocktail Guy, I think that one is Ward. And Brad is Balls Guy. So I guess the third one is Other Guy. Reed? Was that his name? They've traded the cheesy T-shirts and shorts for button-up shirts and dark jeans.

Edison emerges from the bedroom similarly attired, but somehow making it look really stylish. "Hey there. Are you guys getting dressed up?"

"Dressed up why?" Deena sips her Manhattan warily.

"We're going to this Krewe de Loupe 'Halfway to Mardi Gras' party," Edison says, holding out tickets. Nice paper, silver-blue foil stamping. "The frat thing was kind of a bust, but one of the girls there had tickets to this event that she couldn't use. I guess it's a benefit for the ACLU so she bought extra."

"Krewe de Loupe, huh." I stare at the printed ticket with its wolf-howling-at-the-moon motif. This really is a werewolf town. I'm torn between feeling welcomed and not wanting to go at all in case the place is swarming with Varger.

"You girls need to get dressed up too," Ward says, looking us over critically.

"What? We have to get girl-ified? I don't do that," Deena says, in mock indignation.

"You don't have to get girl-ified, you just have to dress up." Edison shrugs. "Wear a tux like Marlene Dietrich if you want."

"It's much too hot for that. I guess I'll put on the outfit I was going to wear to Commander's Palace."

"The dress code isn't super strict. No shorts, no T-shirts, no distressed denim." Ward looks me over critically. "Sorry, that T-shirt dress probably isn't going to cut it."

"Wait, I have something." Edison disappears into the bedroom and re-emerges with a slip dress in a shiny black fabric that looks wet. He hands it to me. It still smells strongly of the woman who last wore it. She was drunk. And kind of horny, probably because she was talking to Edison.

"Ed, why do you have that?" Deena says.

"I don't know, some woman at the frat party just handed it to me." He holds it up in front of me. "I think it'll fit, though. Don't you?"

"Fine." I take the dress into the bathroom, take off the T-shirt dress, put on the slip dress. It is cooler, I'll give it that. The texture is a little weird. It has a built-in boob shelf, so I guess it's designed to be worn without a bra, which is good, since I'm not wearing a bra.

I turn this way and that. It looks pretty good, I guess. But the thin straps do nothing to hide the scars on my shoulder. Do I care, though? Everyone's going to see them soon, when the *Teen Mode* article comes out.

So. No. I don't care. Let other people deal with my scars tonight. I walk out, but almost lose my nerve when Balls Bro sees me and gapes. "Dude! What's wrong with your shoulder?"

"Brad, rude," Edison says.

"But—shit—"

"What, you don't recognize whip scars when you see them?" I snap my head to stare intently, making him squirm in a gratifying manner.

"I guess not." He takes a drink. "Who whipped you?"

"My father. Sometimes my older brothers, at my father's direction."

"Harsh, dude. That's fucked up."

"Yeah. It was." My estimation of him goes up a notch.

"She grew up in that cult," Edison says. "You remember, we watched it on CNN."

"What? That was you?" He goggles at me. "You were one of those New Harmony people? Like, the girls in those pink prairie dresses?"

"I was wearing a Disney princess bathrobe, but yeah. I'm not sure they showed me on TV."

"Briefly," Deena says. "Kinda in the background."

"Whoa." Brad slams the rest of his drink. "That is so weird, dude. You don't think about people you know in real life being on TV and famous and stuff."

"I'm not famous."

"Sure you are," Deena says, encouragingly. "You're the most famous person I know. It's not like I knew David Bowie. Hey, is this a costume party at all?"

"Costumes are encouraged." Edison points to the invitation. "It is a Mardi Gras party."

"Great. I'm giving myself Aladdin Sane makeup. Abby, you want? I'll make you Ziggy Stardust."

Deena paints my face while playing me songs by David Bowie, which are mostly new to me. My musical education comes from Steph's dad, so it leans heavily toward New

Orleans. I didn't grow up with music, not even hymns. Father Wisdom had some scriptural justification for why music was bad, because of course he did, but I think he just didn't like it. He always described it as a bunch of thumping and wailing.

I don't know what has to be wrong with a person in order for them to not like music. Maybe he had no soul. That would be ironic, if most people have a soul, but Wisdom didn't.

I leave the bathroom with pink contouring on my face and a bright gold circle on the middle of my forehead. I like the way it looks, but the feel of the makeup irritates me in a minor way, as if I've got dirt on myself. At some point in the evening I'm going to forget it's makeup and smear it all around.

Deena gives Edison eyeliner and mascara, although the other bros don't want it. I guess Edison's masculinity isn't as easily threatened as theirs, possibly because he's the one who can be at a frat party for an hour or so and leave with a dress, six party tickets, and a couple of phone numbers.

We're ready to leave, and I pause, awkward, not knowing where to put my phone and keys, self-conscious of my bare shoulders. Edison notices. "Abby, you want a jacket or something?"

"I don't know. It's kind of warm for a jacket, isn't it?"

"Wait, I've got it." Edison disappears into the other room and reappears with a men's cotton button-up shirt, in black. "Try this. You can put your phone in the pocket."

"Thanks." I'm trying to be cool, but it's hard. I can't stop inhaling my own shirt.

We leave the hotel and pile into a minivan taxi. "Remember, the plan is that I'm buying the drinks for the rest of you." Reed, the only bro who's twenty-one, reminds us.

"But is that actually going to work?" Deena asks.

"Sure it will," says Brad. "This is a party, not a bar. They don't care."

"You don't know that," Deena says.

"I have faith."

"If we can't drink, we'll just dance more," Edison says, cheerfully.

The van pulls over to drop us off on a dark residential street.

"What's going on?" Ward asks. "Is there a problem with the car?"

"This is the address you gave," the driver says.

"But there's nothing here. Just a thrift store that's closed for the night."

"This is the address," the driver repeats. "If you want me to take you somewhere else instead, the meter is running."

I crack the window and inhale deeply. "I smell alcohol and a food truck, the party's got to be around here somewhere."

"Okay." Ward looks dubious, but everyone piles out of the van.

"Follow me," I tell them. Deena and Edison start following without hesitation, but the bros hang back.

"It looks kinda dark back there. I don't want to get jumped in a New Orleans alley, brah," Brad says.

"Fine, you dudes can stay there all night," Edison says. "You want your tickets?" He holds them up and the foil stamping flashes in the street lights. An unseen door opens nearby, releasing a burst of laughter and music. The bros decide to catch up with us.

"Okay, but if I get mugged, it's your fault, dude," Brad tells Edison.

From the alley side, the building that looked like nothing but a darkened thrift store is revealed as a sprawling complex called The Healing Center, which is the location on our tickets. As we approach, I'm on the alert for other rougarou, but don't smell anyone. We display our tickets and pass muster on our finery, and enter. Although the canned music is playing loudly, the crowd seems sparse, as if the party hasn't really gotten started yet.

"I'm going to find the bar," Reed announces and takes off down the hallway. Brad and Ward follow.

"Well, I'm more interested in the live music," Edison says. "I think it's this way?" He takes off, and Deena follows him. They pause, glance behind at me. "Abby? What do you want, alcohol or music?"

I laugh. "I'm not sure yet. I'll find you guys later."

I decide to go exploring. I've never been to a party like this and it seems intriguing. The space has been divided into many rooms at different levels, each with a distinct theme of decor and music. I see giant wolf puppets, an interactive calendar of moon phases, a series of Little Red Riding Hood paintings. Maybe that's why no Varger are here, because this is way too cheesy for them.

As I circulate through the thumping, increasingly overheated atmosphere, I'm reminded of the first party I ever went to. Deena took me, the day after my wolf appeared. I didn't remember being the wolf the previous night, and had no idea why I felt so powerful, or why my sense of smell had gotten so intense.

But it was awesome. I can't deny that. It seemed like everything was going my way. I had friends, cool people like Deena who wanted to hang around me and take me to college parties. I had a boy, Deena's knockout buddy Edison, who seemed kinda interested in me. I punched a guy for grabbing my breast without asking, and everybody seemed to think I'd performed a great service, because the guy was a jerk who really needed to get punched. Before me, the future opened up with an infinity of possibilities.

Until the next full moon came. It found me at another party, the Howl. Edison tried to kiss me without warning and I freaked out. I even wanted him to kiss me, so I don't know why I reacted so badly. I guess he took me by surprise. Instinct took over and I flipped him onto his back, alienating both him and Deena in the same moment. Later, they seemed to forgive me, and they're here now, so I guess that part turned out okay. But the next morning I woke up in the middle of a partly eaten deer carcass, and remembered exactly how I got there.

Ever since then, I've had much bigger problems to worry about.

Finally, I run into a rougarou woman, not someone I've met before. She's in a small psychedelic room painted with wild glowing designs, illuminated with swirling colored lights. I smell marijuana, no surprise, and alcohol, but other things I can't identify. They leave a bitter, bruised impact on the sweat, similar to whatever Dennis was on.

The Varger woman is wearing a short, tight, silver dress over fishnet stockings and shiny platform boots. She looks like she's from outer space. She towers over me. She's drinking a big daiquiri and talking to a regular human guy who's sexually interested in her. When I enter the room, she turns her face toward me and wrinkles up her nose, then smiles. She approaches me, a little unsteady on the high boots.

"You. You're—*Abby*." She points and laughs, as if she thinks my identity is some big secret she guessed.

"I am." I don't ask how she knows. The Varger have all heard of me by now.

She ruffles her hair, which is long and dark and thick. "Your head's on fire." She leans in, draping an arm over my shoulder like we're old chums, and stage whispers, "I heard you said no to him. To Pere Claude."

I guess she's talking about my refusal to go out to Bayou Galene. "I haven't met Pere Claude. I said no to Vivienne."

"Oh, her." She laughs. "She's weird." She leans more of her weight on me. "I'm Babette. I thought you'd be taller."

"Really? Me too."

She laughs. "Hey you want a drink?" She hands me an open flask of alcohol which smells sweet and herbal, like Jaegermeister.

I sniff cautiously. "What's in this? Just alcohol?"

More giggles. "No. Not just alcohol. It's hard for us loupes to get messed up on just alcohol, you know?" She leans against me, swaying. "Maybe you don't know. You're still a child. But you're —" She toys with my hair for a moment, then leans in to whisper, "I heard you said no to Pere Claude."

She's drunk enough to go into repeat mode. I nod. "Yep."

"That's so—wow." She pauses for a long time, as if she's about to elaborate, and finally says "Wow" again.

The man she was talking to comes up to us.

"Hey, Babs, I wanted to check out the live music, you coming? Earlier you said you wanted to dance."

He hands her a drink. She takes the drink but stays draped around my shoulders. "I wasn't ditching you, Frank. I just wanted to talk to my friend here." She points at me. "She's my friend. My very good friend."

"Actually we just met."

Frank nods. "She's a friendly drunk."

"But you are my friend," she tells me. "Aren't you? You'd share your meat with me."

"Yes. Absolutely. Every last bit of it." She doesn't fight me while I drape her arm around Frank's shoulders instead, and doesn't fight him while he leads her out of the room. I follow them, interested in the possibility of live music.

Deena and Edison are watching from the balcony. The music is so loud they don't bother trying to talk, just smile at me briefly then go back to staring at the performer.

I can't place the musical genre immediately. Some kind of rap or hip-hop I guess, which isn't one of the kinds Steph's dad is really into. Whatever it is, it's heavy on rhythm and syncopation, low on melody. It seems to demand that I dance to it, so I give in to the logic of the rhythm and try to move along. I imitate the movements of the people around me, which seems to require dropping low in the knees, leaning forward, then sort of —popping the buttocks rhythmically? It fits the beat, anyway. After a moment of awkwardness I find the flow and it starts to be fun, until Deena jolts me out of it.

"Oh my God, where did you learn to twerk, Abby?" Deena is laughing, delighted.

"Uh, just now?"

"You're pretty good at it," Edison says, with a flash of lust that makes me too shy to keep moving.

"I was just getting into it. I mean. The music."

"Don't stop," Deena says.

"I lost the flow, sorry."

I listen for a while longer, but now that I'm out of the dancing headspace, the hard stuttering rhythms start to get on my nerves. It still demands that I dance, so if I'm not going to do that, I need to leave. With a smile at my friends, I go out wandering once more.

I circulate aimlessly for a while. It gets hot enough that I take off my borrowed shirt and carry it around like a weird purse. I use the restroom and wipe off the sweaty remains of Deena's makeup job. I run into Reed, drinking in a dark room full of mini-skirted go-go dancers.

"Hey, Abby, you want a drink?" He holds out a cup with what smells like bourbon.

"Sure." I gulp it back, hoping for a distraction. I feel over-heated and unsettled.

Reed nods approvingly. "I like a girl who can shoot her whiskey straight."

I grimace. "That's a thing? Girls who can and cannot shoot their whiskey straight?"

He misses the sarcasm and offers to get more drinks, which I accept. He comes back with two margaritas. "They're out of bourbon." He hands me a red plastic cup and clinks as if toast-ing, although our glasses, being plastic, don't actually make a clinking noise. He leans forward with a grin. "You're sort of weird, you know."

"I guess?"

"I can't figure out if you're hot or not."

"Is that something you need to figure out?"

He laughs, gestures, sloshes margarita onto his hand. "No, I mean, Edison is really into you, you know? And when I saw you, I was like, dude, you're nuts, she looks like a stray dog."

I grab his margarita and drain it. "For that you lose a drink."

"See that's what I mean. Like, that was hot, when you just took my drink like that and drank it. It's almost like, you're hot, but you don't look hot?"

"This is by far the stupidest conversation I've ever had in my life. And I grew up in a cult."

He laughs, pointing at me, as if for an audience. But nobody's watching. "That's it. That's exactly what I'm talking about." He pauses. "You wanna make out?"

I don't answer. I drain my own drink, stand up, and leave. Everything about this evening is starting to get on my nerves. I head back to the room with the live music, hoping it'll sound better to me again, or that another group will have started performing. I spot Edison. He's still in the balcony, he's—

He's—

Standing behind a young woman doing the same dance moves I was trying earlier, only without apparent self-consciousness.

His hands—

His hands are around her waist—

Resting on the upper curve of her butt.

Red bees sizzle along all my limbs and I want—

I want to rip them both apart—

And I could. I could do that.

Terrified by the thoughts in my own head, I run outside, and run, and keep on running.

7

CACHORROS

"Opal, I need your help." I leave a message on her phone. "I have feelings I don't know how to deal with."

Body and brain buzzing, bare feet pounding the pavement, where did my shoes go? I lost them. But tough calluses build up quickly. I'm used to being barefoot. At New Harmony, it was wasteful to shoe children who were still growing. Unless it was really cold, I didn't mind.

I run, and run, and run. I have no idea where I am, but I don't worry about finding my way back. I can always follow my own trail.

Finally, my phone buzzes with a text from Opal.

Where are you? I'll pick you up

I stop at the next intersection and answer.

St. Roche and Urquhart

I wait awkwardly, pacing around in nervous circles. In this slip dress and bare feet I probably look like I ran outside in my underwear. Do I look like a target, a victim? I put the overshirt back on, even though the smell of Edison's body reminds me of why I'm so upset. A car passes and I tense. I do not want to have to fight anybody. I'm worried I'd kill them.

The car slows down, light playing on my face. I crouch, concentrate, try to make my eyes flash. Don't mess with me, you will regret it.

It's Opal's car.

She pushes the passenger door open and grins at me. "I know that look, sister. What's wrong, did you kill somebody without meaning to?"

"Not yet." I close the door and sink into the seat.

"Oh, my, you're serious." She starts driving.

"Yeah. I have—I felt—" I stop, clear my throat. "I need help dealing with a sort of murderously intense jealous rage?"

She nods. "I know just the person to help you, my dear."

We start driving and she hands me her phone. "Find Jaime in my contacts and text him, please? Let him know we're coming?" She gives his name the Spanish pronunciation, "haim-e".

"Jaime? Who's that?"

"Our oldest brother and a key member of the Cachorros. He's been through everything you've been through. But he's not like Pere Claude. He'll help you without trying to force you to do something you don't want to do."

"And the Cachorros are?"

"Like the Varger, only centered around our father. Cachorros is Spanish for wolf cubs."

I find an entry for Jaime on her phone, and send a text.

> This is Abby. Opal and I on our way

> Love to meet you Abby. Say hi to Opal

"Jaime says hi." I try to give his name the right inflection.

"De nada," she says, with a smile. "He always says that. He's from near Los Angeles I think?"

I hand Opal her phone and notice she's changed clothes, into grungy denim coveralls that smell strongly of motor oil, gasoline and other harsh chemicals that I associate with cars.

"Were you fixing your car?"

She grins. "Yeah, doll, I'm a pretty good mechanic. That's how I keep this bucket running." She pats the dashboard affectionately.

"Is that what you do for work?"

She makes a sour face. "Not really. I can't deal with the sexism of most auto shops."

"Is it as bad as it is in the movies?"

"Oh, much worse. The movies always tone things down."

We drive through darkened streets to the edge of town, toward the ruined amusement park that's been abandoned since Katrina. She pulls off to the side of the road and stops. But I'm confused. "This is where the Cachorros are staying? Don't they have to stay out of New Orleans to avoid the Varger?"

"The Varger don't come this way much. You wouldn't want to walk here from downtown and leave a clear trail for them to follow, but in a car, they won't notice. And we won't be here long."

We get out of the car. Roller coaster skeletons are stark against a sky bright with the waxing moon, like dinosaur bones, the remains of some race of great and forgotten beasts. I follow Opal through a twisted fence and around overgrown greenery. We pass—wait—

"Is that a boar's head rotting on a pike?"

She laughs. "It is."

"Why is there a boar's head rotting on a pike?"

"The swamps around here are just full of wild boars. Big pests, to tell you the truth. But they make good eating for the den."

I stare at the head, hear the sawmill buzz of the flies, feel like I've wandered into one of my Father Wisdom's nightmare hellscapes. "Opal, 'good eating for a den of werewolves' explains why a boar is dead, but it does not explain why his head is rotting on a pike."

"It's a warning. For the cops, mostly. New Orleans cops all know about the wolves, or have heard rumors anyway, and would take this as a sign they're in wolf territory. They won't violate that just to bust people for smoking pot or taking pictures."

I follow her through a maze of deteriorating structures, covered with graffiti and reeking of mildew and neglect. There's something especially disquieting about the grinning faces and colorful banners all given over to decay. This is Wisdom's hell, where the pursuit of pleasure ends in rot and ruin.

I pick up the trail of my half siblings, and—that can't be—infected wolves? "Opal, how many Cachorros are there?"

"This den? Nine wolves."

"Infected too?"

"I think you mean bitten, sugar. The Cachorros find 'infected' to be a rather offensive term. We say 'bitten' and 'born.'"

So the answer is yes. I'm starting to get nervous.

The criss-crossing paths of family get stronger, until they converge on one of the abandoned buildings, a restaurant built in imitation of classic French Quarter architecture. It's covered in graffiti just like everything else, made of tattered banners and disintegrating wood. We push through, into a single large room.

"Welcome to the den," Opal says.

In a second, I take in the scene. A ruin turned into a camp-site, with cushions and blankets and a metal fire barrel currently unlit. Smells of marijuana, beer, and pig meat, overwhelmed by the thick peppery smell of three transforming brothers and one sister, plus the quieter sulfur odor of three infected women and two men. Bitten. Right. Not infected.

The Cachorros are shaggy and tattooed, like a Burning Man

camp. They seem mellow and artsy, lounging around on cushions, drinking beer, playing the guitar.

But the instant I enter the room, their demeanor changes. They snap to alertness, directing a sharp, focused attention right at me. I have a moment, not of fear exactly, but of apprehensive awareness, as I feel all that potential force aimed in my direction. Even a werewolf would not want to piss off a bunch of other werewolves.

"You must be Abby." One of my brothers, a man in a blue silk bathrobe, unfolds himself from his cushions to stand and stare down at me. He's about the same height as Dennis, which gives me a flash of déjà vu followed by a flash of annoyance. Men are always trying to look down on me. Sometimes I hate being short.

But the moment passes, and he's nothing like Dennis in any other respect. His expression is appraising but not dismissive. His body language is poised, strung with tension, but not aggressive. I see a family resemblance in the shape of his face, but he doesn't match my coloring, with his long dark hair that has no hint of red, and smooth brown skin without any freckles.

"I am Abby."

"And I'm Jaime."

I stare up at him. He stares down at me. I feel like I'm being challenged, even though he hasn't locked eyes with me the way Viv does. He's sizing me up. Judging me. It makes me feel annoyed, even before he asks, "Was your mother very short?"

"Not especially. I'm probably small because I grew up starving." I deliver this with a hint of a snarl.

He nods. "Protein deprivation can be bad for us. But your wolf is functional, yes?"

"Define functional."

"You transform completely at the full moon? You have her gifts about you at other times?"

"Except for the new moon, yes."

"The dark moon is dangerous for us all. Do you have the red moon and the black, like our father?"

"I'm not sure. Can you explain?"

"The black is despair when she is empty. The red is mania when she is full."

"Okay. Yeah. I'm pretty sure I have the black. I don't think I have the red." Unless I'm feeling it right now, and that's why I'm so restless and unsatisfied and also for a moment wanted to kill one of my best friends and a woman I don't even know because of something stupid like sexual jealousy.

"Do you have the trauma morph? I mean, do you transform only at the full moon, or also when badly injured?"

"Injured. Once when I got shot with silver and once when I got beaten severely. Is that not usual?"

Eyes bright, he shakes his head. "No, sister. Our father had it, and his father, but not me, or any of your siblings here. It's a special gift." He looks thoughtful. "The Varger, they must be ignorant of this gift, yes?"

"Well, I don't know. I, uh, I mean the wolf, she killed a man two days after the full moon, but maybe the Varger didn't know the exact timing."

He narrows his eyes. "Perhaps not. It sounds like you barely escaped."

My gut lurches and I think of Leon's diary, the agnara, the torture. "Escaped what?"

"The Varger do not allow an uncontrolled trauma morph to live in the world freely, among outsiders. Until you mastered it, they would keep you in Bayou Galene under a kind of house arrest. But learning that mastery is grueling. There's no way to do it other than causing extreme trauma again and again."

"What? They can't do that. Keep me there against my will? Do they chain us up? Have they developed some kind of metal we can't break?"

He laughs. "I don't know, sister, but I suspect not. What they do is offer a kind of choice. Stay with them under their terms, or run, and keep running forever. Our father chose to run."

"Does the training involve something called the agnara?"

"The agnara is a traditional weapon used for trauma morph training, yes. It's a small curved knife." He gestures, defining the shape. "Used in cooking and meat preparation, but also easily used against the self."

"So Leon was doing trauma morph training? That's why he writes about getting tortured in his diary?"

"If he mentioned the agnara? Yes." A pause. "Have you created any bitten wolves?"

I sigh, nodding. "I'm afraid so. I mentioned getting shot with silver? The guy who shot me was a bitten wolf, bitten by me. He was terrible. Violent. The Varger made it sound like the bitten are always totally out of control like that, but obviously it's not true." I gesture around the room, indicating the bitten wolves. They stand out among the born Cachorros, partly because they don't share our vague family resemblance, but also because some of them have that slightly deformed look, of features permanently shifted to the lupine.

Jaime nods toward one of the bitten and she comes forward, tall, dark, and completely rocking the lupine shift, with an assortment of piercings on her slightly pointed ears, and smoldering makeup around her eyes that makes their amber glow seem like a fashion choice. She rests herself on Jaime's shoulder in a possessive way, and I realize they smell strongly of each other. Lovers, probably. I feel nervous and overheated. I'm sure I'm blushing.

"My name is Reina," the woman says, through teeth longer and more pointed than they should be. "I was bitten by Jaime, and he helped me through the transformation. Three moons. That's what it took. And now I am one of the pack." They kiss, and I get even more embarrassed, although I'm happy for them, really.

"The first moon is the berserker moon," Jaime says. "This is the hardest. There is a madness on the new wolf, who often must be restrained physically and guarded closely by one of the born. The second moon is the hunting moon. The new wolf requires an experienced wolf to follow, but the presence of an entire pack might overwhelm her and cause a return of the berserking behavior. The third moon is the pack moon. The new wolf hunts with the entire pack for a night, and if she makes it through with no incident, she's one of them."

"That's why the Varger don't do it," Reina says, with a sneer. "They think they are too good to wait, so they kill us during the berserker moon."

"Every time?" My stomach lurches. I don't really trust Vivienne, but I still don't want to see her as a heartless slaughterer of the innocent.

"If you doubt us, talk to your Varger contacts. Ask them what happens to bitten wolves," Jaime says. His arm around Reina tightens protectively, as if shielding her from a vicious pack of Varger.

"I will. I will definitely ask them about that."

"Good." He looks thoughtful for a moment.

Then he flicks his head, and Reina goes to join the others. He makes steady eye contact with me, a challenge. "You say your wolf is with you now. Can you fight?"

"Of course I can fight."

"Do you want to fight me?"

I answer honestly. "I don't think so. You haven't really pissed me off yet."

He laughs. "You don't have to be angry to fight. Sometimes it's just a way of getting to know each other."

I feel put on the spot. If I don't fight him, I look like a dork. But if I do fight him, I already know I'm completely outclassed and he's going to pound me into the floor and I'll look like a dork in a completely different way.

"Fine, we fight." I try to focus on my annoyance, get in a fighting mood for—

He just dropped his robe, and has nothing on underneath it.

"What the hell?"

"We fight nude."

"You expect me to take off my clothes?"

He shrugs, frustratingly casual. "If you would prefer not to fight, you can leave them on."

"Fine. Okay. Your den, your rules." I exhale deeply and shimmy out of my clothes as quickly as possible. But I'm starting to regret this.

Behind me, one of my brothers gasps. I snap my head to look at him. "Your scars," he says, in answer to my stare. "They must be from your childhood, before the wolf."

"They are," I confirm.

"What kind of monster would do that to a child?" His anger flares, a smell I know on myself, as the pepper grows stronger and picks up a hint of ozone, like lightning about to strike.

"The kind of monster who raised me."

"It's time," Jaime says. We face each other. A little nod from him. I nod in return. Then he starts it.

8

JAIME

My brother tosses me across the room. Literally, across the whole room. It's kind of exciting for a few seconds, until I crash-land into some broken furniture and it hurts like hell and I feel like an idiot. This is not going to go well at all.

But the throw gets my adrenaline going, which masks the pain, and I rush back at him with an inelegant head-butt that sends him sprawling to the floor, which shakes with the impact. A cheer goes up. Are they rooting for me, then? Or just for a good fight?

A part of me is watching myself do this, taking notes. When I got Dennis on the ground, he stayed on the ground. Not true of my brother. He gets back to his feet quickly, grabs me and slams me into the wall as if I'm a big, awkward, baseball bat. The wall splinters and another cheer goes up. So, it's the destruction they like.

And why not? Everything in this place is destined for the wrecking ball. There's nothing to protect, nothing to preserve. We could reduce this whole building to rubble and be doing the world a favor.

I leap into the air so I can use momentum to send my

brother crashing into a pile of furniture, me on top of him. Our combined force shakes the floor again, the furniture clattering and splintering, the crowd cheering as they duck flying bits of chair.

Damn. That was—that was—

Satisfying. Like being thirsty and finally getting to drink as much cool water as you want. For half a second I just want to keep slamming the chairs around over and over and listen to them make a big racket. But my brother is coming at me again, flipping me into the air toward a snack counter that still smells faintly of hot dogs and mustard. But this time I'm ready for it and adjust myself so that I land in a crouch, ready to move again instantly.

Thinking of thirst has reminded me of the prayer closet, of Wisdom, of all the helpless anger I feel when I remember everything that happened, when I find myself wanting to destroy an enemy who's already gone. I can take it here. I can turn it into this. Violence and destruction, but in a safe environment where I don't have to hold anything back. This landscape is already ruined. There's nothing I can do to hurt my wolf brother in any serious way. I can pick him up and throw him across the room, where he lands on a grill hard enough to tear it from the wall, and he's fine. He can topple a refrigerator onto me and I'm fine. We can take turns slamming each other into a counter until the counter disintegrates, and we're fine, everything's fine, nothing matters.

We slam, leap, pound, wreck and occasionally snarl for what seems like hours, and I feel like I could do this all night, like I've been waiting my whole life to do this. That wall there, it's the prayer closet—I drive my brother's head through it and now it's gone. I think about Wisdom, with his deep voice, his cold certainty, his lack of human feeling. I think about how many times I wanted to pick him up and throw him into the swamp and never see him again. I felt wicked for such thoughts, at the time. Guilty. I let him punish me. But now I can pick up my brother, and throw him into a pile of chairs, and imagine every time that I'm throwing Wisdom into the swamp. I'm saving my mother. I'm saving my sister. I'm saving everybody.

Jaime stops. On his back in the pile of chairs, reduced now to a heap of undifferentiated rubble, he doesn't get up again right away. I wait, but can already feel the adrenaline draining away, bruises and strains making themselves felt. But they'll heal so quickly, I'm not worried.

"That was fun, but I'm getting thirsty," Jaime says.

That ends it. There is much cheering and clapping us on the back, while people bring our clothes and somebody offers me beer from a keg. I drink it, because I'm thirsty, even though beer smells like rotten grass to me. It tastes a little better than that. I meet, officially, my other siblings: Arden, Seth, and Tammy. Andrea, bitten, is Seth's ex-girlfriend, but now she's dating Seamus, one of the bitten men. He's Tammy's ex. Gabrielle, bitten, is currently dating Seth, and Arden is dating Henry, a bitten man. Tammy isn't currently dating anyone, I don't think. It all seems a little confusing. Did my siblings start dating bitten wolves because then they wouldn't have to worry about infecting them? Or was it the other way around? Did they infect their lovers on purpose? But I feel like it would be rude to ask that, so I ask a different question.

"Are you all the Cachorros there are? Or are there more elsewhere?"

"No, this den is not the full extent of the Cachorros. We have sisters and brothers scattered all over."

"All over? How many kids are we talking about?"

"Fifteen, counting you and Opal."

"Fifteen? Good Lord, he's worse than Father Wisdom."

Jaime laughs. "Bad? Just because he had many children? How is that evil?"

"I just don't trust men who try to fill the world with their own personal offspring." I shrug, change the subject. "How have you all avoided the Varger for so long?"

"Easy enough. For the older children, Leon prepared us for what was going to happen. For the younger children, the older children prepared them. The Varger watch the news for certain events that signal a newly awakened wolf. But if you know what to expect, if you have mentors, those events are rare."

"Makes sense, I guess. Wait, that means Leon must have kept in contact with your mothers. Do you have a list of siblings and their contact information?"

"Did. We did have such a list. But you would have been the last name on it. I'm sorry. If we had known about you earlier, maybe we could have helped you."

Oh, the thought of that. The thought of my nice werewolf brother coming to bust me out of New Harmony—to bust up the cult long before—before all the horror—it's too painful to think about.

He sits down, lounging back into the cushions, which seems to be a signal of some kind. The barrel flames up. Henry starts playing the guitar. The sense of laughter and merriment increases. Jaime pats the cushions next to him, indicating I should sit down. I do, as the padding exhales memories of dust and incense and spilled beer and sex. He tries to hand me a jeweled flask. "Something stronger than beer?"

I sniff the flask, smell herbs and alcohol. "What's in it?"

"A soothing compound. Very traditional. The olvhetnar, the wolf-berserkers of old, they used to take it to calm down after their battles." He takes a sip himself. "It dulls the pain during healing and helps quiet the mind."

"Yeah, but what's in it?"

"Opium, among other things." He sees my look and shakes his head, with a smile. "What are you worried about? Addiction? That won't happen to you."

"No? Werewolves don't get addicted to things?"

"Not drugs." He pauses, thoughtfully. "Not opiates, anyway."

"I'll pass." I hold up my second cup of beer. "One vice at a time."

"It's your pain. Do you need anything pushed back into place before it finishes healing?"

"Well—I think I might have broken or dislocated something in my shoulder here." I show him. He nods, and pushes things around a little bit until, with a jolt and a stab, they go back to the right place.

"Dislocation," he says, nodding. "If you work to land on your muscles instead of your bones, that should help keep that from happening." He smirks and punches me in the arm, lightly. "Of course, you need a little more muscle before that's going to work very well."

"Hey, what did I say about growing up starved?" But we're just teasing each other now. I'm no longer genuinely annoyed with him.

He turns serious. "You're not trained. You don't know how to fight. But you do have a lot of fight in you. A lot of rage."

"I guess you could say that." I think back, about all the things that went through my head during the fight. Rage, as a word, hardly seems adequate to describe it. "But that's also what I wanted to talk to you about. I came out here because earlier tonight, I had a moment of jealousy so strong that I seriously thought about ripping both of them apart, the guy I like and the woman he was flirting with. But I didn't want to feel that way. My father—Father Wisdom I mean—my rage against him feels righteous, you know? He was evil. He did evil. He needed to be stopped. I should have stopped him sooner. But my friend, he didn't deserve it. My jealousy was wrong. I know that. But I felt it anyway. How do I—" I stop, realize I'm starting to cry a little, and my voice trembles. "How do I deal with that? We're not even dating in any official way and I wanted to kill him because he was flirting with somebody else."

Jaime folds me into his arms and it's probably the closest I'll ever come to being held by my real father. Maybe it's better.

Jaime seems like a good person, not a monster at all. "Sister, you feel what you feel. But you can feel something without acting on it. You said it yourself in the article. You were raised by Father Wisdom to think your emotions themselves were wicked, just having them. But no feeling is wicked until you act on it."

"I guess not. But—" I frown, pull away from his embrace. "What was that you said about the article?"

"The *Teen Mode* article." He's smiling, but his eyes hold a hint of a frown. He doesn't know why I'm suddenly upset. "That's how we knew to look for you here in New Orleans."

"But that's—the article—it's not coming out until September."

He laughs. "Is that what's bothering you? Most periodicals are available well before their official release date. Just like the Varger, we watch the news carefully. The New Harmony coverage of a month ago piqued our interest, but didn't focus much on you. The *Teen Mode* article left us almost certain you were one of us."

"So. Wait." A memory of a purple bra flashes in my mind. "That means Opal was trying to get my attention? On purpose?"

"She was living in New Orleans already." He studies my face, his frown deepening. "I don't understand why this seems to be upsetting you so much. Surely when you gave the interview, you knew other people would read it? And you must have known some of those people would be your wolf kin?"

I stand up, start pacing around. Briefly the aftermath of the fight made me tired and peaceful, but now I'm all stressed out again. "No, I didn't know that! Until today I didn't know I had any wolf kin beyond the Varger. But that's not what's bothering me. It's Opal. She left a bra of hers in a trash can, and that's what led me to her. Now I know she left it on purpose for me to find."

"Is that so ominous? If you were who we thought, you'd pick

up on it, and find her. If you weren't, nothing would happen, no harm done."

"That's not why I'm upset! She lied to me about it. She made it sound like an accident. I mean, she didn't mention you at all."

"She was protecting us. Because of the Varger presence in New Orleans we have to be cautious." He stands up and gathers me into a hug. I fight it for a second, then relax. "I know you aren't inclined to trust people. But you can trust me."

I sigh, but sink deeper into the hug. He's right. I'm not inclined to trust people. I probably said exactly those words right there in the article. I do trust Jaime though, almost in spite of myself. Maybe you really can get to know somebody by fighting them. I roll my shoulders, feeling the tingle as the flesh heals. "Be honest, Jaime. Rage or not, if we had been fighting to win, you would have kicked my ass, right?"

He laughs. "Does that matter to you?"

"Maybe a little bit."

"All right. The answer is yes, probably, but I kick the ass of most people I fight with. That includes other wolves, my size, who are trained in this. You have nothing to be ashamed of. I really did give up because I was getting tired and thirsty. You earned that."

"Thank you." I pause, think about how to ask the other thing on my mind. "Jaime, did you know Leon well? Did he raise you when you were young?"

"When I was young? Yes. He tried to be a good father to me and my little sister."

"He tried. But was he a good father?"

"He seemed that way to me." Jaime shrugs.

"Would your sister agree?"

"My sister? I think so. It's my mother who—" He shakes his head. "I don't need to go into all that right now. Leon would be the first person to tell you that he was a better father than a lover."

"Was he abusive? Did he ever rape anyone?"

Jaime reacts with shock. "No. He would never do that."

"Never? How can you be so sure?"

"Because of what he taught me. He taught me such things are wrong." His expression is firm, and I'm pretty sure he believes what he's saying. But he also told me that his mother saw a different side of Leon than he did.

"Would you say—" My phone buzzes, and I jump. I'd forgotten phones exist. But mine is still right where I left it in the breast pocket of the borrowed shirt. "Excuse me." I pull away from Jaime and look at my phone. It's only been a couple of hours since I left the Krewe de Loupe party. It's about three in the morning and the others are texting that things are shutting down and where am I? I text the group.

> Got lost sorry. I'm ok. What's up?

Deena responds.

> We're going to cafe du monde it's 24 hours

> Ok. Meet you there

I stand up, look around for Opal, find her in the corner, smelling freshly of motor oil and sharing a video of the fight with some of the Cachorros.

"Oh, my, Miss Abby, that was glorious," Opal gushes at me. "I've seen the wolves fight before, of course, but I have never seen anything quite like that. He's so much bigger than you that it keeps looking like you're about to get crushed, and then when you hold your own, it's beyond thrilling. You're so creative, and fearless, and, oh my goodness, so full of rage. Of course, you're both naked, so I can't post this anywhere."

I'm horrified. "What? How could you think of posting it?"

She laughs. "Oh, sugar, don't worry, no, I was just making a little joke. We couldn't possibly post this sort of thing online for all the world to see, now, don't be ridiculous."

"Well. Good." I'm a little mad at her, but I need her to drive the car back to the French Quarter, so I try to dial it back. "Are you ready to go? I'm supposed to meet my friends at Cafe Du Monde."

"Oh, sure." She glances at Andrea. "I think I got it, but let me know if your bike starts making that noise again."

Andrea nods. "Will do. Thanks."

"One thing before you leave." Reina takes Opal's phone and shows it to me with a serious look. "You have this one move right here, see, where you lower yourself like a little bull to ram your head into your opponent's abdomen? You take too long with it. We call that telegraphing. An opponent would have the time to see what you were doing and could get you into a lock, like this."

She leans over me, demonstrates. Yes, I am locked. But it doesn't last long. I flip her around easily to the floor. In fact, I seem to be much stronger than she is, which surprises me. It clearly surprises her, too. She hops back to her feet and gives Jaime, who is watching us, a quizzical look. He comes over, laughing, to kiss the top of her head. "I told you the born are stronger, love. But you should have known that already. You watched her fight me."

She butts her head into his shoulder. "I did. I assumed you were going easy on her."

He gives a huge joyous laugh, scoops her up into his arms and spins her around. "You think that because I go easy on you."

"Don't," she says, and it comes out in a breathless growl and a rush of desire sweat. She nibbles on his neck with her unnatural teeth. "Don't you dare go easy on me."

I blow out my breath, nervous and hot. I'm extremely relieved when he carries her out of the room off—somewhere.

"Okay, Opal, come on, let's get out of here before the howling starts," I say, my voice tight and shrill.

Opal laughs at me. "It's den life, hon, you get used to it."

"Can we please just leave?" I spit it out more aggressively than I meant to. The supercharged sexual atmosphere is upsetting me again.

No, it's okay. Breathe. I have feelings. I can just let them go.

Just.

Let.

Go.

"So what did you think?" Opal asks me, when we're back in the car.

"About Jaime? I liked him. Reina too. I want them to be my werewolf mom and dad." I take a deep breath. "But why didn't you tell me that you were out there actively looking for me? That the bra was bait? That you'd already read the *Teen Mode* article?"

She smiles brightly. "Sugar, I think you know. What did I tell you about the Varger?"

"You couldn't mention the article because of the Varger?"

She sighs heavily, rolling her eyes. "I couldn't mention the Cachorros because of the Varger. We had to feel you out a bit first. We didn't know how deep you were in with Pere Claude and his people."

"Huh. I guess that makes sense."

"Of course it makes sense. You know how pushy they are. What do you think they'd do if they knew about the Cachorros? About the bitten wolves?"

"I guess I don't know."

"You do know. They'd kill the bitten and maybe the born Cachorros as well."

"But why would they do that? The bitten are already fully integrated and the born Cachorros are Pere Claude's grandchildren."

"They're ruthless, sugar. You know that. You told me you don't trust them."

I feel suspicious of Opal again. "Yeah, but one of the reasons I don't trust the Varger is because I can tell they haven't been totally honest with me. And now I find out that you haven't been totally honest with me either."

"We're werewolves, sugar, a little deception comes baked right into the pie."

We. We are werewolves. She doesn't have a wolf, but she thinks of herself as one of us. I don't know if that's important. It seems briefly that it might be, but maybe I'm too tired to figure out why. I fold my arms, sink into the seat, don't say anything. Apparently I'm correct not to trust anybody, because nobody can be trusted.

"Ah, come on now, don't you pout. What's getting you so riled? It can't really be because I didn't tell you about a little magazine, now? Maybe you got that red moon after all."

My gut clenches. I probably need to include myself on the list of people who can't be trusted. "I guess."

"Well, don't you worry about it too much. If you do have the red moon, you did just the right thing by going out there to have that fight with Jaime. What you need is more safe outlets for your violent and predatory instincts."

I don't say anything, just fold myself tighter around the knot in my stomach.

Opal keeps talking. "You want to know what I think, if you do want to talk about that article now, I read that thing and I thought, why, this is a wolf who was taught to pretend to be a sheep by that messed-up religion her father had. You were taught it's bad to be a wolf. But it's not. You can't be bad just being what you are. The wolf and the sheep need each other."

I say nothing. I've had these same thoughts myself, trying to tell myself it's okay, I'm not a monster, not the ravening Beast of Wisdom's ranting sermons. But hearing my thoughts from Opal makes them sound smarmy and self-serving. Of course, the wolf would tell the sheep they need each other, but what does the sheep think?

"What you need to do is, you need to let yourself enjoy being what you are. I know you did while you and Jaime were fighting each other, didn't you? Didn't you enjoy that? It certainly looked like you did."

"I guess."

"See, there now. Just think about that. Enjoy knowing that you could eat the faces of your enemies any time you wanted. Then enjoy choosing not to."

9

WAKING UP NAKED

Opal lends me some flip-flop shoes, and decides to join us at Cafe Du Monde. We find everybody clustered around a small table in the inside portion. Deena and Edison are still perky but the bros are drooping and ready to pass out. Reed looks up when I enter and rouses enough to give me a vague drunken smile. "Hey. Abby." If he remembers awkwardly asking me to make out after telling me I'm not so hot, he shows no sign.

"Who's your friend?" Deena asks.

"Sister. Half sister. Opal, this is Deena and Edison. And the bros."

"Pleased to meet y'all," Opal says, shaking hands with Deena and Edison. The bros aren't really up to shaking hands right now. Her eyes linger on Edison's face longer than I like.

No, no, no. No jealousy. Not against my own sister. I am not going down that road.

"Where did you go, anyway? Were you at the party that whole time?" Deena asks.

"No, I, got kinda claustrophobic, so I went out wandering with Opal."

Opal squeezes my arm enthusiastically. "We just met. It's so exciting to find out I have a sister. Do the two of you have any siblings?"

"I have a big brother and a little brother, and Edison has two big brothers and a little sister. They're pretty cool. The younger ones are starting to age out of that screeching hellion stage. Now they're into making me play the villain in their home movies and stuff. Turns out, everything I know about sword fighting I learned from the Star Wars movies."

Edison nods. "She does the noises and everything."

They exchange glances, then they're on their feet, having a slow-motion light saber battle, complete with sound effects.

Opal gives me an amused look. "And these nerds are your friends, hon?"

I nod, with pride. "These nerds are my friends."

Coffee and sugar consumed, Deena and Edison shepherd the bros back to the hotel room, while Opal drives me to the house.

"Have you thought about what you're gonna do for the full moon?" she asks. "It's already the day before, my goodness."

"I don't know. Go camping and hope for the best, I guess. That's what I did last time."

"Well, you might want to contact Jaime and find out what the Cachorros are doing. Here, let me give you his number." She types it into my phone and hands the phone to me.

"Thanks." I get out of the car. It feels like weeks have passed since I last walked up this porch, but the sky is still dark.

Inside, I find Steph on the couch, asleep, Terry at her breast, also asleep, as if they both nodded off in the middle of nursing. They look very peaceful together, like a classic Madonna and child painting. Tattooed Madonna, I think, and sit down to hug them both. "Hey. You weren't waiting up for me, were you?"

Steph wakes enough to give me a sleepy look. "You? Nah, it was Himself here who got me up. Did you have fun with your friends tonight?" She yawns. "What time is it, anyway?"

"About four in the morning." I check my phone. "Okay, closer to five now. When does the sun come up?"

She yawns again. "Too early. I'm going to put us both to bed for real." She smiles. "You did okay, though, right? Nobody drove drunk?"

"No. No, they didn't."

"Good for you."

She leaves me alone and I'm sinking, too tired to bother going upstairs to the loft. Instead, I open my father's diary to read a little more while falling asleep here on the couch.

I flip through, scanning for the words "red moon," and find a passage:

> The pull of the red moon is getting stronger, and it fills me with a savage joy, so powerful I can barely sit still enough to write these words. My father tells me to resist, to control, to hold back. But he doesn't know what it is to feel these things the way I do. His wolf is already tamed, like a dog, to do the bidding of his human master. But my wolf is wild still. I don't want to tame him. It feels wrong, like a violation of the very soul of what we are.

And then, a few entries later:

> Each black moon regrets the last red moon's excess.

It's written out in large, fancy letters, surrounded by doodles and flourishes, almost as if he intended to turn it into a T-shirt. The doodles include a fairly detailed drawing of a wolf, jaws open and dripping blood. Not bad, I think. My father could draw. I guess that's one thing I didn't inherit from him. If I have any artistic talent, it has yet to reveal itself.

There are other references to the red moon, but even here, in his diary, he doesn't go into details. He alludes to having done terrible things that he regrets, but he doesn't mention what those

things were. Did he not want to face them, even to himself? Or
did he not trust the secrecy of this diary?

My eye is caught by an entry with no date, just a title:
Berserkers & Olvhetnar & Varger Origins

Jaime mentioned them, didn't he? The olvhetnar? I read:

Studied everything in the books about the warriors, but so
many mysteries remain. Were there really bear-shifters, or was
Berserker just a nickname for Olvhetnar of burly stature like
my father? What was in the sacred drink? Amanita Muscaria
and Devil's Trumpet are mentioned by the names we use
today, but what is Mother's Howl and Odin's Breath? The
story as we tell it is folklore, not history, and full of holes. This
is as I heard it from my father:

Before the exile, in the northlands, there were bear-shifters
and wolf-shifters. They were honored for their bravery and
fierceness, and for many years were the most honored of all
the people of the north.

In time there arose the cult of the Berserkers and the
Olvhetnar, young men of these shifter clans who used drugs
and prayer to derange themselves into a mania for battle so
pure and strong that nothing could stop them, no pain or
weakness or fear. Cut off his foot and a Berserker would kill
you while standing on the bloody stump.

As honored as all the shifters were, the Berserkers and
Olvhetnar were honored even more. In battle they brought
victory upon victory. Just the rumor of them could make an
army scatter. There were families that specialized, producing
Berserkers and Olvhetnar for many generations.

But this power and glory was their undoing, for it made
them arrogant and lazy. They embraced a certain Berserker
Way, swaggering and hostile and aggressive, starting fights,
taking what did not belong to them, ignoring the voices of
civilized authority.

One day, an Olvhetnar took liberties with the daughter of

the King. Our own people passed judgment, Rending him, but still the tide began to rage against us.

At the new moon, mobs drove us from our homes and seized our property. Some of our people wanted to stay and fight, but others came here to the New World, to the lands that are part of Canada today. We took the name Varger then, for it means stranger, exile, outlaw. For many generations we were there, until, once more, we were driven from our home, along with the Acadians, in the diaspora they call Le Grand Derangement. This is when we became also the Rougarou, the Acadian name for us that comes from the French Loup-Garou, meaning Wolf-Man.

We attempted colonies in places other than southern Louisiana, but they ended badly. The world was changing, becoming more crowded, more connected, more tamed. Less tolerant of wilderness and wild things. People began to claim ownership of every scrap of land, seeking to make a profit off it.

Nobody hates the Wolf quite so much as the Shepherd.

So today we stay in our own territory, this land which is ours, purchased long ago according to the laws of this nation. And here we stay, and here we keep our secrets.

Makes a neat story, no? But the timeline isn't quite right. Fails to explain why Wolves are only here, none left in the Norselands. Why are there no Pere diaries dated before the exile? Why is Datura, a North American plant, listed as a key Berserker ingredient? Etc.

Theory: we are the descendants of Norsemen exiled for other reasons, and the Wolf entered our bloodline only once we arrived in North America.

Plan: I must go back to the Acadian territories where we first lived, and see if there are any wolf or other shifters to be found.

I close the book, head spinning, eyes drooping. So much to

wonder about. Where do we really come from? What is our true nature? Leon knew so many secrets.

I replay the fight with Jaime in my mind, and it morphs and changes. Sometimes we're fighting in wolf form, sometimes human, sometimes only one of us is a wolf.

I hear the music of a distant brass band, like a siren calling, pied piper, leading me into hell. I begin to walk toward a ruined, half-drowned city, silhouetted against a sky bright with a nearly full moon.

The wolf walks beside me, a red-furred companion, but as she nuzzles my hand, I realize, she's not my wolf. She belongs to my grandmother. She runs up ahead of me, into the broken city that smells like DANGER and I try to scream, to warn her what's to come, but my throat won't make any noise, I can't howl, so I run and run but I've lost her trail already, we're swept up in a big parade, a parade for Mardi Gras.

Now I'm in the parade, walking through town. I'm naked. I don't remember choosing to be naked. This is the kind of parade where you're supposed to not be naked, and I start to look around for clothes I could put on, for somewhere to hide.

I crouch, covering myself, and now I'm down on all fours, in the mud. My head hurts a lot. I think somebody hit me. I don't remember who it was. Maybe Father Wisdom? My teeth feel like they're going to fall out. I loosen them with my tongue.

One by one, every tooth tumbles out of my mouth to lie on the ground in front of me. I thought I was in human form, but my lost teeth are wolf fangs, pointed and white and long as little daggers. But of course my fingers are paws now. When did I change shape? I don't remember it. Usually I notice. I walk forward, limping on an injured paw.

My friends are around here somewhere. Go ahead and eat them, my father tells me. Father Wisdom tells me this. Father Wisdom tells me, it's written down in the book. A wolf will come to eat the world at the end of time.

No, we say. Eat YOU.

We flip him over, tear out his throat, drink his blood. We chew into the soft cavity of his intestines and organ meats. He's alive while we do this, screaming in fear and pain. This is hell, and that's how we do it here.

But we made a mistake. I made a mistake. The body beneath me belongs to Edison.

I scream, but I'm inside the wolf and she doesn't listen. The wolf knows her destiny now, and tastes it with a powerful delicious rightness.

We chase down another victim, Deena. And another, Steph's mom. Then her dad. Then her brother.

The wolf crushes cities when she runs through them, and her howl shakes the earth. Her hunger will never be sated. Everything consumed, every steaming slobbering bite, disappears into infinite darkness inside her.

I shiver and quake and sob but also feel her savage joy in the purity of slaughter and destruction.

We will devour everything down to the last, until we eat Steph, then finally the baby. Then the world will end, in fire and flood and darkness…

I WAKE UP.

The nightmare shudders across my mind, fading with the return of consciousness, the return of sunlight.

Sunlight. Wait.

I'm outside.

I'm naked.

It's first thing in the morning.

I'm in the courtyard at CharliQ's, near one of the smokers, where a duck smolders over fragrant coals.

Behind me, I hear someone emerge from the building—Isobelle. I can smell that she's got a firearm of some kind.

"You know, you're not the first naked white girl I ever found here early in the morning," she says, her voice casual. "But I think you're probably the first one who was sober."

I inhale deeply, for any sign of blood or death or injury. Did I go to wolf form, based on the trauma of the nightmare, or only dream that I did? I don't seem to have killed any pigeons or other urban wildlife. There's no way I would miss the smell of that. But why am I here? Was it the smell of the meat in the smokers that drew me in my sleep? Or was it the scent trail of the other rougarou? "Isobelle? I think I—I must have sleep-walked over here. I'm sorry."

"Just a second, let me get you something to wear." A moment later, she comes back without the gun, but with a bright yellow T-shirt, which she tosses toward me. It's XXL, long enough to be a short dress on me. It seems to be for a place called Frere Jack's, which apparently sells hamburgers. The design of the logo isn't very attractive, especially compared to the current CharliQ's sign. "So, Abby, do you sleepwalk a lot?"

"It's my first time." Now that I'm dressed, I sniff around the courtyard a little more, trying to make it look casual, like I'm just stretching out. No sign of blood, no injured animals. It must have been a dream. I didn't really become the wolf. It's probably not possible, not from emotional trauma only.

"You want to come inside for coffee?" She beckons, leads me through to the deli portion of the restaurant. "I've been working the night shift this summer since I graduated high school. The gun is my dad's idea."

"You ever use it?"

"Well, I scared away a couple of homeless people who were thinking about sleeping here. But I probably could have done that with a frozen chicken." She grins. "Good thing too, because I have no real idea how to use this thing. Your uncle Morgan, he's handy with a gun, right? You think he'd teach me?"

"Without a doubt." I think back to the time when he brought me out to the gun range to celebrate my sixteenth birthday. "He lives to teach people how to use a gun properly."

A carafe is sitting on the burner full of coffee already mixed with milk. She pours me a mug, and refills her own, which is black with a red CharliQ's logo. She sits down at a tiny table and glances at her laptop, types a few things. "Sorry, just chatting with some of the other hackers." She closes her laptop, then gestures for me to sit down across from her.

I sit down and sip my cafe au lait. "Hackers? That's a computer thing, right?"

She laughs. "Yes, it's a computer thing."

"You're good with that kind of stuff, aren't you?"

"I am." She sips her coffee. "That's part of why Seattle was on my list of schools."

"Does that mean you know how to do algebra?"

"I do. Why, do you need help with algebra?"

"At some point I will." I sigh, sip my own coffee. "At the cult I learned how to be very good at what turns out to be, I guess, about the level of math skills a ten-year-old should have? Arithmetic. Nowhere near algebra. I took a pre-algebra class last spring, but I don't think I was really getting it."

"You might need a tutor."

"I think so. Is that something you're good at? Math tutoring?"

"I am. Too bad you're not going back to Seattle."

"Yeah. Too bad."

We both sit in slightly depressed silence for a moment, then she brightens. "Your friend Deena. Are you two very close? Have you known each other a long time?"

"A few months, I guess. So, not too long. But she likes you, if that was your next question. You should totally ask her out."

She looks down at the table, trying to suppress a big, embarrassed smile. "Was it really that obvious?"

"To me. And to her, I think. But Morgan didn't seem to notice. Still not sure about Steph."

She sighs, nodding. "Good. I do want to be a little discreet while I'm still here in town. I haven't told Grandma Charli yet, to be honest."

"Haven't told me what?"

And there she is, Charlotte Quemper, in the doorway. She looks an awful lot like an older version of Izzy, including the thick-framed eyeglasses. But her hair is short and gray.

"Jesus, Grammy, how do you do that?"

"The Lord is with me at all times," she says, with a wink. "So, you're that girl Abnegation staying with the Marchandes up there?" She gives me an appraising look.

"Yes. People call me Abby."

"And I'm Ms. Charlotte Quemper, known as Charli, and pleased to meet you." She shakes my hand. "You one of them rougs?"

"I—what?" The floor feels like it's dropping out from under me. "You mean—you don't mean the rougarou?"

"Of course that's what I mean." She makes eye contact, hard, dominating. This is her territory, so I'm not going to fight her on it. I blink. I look away. She grunts softly in satisfaction. "That's right. You know who's boss here. You coming in on the full moon with the rest of your people?"

"Grammy, please." Izzy laughs. "Abby isn't a tourist, you don't have to tell her those goofy New Orleans monster stories."

She shrugs, and adjusts her glasses in a gesture that looks just like her granddaughter. "Izzy, you're smart enough, you're going to figure it out sometime. More things in heaven and earth, baby." To me she says, "One warning and I'm done, I've got cooking to do. Now, you know I'm a friend to you loup-garous, my family has been for generations. We feed you and keep your secrets, and you pay us well and protect us. But if you hurt my Izzy, or allow her to come to harm because she got mixed up in that roug business of yours, I'll have your head. And I know how to do it too. Go in there with an axe on the new moon, take it right off your neck, I don't mess around."

She smacks her palms together in an imitation of an axe taking off my head.

I gape for a moment, in awe. "Ms. Quemper?"

"I mean every word."

"I know you do. And you would be right to do it if I let your baby come to any harm."

"That's my girl." She gives me a brief one-armed hug, then disappears into the kitchen.

Izzy gives me an embarrassed look. "Uh. So, now you've met my grandma. She's a little intense, but she's not crazy. That loup-garou stuff…" She trails off, shrugging. "I mean, she's been telling that story my whole life. She says it's part of our Creole heritage."

I nod, then inhale deeply, catch a whiff of something troubling from outside. I go to the front door, open it, put my head out, inhale.

Another dead man. Here, in Bywater.

10

A DEAD MAN IN AN ABANDONED
NAVAL BASE

y gut freezes. I dreamed this. I dreamed I killed people last night. Maybe I really did. "Izzy, I'm so sorry, I have to go, thank you for everything."

She looks concerned. "What is it? What's wrong?"

"It's something—I'll tell you later if I can. I'm sorry, I really do have to go right now."

I follow the smell across the street to the fenced-off abandoned Navy facility. There's a place where the fence has been bent enough for somebody to climb under. The air tells me that my sister Opal passed this way not long ago, not more than a day or two. Tiny insects of some kind leap up from the wet grass to bite my ankles, making my legs itch.

I close my eyes briefly, to make the peacock ribbons of Opal's scent come clear, then follow the trail across cracked pavement and around to the side of a squat office building that was a grim concrete box even before it was given over to graffiti and dampness.

A door rests off its hinges, easily moved aside, letting me into a hallway filled with scattered debris and remnants of a fresh party. Just like the man yesterday—was it only yesterday? —the dead man is laid out in repose, in a pool of blood and water and alcohol. Like the other man he's young, tall, strongly built, wearing a T-shirt. This one is also for a fraternity, I think, with a different collection of Greek letters on it. He reeks of alcohol and other drugs. Even though he appears to have bled to death, there's no sign of a struggle or violence. It looks like an accident, like he broke a beer bottle and cut a thumb artery on the shards, bleeding out while unconscious.

I couldn't possibly have killed him last night. He's been dead a day or two already. I didn't notice the smell earlier because he was so far from the street. His body, rotting, finally reached the point where it cut through the background smells. That could mean Vivienne or one of the others will notice him now.

I try to examine everything carefully, with my nose, not my fingers. Who was here, other than my sister? People who were at the other death site? I inhale deeply, catch memories of at least three men and four women.

I sniff around, trying to get a clear scent picture of all the places people left themselves, on the dead man's skin and cloth-ing, where saliva and sweat touched now-empty bottles and cans and cups, where lipstick clings to discarded cigarette butts.

Embarrassed, I realize the dead man had sex with two of the women. Not my sister. I'm glad of that even though it shouldn't be any of my business.

I continue to sniff around. I see a sprinkling of white powder, wonder what it is, inhale deeply of it a split second before it occurs to me that was probably a very bad idea.

It feels like a sledgehammer to the back of my brain. My heart is racing. My head is racing. I start to tremble.

Well, damn. I think I just inhaled a bunch of cocaine.

The world stutters, and now Vivienne is here, seizing me by the shoulders, yelling into my face. "Bon Dieu, what on earth are you doing here with a dead man yet again?"

"Viv." Swallow. Resist the urge to repeat her name over and over. Squeak out normal-sounding human words. "My neigh-borhood. Of course I'm here."

But she's not fooled. She takes a hard look into my eyes and says, "You inhaled some of the cocaine, didn't you?" Unexpectedly, her face softens in sympathy. "See, little one, this is why you need to leave these investigations to the senior wolves." She sniffs my neck, my face. "Well, it wasn't too much, the effects shouldn't last long. There's a gym on Rampart, you'll know it. They have a special room for us. You can run around in there, not hurt anybody, burn it all off. Ask for the red room. The clerk will know."

She pauses, observes my outfit with a smirk. "You also had a sleepwalking incident, didn't you?"

I open and close my mouth, unable to think of anything intelligent to say.

"Let me guess. Your teeth fell out. You killed the wrong person. You found yourself naked in a really public place." I just stare at her, and she smiles. "We all have those dreams, little one. When you go to the gym, ask for spare clothes. They will have some to give you."

Before I can leave, a police officer arrives, and I freeze, shaking. Is he going to know about the cocaine? Am I going to get in trouble? But he barely notices me at all, smiling broadly when he sees Viv, exhaling a rush of sexual pleasure that feels disturbingly personal. "Hey, my beautiful rougarou," he says in a heavy Cajun accent, and kisses her cheek.

"Don't call me that, Régnault," she says, but she's smiling. She likes him too, although maybe not quite as much as he likes her. "We found this." She gestures at the body. "My young niece Abby was just leaving." A pointed glance back at me.

I inhale. Exhale. Standing still right now is the hardest thing I've ever done. She's right, I have to burn this off somehow.

Régnault studies me for a moment. "She is your niece, so, like you?"

"Like me." She nods. "But too young to help us here."

He takes my hand. His is rough and warm, mine clammy in comparison. "Pleased to meet you, Miss Abby."

"You too," I say. Breathe in. Breathe out. Act cool. It's okay. It's okay.

"We've got this, Abby, please," Vivienne tells me, with an amber flash to her eyes so I know she's serious.

It's time. I take off.

THE GYM IN QUESTION IS IN AN UNASSUMING TWO-STORY BRICK building from the 19th century. The reception area smells strongly of Varger, but not only Varger. There seems to be a "regular" gym in addition to the special gym. The receptionist, a young Varger man, has the laid-back boredom of somebody who has been working the night shift and doesn't really expect anybody to show up and make him do his job. He has to pull headphones out of his ears, and it seems to take him forever to get his attention away from whatever he was looking at on his phone. When he does notice me, he inhales deeply, nostrils flaring. "I don't know you," he says. "Are you Abby?"

"I am. Uh, Vivienne sent me? I'm supposed to ask for the red room. And clothes."

He nods, and hands me a bundle of dark gray clothing, then points at one of the doors. "You haven't been here before, so I'll give you the rundown. The room is reinforced, so you don't have to worry about breaking anything. It'll withstand a category five hurricane, or a couple of Varger really going at it. When you're alone, do whatever you want. If you're joined, be polite. Don't fight anybody who doesn't want to fight you." He smirks. He can smell the drug in my sweat. "When all that excitement burns off, you'll want this." He sets a plastic bottle full of purple liquid on the counter. "I'll leave this out here."

The red room is large, padded, and mostly empty. I was expecting a plastic surface, but the red walls, floor and ceiling are all covered in leather, studded like a fancy sofa. Is the leather because this particular gym predates plastic? Or is it because we don't like the way plastic smells? Whatever the reason, that's a lot of leather.

I put on the clothes, sweatpants that are a bit too long, some kind of oddly stitched compression tank top, and a sweatshirt. I realize I'm too warm for the sweatshirt and leave it piled in a corner along with the yellow T-shirt, while I explore the room.

One part of the wall does have some plastic, small nodules of a type I recognize from the REI climbing wall in downtown Seattle. Leather spheres of various sizes squat in the corners. Are those what you call a medicine ball? I pick up one of the larger spheres. It seems to be padding around a weighted core, and is a lot heavier than it looks like it should be. Not as heavy as a person, though. I throw it across the room. It's fun, but not as satisfying as throwing Jaime into a bunch of chairs.

I toss the medicine balls around for a while, but it doesn't seem to abate the red sizzling in my nerves. I try the climbing wall instead. It surprises me to find that holding up the weight of my own body is harder than picking up a medicine ball and throwing it. The difficulty makes it more effective at eating up some of my tension, so I climb. It's almost as if I can feel my muscles in the process of breaking down and reforming, stronger than before. It happens so quickly that by the top of the climbing wall it's already easier than it was at the bottom, as if I have compressed weeks of training into a few minutes.

Is this normal? Is this how we work? Because it's kind of amazing.

I make the climb harder, moving sideways and upside down, stressing new and different muscles. Eventually I move off the official climbing wall and try seeking purchase on the irregular places in the leather. I climb up beyond the end of the little nodules, up to the ceiling. And then, why not? I try crawling on the ceiling. I manage a few feet before losing my grip entirely, falling all the way to the floor and losing my breath for a few moments. But it's exciting, almost as exciting as the clattering chairs. I try again. I'm midway across the ceiling when a new brother enters the room, which startles me so much that I drop immediately.

"Whoa," I say, by way of greeting, from the floor. He's a tall, light-skinned black man with freckles and coppery hair.

He extends one hand to help me to my feet. "I'm Nicolas," he says. "Nic. Vivienne sent me."

"Nice to meet you, Nic. Sent you to do what?"

"Spar, if you want. She said you had, uh—" he taps the side of his nose. "Something you needed to get out of your system."

And that's how I end up fighting a second half brother just a few hours after fighting the first one. Nic is similar to Jaime in some ways—tall, athletic, and a trained fighter—but the fight itself couldn't be more different. The fight with Jaime was a complete free-for-all. But Nic seems to be giving me lessons, saying things like, "I'm going to try throwing some punches, see if you can block them." Or "I'm going to try to get you on the floor, and you do the same to me."

It's fun, I guess, although it's less fun than it would be to just throw each other around.

Eventually he seems to notice my underwhelmed reaction, and says, "You need something more intense, don't you?" I nod. He takes a deep breath, positions himself into a fighting stance. "Okay. I'll let you set the pace. You don't have to worry about hurting me." An awkward smile. "You probably already know that."

I throw him into the leather padding as hard as I can. He hits, falls in a tangle of limbs, then quickly rights himself with a smile. I can smell that his adrenaline ticked up. He nods thoughtfully, tenses, then comes after me with approximately the same amount of force. Now we're getting into it properly, slamming each other into the leather padding until we can feel the reverberations of the metal supports deep in the walls.

Then, all at once, I'm done.

My energy and motivation drain out and I sink to the floor. Nic nods, giving me a slight smile. "That's it?"

"That's it." Even my voice seems to come in slow motion.

"I'll get you a drink."

He hands me the sweatshirt, then disappears. I stare at the ceiling. I crawled on that ceiling. It was probably weird and maybe a little bit creepy, if you happened to see it. Like I was a giant insect or something.

Nic returns. He hands me a bottle full of purple liquid, the smell of the receptionist's fingers still clinging to the plastic. . I can still smell his fingers on the plastic. I take the bottle from Nic, astonished that my arm has even that much strength, and sip.

"It's funny. I thought people took drugs because the drugs felt good, but the cocaine made me feel terrible. I only feel good now that it's wearing off."

Nic sits beside me, drinking his own purple. His face is serious. "Drugs will not affect you the way they affect a normal person. Not even ibuprofen."

"Ibuprofen? What does that do?"

"Not much." He grins, and looks an awful lot like Jaime. "But we heal so fast, most of the time it doesn't matter."

A long, silent pause, while we sip and breathe. "So, Nic. Where was your wolf birthday?"

"Right here in New Orleans."

"And you're—how old are you?"

"Twenty-seven."

"What was it like for you? When your wolf came?"

"Nothing too dramatic. My mom and dad—I mean, the dad who raised me, married my mom when I was little—had recently moved back to New Orleans after teaching in Berkeley for a few years. I always knew my birth father was from here. My mom described him as a Mardi Gras fling. She even told me he was a loup-garou. I thought she meant his costume." He chuckles. "I was seventeen when the wolf came. I woke up in Bayou Galene, my parents became loufrer, and that was it."

"Loufrer means what?"

"Friend of the wolf. My parents are honorary members of the pack. They're welcome at Bayou Galene. They keep our secrets and we protect them. Your Steph could have that."

"Is that a good thing to have?"

"It's a very good thing to have."

He seems so sincere, it causes me to think about it seriously. Steph and Terry as honorary pack members. I've been thinking I don't want to drag them into all this wolf business any more than I already have. But the idea of having them protected by a whole pack full of people with my power or more? That seems a little tempting. "So how do you get to be loufrer anyway?"

"Ask Pere Claude. That's all you have to do. He'll say yes for one of his grandchildren."

"Seriously? That's all there is to it?" I close my eyes, slip into a semi-conscious state. We're in Bayou Galene, where everything is a bright emerald green, and Steph and Terry sleep within a circle of wolves. The wolves are all sitting at attention, facing out, ready to take apart anything that looks like a threat.

"That's it. You're the fourth of Leon's children to be found, and all three of us made our closest family members loufrer."

"All three of us?" I frown at him. "Three?"

"Four, now, including you. You have three half siblings."

I start laughing. "Three? I've got a lot more than three half siblings, Nic."

He frowns at me. "What are you talking about?"

I stop. I was about to tell him about the Cachorros. That would be bad. I can't believe I was about to tell him. "I, uh, New Harmony?"

"Oh, right, of course." He pauses for a while, then says, "Your grandfather wants to host you and Steph for a meal today at three. The location is near Commander's Palace." He hands me a business card. "If you can't make it, call that number. Otherwise, be at the Bywater house at three p.m. and I'll have a car for you."

I stare at the card. My brain feels so sluggish that even ordinary things like figuring out what to do with a phone number seem ridiculous. I know this is a trap. Get me when I'm tired, bribe me with food and promises of protecting the people I love, make one last pitch to get me to face the moon their way.

But I don't have quite as much reason to fight as I once did. I still don't know for sure whether Pere Claude is a monster, but I do know that his torture of my father, as described in the diary, had a real practical purpose. Stabbing yourself in the gut repeatedly probably hurts just as much as what Father Wisdom used to do to us, maybe more. But the physical pain Wisdom inflicted was never the worst part. That's something I realized during the *Teen Mode* interview. The chastisements were *humiliating*, engineered to prove to us that we were lowly sinners who didn't deserve any better, to make us feel degraded and beaten down and helpless.

But trauma morph training is intended to give you power. To make you the master of your own wolf. It still sounds pretty hellish, and I don't want to get stuck in Bayou Galene forever if I fail. But at least I can forgive Pere Claude, maybe, a little bit, for thinking it was the right thing to do.

"Okay." I put the card in the pocket of the sweatshirt. "I'll do it. We'll be ready at three."

11

THE COVER OF TEEN MODE

When I get back to the house it's only about nine a.m., which astonishes me, because I feel like I've had a full day's adventures already and I'm ready to go to bed. But I don't get the chance. When I enter, the whole family is up, Steph feeding Terry, Morgan drinking coffee, their parents reading through the Sunday Times-Picayune.

"Abby!" Steph's mom says. "Where were you?"

"I went to CharliQ's for coffee." I hold up the yellow T-shirt as if in evidence.

"Uh-huh." Steph folds her arms. "First thing in the morning, without your phone, in an outfit you didn't own yesterday?"

Shoot. Steph is sometimes way more observant than I give her credit for. "Okay. I guess I had a little sleepwalking incident, no big deal. I just ended up in the courtyard at CharliQ's. Izzy gave me some spare clothes to wear home."

"Sleepwalking? That could be dangerous," Morgan says.

"I just went a few blocks."

"Yes, but in your sleep and without your clothes!"

"It's a problem, sweetie." Steph squeezes my shoulder. "During my worst drinking periods, I would sometimes black out a lot of time and end up someplace with no idea how I got there. It was scary. It had to stop."

I think back to Izzy's joke about finding naked white girls in the courtyard. Was Steph one of them? "But nothing happened."

"Nothing happened?" Morgan practically spits out his coffee. "You woke up in the courtyard at CharliQ's without any clothes!"

"But nothing else happened." I find the business card from Nic in my pocket, hold it out toward Steph. "Are you free this afternoon? My grandfather, I mean my biological grandfather, wants to buy us dinner. Or lunch. I don't know, what do you call a meal at three pm?"

She laughs. "Depends on when you get up, I guess. Sometimes I've had breakfast at that time." She takes the card, studies it. "I didn't realize you were in contact with your grandfather. How long have you two been speaking?"'"

"We haven't technically spoken yet. I met a half brother named Nicolas, he's the one who gave me the card? My grandfather's lawyer set it up. You've met her. Vivienne?" Steph continues to look perplexed. I raise my hand to indicate Viv height. "She's tall, has dark red hair, and you always really like her outfits?"

"Oh, right, her." Steph nods thoughtfully. "I've seen you talking with her but I didn't realize she was your grandfather's lawyer. Did you tell me she was?"

"I thought so, but maybe not." Now that I have to explain all of this to Steph, in front of the rest of her family, I realize how weird it all seems. *We track each other by scent, Steph, it's not as weird as you think...*

She sighs and hands back the card. "Well, if we're eating at three, we should probably get a move on."

"A move on where?"

She laughs. "We're getting your ID, kiddo. Don't tell me you forgot? A couple of days ago you thought it was the most exciting thing you'd ever heard of."

"I guess I lost track of the time. That's today? Shoot, I need to take a shower."

"As long as you make it quick. Just a second, I picked out a dress for you." She goes to the coat closet and pulls out a dress in dark blue, a thin knit fabric with a heavy swing to it. "I used to wear this to church when I was twelve or so. I know it's old, but it's sort of a timeless style, don't you think?"

"I grew up wearing weird prairie dresses, so I'm sure it's fine." I laugh, but Steph looks uncomfortable.

"If you don't want it…"

"No, it's fine, I'm serious. Thank you." I take the dress from her and carry it up the spiral staircase into the sweltering loft. The shower in the loft bathroom turns everything even more warm and steamy. It feels impossible to dry off when I get out, and the dress clings to my skin. It smells strongly of Steph, in church, years ago: perfume, hairspray, incense, boredom.

Downstairs, Steph looks me over and nods. "Very respectable. But still flattering from behind." Her eye gets a little twinkle and I start to panic.

"From behind? Who's looking at me from behind?"

"Everybody, kiddo. Important mom lesson: don't go out on the town unless you've had a trusted friend inspect your outfit from the rear, because you might be wearing see-through pants and not know it."

"Wow, that is important mom stuff. But you said it looked good?"

"It does. Let's go."

We start heading out to the car. I ask, "What happens when we go in to see the judge?"

"Well, I show them a notarized piece of paper proving your lack of a birth certificate. And then I offer some paperwork proving your actual real life existence. Documents from Saint Sebastian, that sort of thing." She holds up a folder that presumably contains said documents. "I testify that I've been taking care of you and know for a fact that you exist and that you're approximately sixteen years old."

Deep breath. "Um, yeah. About that. Can I be eighteen instead?"

She frowns. "Why do you want to be eighteen? You're not planning to start smoking, are you?" She grins. "Or do you really, really want to vote in the next election?"

"Well, maybe. But you remember that interview I did a couple of weeks ago with the *Teen Mode* reporter?"

"I do."

"Well. I kinda maybe just might already have signed something testifying that I'm eighteen? For the reporter, I mean. It was like a release form."

Her eyebrows shoot up. "And why exactly did you do that, Abby?"

"Because otherwise I had to get somebody else to co-sign it for me. Like, a legal guardian. And I started to think about it. Who would that even be? I have three parents and they're all dead. You're my acting guardian, but I know you've never done any paperwork."

She looks thoughtful. "Huh. I suppose I never thought about it like that. If you're a minor, your legal status is sort of in limbo, isn't it?"

"There's more. My grandfather, the one we're meeting later on, is going to want me to go out and live with him."

"That's what this is about? You going to live with him?"

"He wants me to. But I don't know if I want to yet. And if I'm under eighteen, he could use the law to force me."

"Oh." Her eyes get wide. "I hadn't thought about that." She takes a deep breath, exhales. "All right, you've sold me. Let me look through my paperwork and see if I have anything that contradicts the fact of you being eighteen." She starts rifling through the folder. "So, June 16, eighteen years ago? I think we can manage that."

BECOMING AN OFFICIAL ADULT CITIZEN OF THE UNITED STATES of America turns out to involve a lot of waiting and signing things. Steph signs a thing, I sign a thing, the notary (I think she's a notary) signs a thing. We go to one room and wait, then another room and wait, then another room and wait some more. Then we sign some more things.

Our conversation is subdued, almost as if we're afraid of giving something away. The fact that we both know I'm not eighteen for real? A more generalized fear of authority figures? I mean, I was high on cocaine earlier today, and it's not like I expect anybody here to smell it in my sweat, but it still makes me feel vaguely threatened by all the suits and uniforms and stern-faced people.

"This is not quite as boring as the prayer closet," I mention, at one point when we're sitting in some wooden chairs staring at a hall of the faces of (I think) judges going back more than a hundred years. I make note of when some of the faces start being female, and it's not until the 1980s.

Steph was zoning out and gives me a startled look, then laughs. "The prayer closet, huh? That was solitary confinement for three days, wasn't it?"

"Yeah. Three days in a concrete bunker. That was even more boring than this." I pause. "But not by a lot."

She laughs again, but her forehead is knitted into a frown.

We get called in at last. A judge makes a final ruling. An eighteen-year-old citizen of the United States of America named Abigail Marchande now has a legal existence. I have an official birth certificate substitute. I will be getting a Social Security card and a voter registration card in the mail. I head to another room and walk out with a Louisiana state photo ID, which is the size and shape of a driver's license but has NOT A DRIVERS LICENSE printed prominently on it. In the photo I look pale and haggard, which makes my claimed age seem more plausible.

Steph hugs me. "Welcome to adulthood, kiddo. I think you'll find it's okay. Maybe not everything you dreamed of. But okay."

I sink into the hug, letting some of my weariness show. "Does this mean I'm all on my own, then?"

She kisses the top of my head. "Sweetie. I'm almost thirty years old, and I'm still fighting to get my mother to let me make my own decisions. When people love you, you're never really on your own."

BACK AT THE HOUSE, STEPH'S FAMILY POPS OPEN SPARKLING apple juice to celebrate my new legal existence.

"Eighteen? I thought you were only sixteen." Steph's mother squints at my ID, seeming confused and a little hostile toward the notion of my legal adulthood.

Steph jumps in to explain. "Well, Mama, we talked it over. You know Abby doesn't have any living parents. And I could adopt her, of course, but we thought it seemed a little silly to go through all that paperwork for somebody who's so close to eighteen anyway. So, we made her an adult. It was just simpler all around."

A knock on the door, not Varger and not anybody I know. Steph's dad opens to a UPS driver who wants a signature. He signs for a big box that smells of paper and ink. I'm pretty sure I know what it is even before he turns it around and I see the *Teen Mode* logo printed on the side.

"Oh, it's here!" I rip into the box eagerly and then stop, taken aback by the cover photo. The thought that goes through my mind is, *wow, who is that, she looks just like me, is it another one of Leon's kids?*

Wait, that *is* me.

Somehow I didn't envision ending up on the cover.

The lighting and color balance make me look a little artificial: skin paper-white except for brown inkblot freckles, hair bloody red, eyes bright green. My lips are pale and set in a firm line. The blurred-out background behind me is recognizable as the bricks and black iron lace of the French Quarter.

Amid headlines promising to talk about SMOKY EYES FOR FALL and TAKING STYLE BACK TO SCHOOL, the largest type, in red, says ESCAPING CHRISTIAN PATRIARCHY, and below that, smaller, in black, SELF-ABNEGATION IN THE SERVICE OF THE LORD TALKS ABOUT NEW HARMONY AND MORE.

"Wow, they put you on the cover," Steph says.

"Good on you," says her dad.

"Oh my goodness," her mother says, fluttering with excitement. "The cover, my goodness. You mentioned you were talking to that reporter, but I had no idea. No idea at all."

"How the hell did you end up getting interviewed by *Teen Mode*?" Morgan asks, frowning. He picks up a copy of the magazine, suspiciously, like I've been running around behind his back. "Did they call you?"

"No, I called them. I happened to catch my stepmother Meekness and my older brother Justice on some religious talk show, and they were trying to make it sound like what Wisdom did wasn't so bad. It made me really angry, so I contacted a bunch of magazines to offer an interview, and *Teen Mode* was the one that took me up on it."

I flip to the article itself, which takes up several pages, with pictures and pull quotes and a couple of short related articles, "What is Christian Patriarchy?" and "Abby's DIY Two T-Shirt Dress."

There's a picture of me that takes up the whole page, with no text other than a quote:

The chastisements were supposed to break our wills, but I

don't think it worked. I think they broke everything but my will.

The image shows me from behind, at an angle, in a backless two T-shirt dress I made specially for the interview, revealing the whip scars. In the high-contrast photograph, they look particularly brutal and ugly.

That's what people see, when I take off my shirt. When they gasp. That's what they're seeing.

"My goodness, I never knew those scars of yours were so bad," Steph's mom says.

My phone buzzes. It's the reporter, Janelle Barker.

> Hey, Abby, the UPS site says you got the delivery?

I did, thanks

> You okay to talk now?

Sure

My phone buzzes again, with a phone call.

"Hey there," Janelle says. "I just wanted to give you a little heads up about what's been going on here. The article is making a pretty big splash on social media. We're all excited here at the magazine. It's really great."

"Okay." I swallow, feeling nervous. A big splash. That seems scary. But isn't that what I wanted? To really get the truth out there? Why does it make me feel threatened?

"It's a little bit—well, it's a little controversial. That's good. Controversy is good! Honestly with a subject like this, if there weren't any controversy, it would mean you didn't hit hard enough. Just, if you encounter it, please don't freak out. People can be really mean, especially online."

My insides turn to ice. "What exactly are we talking about here?"

"Just—don't read the comments, okay? And if you need any help, call me."

"Okay. Thank you."

"Thank you! And the article is great. It came out great. Don't worry about a thing."

So of course the first thing I do is go to my phone and read the comments. They lean heavily toward DEMON WITCH FEMINIST AGENDA with a side order of WHORE and a sprinkling of DOG. Which in this case means "not terribly attractive young woman" but it still makes me laugh. Oh, dudes, you have no idea.

I could eat your faces off. Every last one of you.

But I won't.

Huh. Opal might be right. Maybe that is fun.

STEPH EXCUSES HERSELF TO RUN SOME ERRANDS BEFORE WE SEE my grandfather. Steph's dad goes to rehearsals for his evening shows. Morgan takes off to spend time with one of his old friends from the neighborhood. Steph's mom and I are left at the house alone. I half-drowse on the couch, reading about myself online with horrified fascination. Steph's mom turns on the TV to the weather channel and pulls out her knitting.

"The ladies at church are going to read that *Teen Mode* article," she says. "I'll make sure they do."

"Oh. Okay. Thanks?" I'm not sure why she's telling me this.

She puts down her knitting and looks at me seriously. "I'm sorry, Miss Abby. I really am. I had no idea what a torment it must be for you to be sitting there in that church."

Oh, this is about the fight we had yesterday. Was it only yesterday? It must have been. I let her take my hands. I nod. "It's okay."

"Are you going out with those friends of yours again tonight?"

"You know, I really don't know. Probably? But we don't have firm plans. Steph and I are having dinner with my grandfather first. Or late lunch. Whatever it is."

"You going to stay out all night again?"

That had an edge of hostility to it, more like the Steph's mom I'm used to. "I don't know, Mrs. Marchande. Maybe."

"Hm." She makes a grunting noise, nods, sighs. "When Steph was your age—your real age, not the age on that new ID you got—I would never have let her stay out all night like you did. She did it. But I didn't let her."

I'm too drowsy to figure out where she's going with this. "What does that mean?"

"Well, I don't know." She goes back to her knitting and the needles clack furiously for a few moments. "Steph seems to trust you. She doesn't seem to care where you go or what time of the night or whether she knows the people you're with. I cared. I cared a lot. I made her tell me everything. Are you going to be with a boy, Steph? Is it that Gallagher boy? You know I don't know his family. I don't want you seeing that boy. Is there going to be drinking at that party? I don't want you going to a party with drinking."

She pauses and I make a vague, encouraging grunt. She's upset but I don't think it's directed at me.

"I made her tell me everything, but she lied. I told her all the places she couldn't go and all the things she couldn't do, and she snuck around behind my back." She drops her knitting, looks me in the eyes, almost as intense as if she had a wolf. "Miss Abby, do you lie to Steph the way she lied to me?"

"No, Mrs. Marchande. I don't think so." Although as soon as I say it, all the lies I have told to Steph start clamoring for attention. I haven't told her about Opal. I didn't tell her about the dead men. I lied about my father's diary.

Steph's mom takes a deep breath. Her eyes fill with tears.

"That's what I thought. You kids do whatever you want, don't you? Doesn't matter what we say."

She seems so upset that I try to comfort her. "Steph turned out okay, Mrs. Marchande. And I will too."

She pats my hand. "I know that. I know." She wipes away a tear. "It just brought everything right back, seeing you in that dress Steph used to wear. All the fights we had."

I hold up my freshly minted ID. "Anyway, Steph doesn't really have to be my mom anymore, right? This certifies that she has successfully raised me to adulthood."

She nods. "Good for her. Are you going to be getting a job, then?"

I laugh. "I guess I'll think about it."

NIC IS ON THE FRONT PORCH. I MUST HAVE FALLEN ASLEEP. I check my phone. It's not three yet. Steph's mom is no longer on the couch.

I open the door. "What are you doing here?"

"I need to talk to you." He's tense. He holds up a copy of the *Teen Mode* issue.

"Abby, who is that?" Steph's mom calls, from the kitchen.

"It's just my half brother Nicolas. We're discussing the visit with my grandfather, it's okay!"

"Your half brother?" She gets off the couch and comes to take a look, adjusting her glasses. "Hello, I'm Mrs. Marchande, Stephanie's mother?" They shake hands awkwardly, as Nic clearly wasn't anticipating somebody being here who wasn't in the know. "Nice to meet you, Mr. Nicolas. But you're not from New Harmony?"

"No. No, I'm not. We share a father, not a mother."

"Well, now, I think I saw that in that article there. Abby's real father wasn't that awful cult leader, right? It was another man?"

"That's right," Nicolas says. He's almost physically squirming in his desire to get away from this conversation.

I take pity on him. "Mrs. Marchande, my brother had something to show me, I'll be right back, okay?"

I slip outside and close the door behind me. We start walking, our voices low.

"What were you thinking, Abby? Talking to a reporter like that?"

"I was thinking I would tell the truth in a public forum. That's what I was thinking. I didn't say anything about being a werewolf, did you actually read the article?"

"Of course you didn't say anything about that! But anyone who knows Leon's history could make a good guess about where you come from. You even talk about the beast."

"So what? Anybody who knows the significance of me being Leon's kid already knows about werewolves, right? So what's the big deal?"

He sighs. "I'll be honest. Vivienne sent me."

"Obviously."

"She's furious. She's sure you did something wrong."

"And you're not?"

He shrugs. "I just don't know that it makes much difference. The New Harmony meltdown was already a major news story. The other survivors are out there telling their stories. Did any of them see the wolf?"

"All of them saw the wolf. But like I said in the article, they also 'saw' the beast with its claws in my heart, long before the wolf was real. When I said the beast in me was my father's way of demonizing another man's DNA, I totally meant that."

He nods, looking around thoughtfully, as if he's coming to some kind of decision. "Right. So your article might even have helped create an alternate narrative. It might be exactly what Pere Claude would have told you to do."

"But I didn't let him tell me first. That's why Viv is mad, isn't it?"

A woman jogs past. Her leashed dog stops briefly to bark at us, but he heels at her command and they jog on. Nic nods. "I think you're right."

"So is that whole 'alpha' thing for real? Viv said it wasn't. But when we argue, we always end up in a dominance contest. You know, growling at each other, doing the flashy-eye thing?"

He laughs. "And you win, don't you?" I nod. "Yeah. See, it's complicated. Your wolf is instinctively very dominant. Mine too. I think we get it from our father. When they first brought me in, I was just like you, always getting into it with the senior wolves. They smacked me around, and eventually everything worked itself out." He smiles, obviously remembering the experience fondly. Getting smacked around in werewolf culture obviously does not mean the same thing as getting smacked around in regular human culture. Maybe that's normal. When dogs play, a lot of it is pretend fighting.

"So why am I getting into so much trouble with Viv? If it's exactly what they expect me to do?"

"But it's not what they expect, not really. I went out to Bayou Galene and stayed there, let them teach me their ways. That's the thing you're refusing. From their perspective it's the ultimate dominance move, way beyond anything they're ready for. So nobody knows what to do. If you simply won't accept the authority of a senior wolf, it's..." He sighs, mood dimming. "Well, it's what our father Leon did. So they've seen it before. And it didn't end well."

"Didn't end well how? I mean, I know Leon is dead, but I don't know any details."

"You have to ask Pere Claude about that. It's really his story to tell."

We circle the block and start heading back to the house. "Is that really all you had to tell me? The Varger are officially upset that I went to the media without consulting them first?"

"I guess that's it. I think Viv was hoping that if I pointed it out to you, you'd instantly see why it was a mistake to go so public with your life story, and have your picture circulated." He flicks his eyes off in the distance, obviously getting an idea. "You don't actually know what Leon looked like, do you?"

"Uh. No. Kind of like you, kind of like me, I guess."

He stops walking, takes out his phone, calls up a picture, holds it toward me. "One of my mother's girlfriends took this, during a fateful Mardi Gras nine months and twenty-seven years ago."

I take the phone and study the photo. It shows a smiling, drunk, black woman posed next to a smiling, drunk, white man. Both of them are beautiful and young and healthy and covered in glitter, face paint and Mardi Gras beads. It's easy to look from the people in the photo to Nicolas and say, those two people, those are your parents. But it's even easier to look from the man in the picture, to the girl on the cover of the magazine, and say, that man, he's her father.

"Thanks." I hand back the phone. "Your mother was very beautiful." And she looks happy to be with Leon. Could my father really be as evil as I think, if he made Nic's mom look so happy? What if my mom was once that happy with Leon, and Wisdom was just lying to me?

"She still is beautiful," he says, with pride, pocketing the phone. "All right, I've said my piece. Let's get back to the house and take you all to meet our grandfather."

12

DINING WITH PERE CLAUDE

I invite Nic inside and we make conversation with Steph's mom for a few awkward minutes until Steph gets back from her errands. We both stand up. "Steph, this is my half brother Nicolas. He's going to escort us to dinner?"

Nic nods, takes Steph's hand. "Pleased to meet you."

"Half brother, huh?" Steph looks up at him speculatively, with obvious appreciation. When we first met, Steph told me about her Cajun grandmother's rougarou tales, and her teenage dream of finding a fais-do-do full of shirtless werewolf boys. I have a brief, dumb fantasy: it would be cool if Steph and my brother hooked up romantically, wouldn't it? Then they could also be my werewolf mom and dad. Except, no. Steph can't become one of the bitten. Way too risky. "Well, it's nice to finally meet you."

He leads us outside where a black limousine has pulled up. We climb in. It smells strongly of its many passengers, Varger and non-Varger alike. I'm starting to get the impression there's a whole shadow Varger economy in New Orleans. This is probably a regular limo company that anybody could call, but if you're Varger, it's the only one you call. A secret society that exists alongside the regular society. Two faces. Deception baked into the pie, wasn't that what Opal said?

Opal. I need to talk to her about that other dead man. But there's just too much going on right now. My head is spinning.

We roll along the streets toward the Garden District, past grandiose mansions, many of them very beautiful, set back from the sidewalk with big showy gardens in front. Some have been turned into condominiums or apartments or businesses, but carefully, preserving their outward appearance.

The limo pulls to a stop next to what appears to be one of those mansions. "Here we are," Nic says. We all get out and he points. "Just follow that brick path to the courtyard."

"Is this a restaurant?" Steph looks around, confused.

"It is, but it's not open to the general public. Members only."

"Oh, I've heard of these." Steph looks impressed. "They're supposed to be very good."

Nic smiles. "I think you'll enjoy it. Pere Claude selected the menu himself."

I inhale deeply and pick up Pere Claude's own trail, a ribbon of dense, warm, reddish brown. Some part of me is eager to meet him—wagging her tail, panting, running around in circles, shouting family, family, family. I try to clamp it down. I don't want some dumb animal instinct overwhelming my judgment.

We walk through a green tunnel of live oaks, while rich cooking smells waft over us. The passage opens up into a small brick courtyard. Steph gasps in delight. "Oh my God, this place is gorgeous."

It feels like a jungle oasis, crowded with lovely, fragrant plants that have attracted birds and butterflies and bees. Three different half-hidden fountains trickle musically as a backdrop to the peaceful chirp and buzz. It's just as humid and hot as it was out on the street, but it feels cooler, shaded and gentle and safe.

But it's hard to think about any of that, when the presence of Pere Claude threatens to overwhelm all my other senses.

He's a big man, tall and broad-shouldered. His hair is gold with a hint of ruddiness to it, fading almost imperceptibly to gray. His eyes are grayish blue. He has the tawny skin of a white man who spends a lot of time outdoors, but no freckles. Did Leon get those from his mother? The fabled, mourned Evangeline?

Pere Claude's scent dominates the air, overpowering even the flowers and the food, but beyond that, he exudes a sense of presence. He owns this space, as he probably owns every space he inhabits. A part of me is comforted by knowing that, knowing who's in charge here, and just wants to sink into it, like a warm bath on a cold day. But another part of me starts snarling in resistance, wants to run away, wants to be free. He smells like family, like home, like father. And that's never going to be a simple thing for me.

"Granddaughter, welcome," he says, in a deep, resonant voice. He opens his arms and I go into them without hesitation or shyness. It looks like a warm, touching, happy meeting. But it feels more complicated than that. I don't really trust him. He senses this. He pulls away, looks at me with a frown. "Is something wrong, granddaughter?"

"I—no, everything's fine. I just, um—this is all—" I wave a hand, vaguely. "It's strange, you know? Anyway, this is my guardian, Stephanie Marchande. She goes by 'Steph.'"

"Pleased to meet you, Miss Steph. I'm Claude Verreaux." He takes her hand, clasping it between big, square hands that swallow hers up. I notice how fine and tapered her fingers are, how perfect the arch of her scarlet nails. She got a manicure the other day and the varnish smell hasn't fully dissipated. I notice that my own hands, though tiny compared to Pere Claude's, are shaped like his: squared off and blunt. Now that I look at them they seem outsized, like the paws of a puppy that's going to grow into a much larger dog. Maybe I really was meant to be taller. Suddenly I want to cry for no very good reason.

"I understand you believe you're Abby's biological grandfather? Are you certain of this? Has there been a DNA test?"

He smiles. "We are certain."

Steph frowns and looks to me to explain. "Yeah, Steph. It's, um, it's a werewolf thing. We can tell we're family by smell."

Her expression says, "you've got to be kidding me," but she just shakes her head. "If you're both sure."

"Would you like some wine?" Pere Claude gestures toward the table, a sturdy and elaborate wrought-iron affair, laid out with a selection of vegetables, both fresh and pickled. It also has a pitcher of iced tea flavored with basil, and an open bottle of red wine.

"No," I jump in to say. I'm lying—the wine smells amazing and I do want some—and he can probably tell that.

Steph pats me on the shoulder. "It's okay, Abby. Mister Verreaux?"

"Please call me Claude."

"All right, Mr. Claude. I'm not drinking tonight. But Abby, if you want a glass, go right ahead. I'm from New Orleans, I'm not going to flip out if a teenager has a glass of wine with her grandfather."

He smiles. He pours wine into two thick, hand-blown glasses without stems, and hands one to me. "Many people would say, 'to your health,' but our people have no need to wish health to each other. So we say, 'to your next hunt.'"

Ominous, I think. Then, what the heck, I say it out loud. "That sounds a little ominous."

"In the modern world, perhaps." He shrugs. "Many of our traditions are very old. To our ancestors, in a harsh northern landscape, a good hunt meant prosperity. Our people fear very little, other than starvation."

Now I feel embarrassed. When I hear the word "hunt" I don't picture people hunting, of necessity, for their own food. But of course that's what the Varger would mean by it.

I focus on the wine. This is the first time I've ever had a

glass of wine, or, let's be honest, even a sip of wine. At communion, at New Harmony, we had grape juice and called it wine. Sometimes it was real grape juice and sometimes it was an artificially grape-flavored powdered drink mix that we called juice anyway.

This is nothing like any of that. This is like if you took the best of the real grape juice, and kept making it thicker and more strongly grape-flavored, until it's like concentrated grape syrup, but that's too sweet, so you let everything mellow out a bit, let the sugar change to alcohol, but somehow there's more to it than that. The wine has layers of flavor, just like it has layers of scent. And I can either sit here and think about that, or I can think about something else and just keep drinking it because it's so easy to drink, almost thirst quenching.

"Do you like the wine?" Pere Claude asks. He's just being polite. He can tell that I do.

"Oh, it's good." I downplay its deliciousness for Steph's sake. "So, food, what are we eating here?"

"Hors d'oeuvres de légumes. Miss Steph, do you have allergies or dietary restrictions I should be aware of?"

"Nope," she says, taking a little tart topped with curried cauliflower. "I can eat anything. Oh, that's fantastic. Abby, you have to try these."

I take one. She's right, it is delicious. "I do. I'm a vegetarian."

Pere Claude stares at me as if he doesn't know the English words I just used. "Excuse me, granddaughter?"

"I don't eat meat."

"I'm sorry, I don't understand."

"It's not that complicated. I don't eat animal flesh."

"But, child, the wolf is a carnivore."

"Sure, the wolf eats meat. I don't."

He looks troubled. "But the wolf is you. You cannot separate her."

We stare at each other for a moment, not quite a locked-eye

challenge, but close. "It doesn't matter," I say. "I don't eat meat when I'm human."

"But don't you want to eat it?"

"That doesn't matter. I don't."

We stare at each other. He blinks. Slowly. Deliberately. He's trying to calm me down, not really giving in. "Child," he says. He makes a gesture with his hands, a kind of pushing-down gesture. "Granddaughter. There is a danger you may not realize. During the full moon, when your wolf dominates, you do not want her to be hungry. Do you understand this? A hungry wolf can be dangerous."

"It's not the full moon tonight, is it?"

"You know it's not."

"So today I'm not eating any meat."

"What about seafood and poultry?"

"Those are animals, aren't they? So, no."

He nods, still looking troubled. "Very well. As you choose."

Steph tries to lighten the mood. "Well, I haven't eaten all day, so let's get going. I'm starved."

Pere Claude goes over to talk to the servers, then sits back down at the table with us. A jazz trio sets up in the corner and plays softly. The servers bring the first dish: some kind of tomato relish on toast, topped with tiny shrimp. "Heirloom tomato bruschetta topped with wild gulf shrimp," the server says. She presents me with a separate plate. "Shrimp-free, for the mademoiselle."

This goes on. And on. And on. "Wild mushrooms sauteed in beef consomme" vs "Mushrooms in butter for the mademoiselle" "Frites seared in duck fat" vs "Frites in olive oil for the mademoiselle" "Mustard greens wilted with smoked wild boar bacon" vs "Wilted mustard greens in sea salt for the mademoiselle." It's all very respectful, but on some level I feel like they're making fun of me. It's obvious that the versions I'm getting, while perfectly great food, are missing something.

Steph, at least, seems overwhelmed with pleasure. At a

certain point she stops remarking on how wonderful everything is, and just eats it.

We chat about innocuous things, mostly food. Food we're eating now, food we're not eating, food we've had in the past, food we want to try in the future, food in general. It seems to be a New Orleans thing. When in doubt, talk about food. Pere Claude is familiar with CharliQ's. In fact, some of the smoked meat in this meal comes from there.

I know nothing about food, and don't really like talking about it anyway, so I'm getting a little bored. That was not something I expected to happen, when we finally met the famed Pere Claude. That I would get bored because he spent the whole time talking with Steph about food.

13

THE RED MOON AND THE BLACK

Cheese and fruit appears, moving us toward dessert. Pere Claude pours the last of the wine into my glass, and Steph frowns.

"Mr. Verreaux, it's her first time."

He smiles. "It will not trouble her. Our people are not overly sensitive to alcohol."

Well, that answers that question. A new bottle of wine appears, much smaller and sweeter. Dessert wine. Its flavor is amazing, intensely sweet without losing complexity. It seems clear on the tongue somehow, like spring water, like drinking sunlight. I would gush about it, but I feel bad doing that in front of Steph. Instead I gush about the cheese, which is also delicious. At least here I'm getting the same thing everyone else is getting.

I realize I'll never think of a smooth way to bring it up, so I dive right in. "Pere Claude. Tell me about my father."

His surge of mixed emotion—sorrow, rage, even a little fear —is so powerful it seems I could touch it. I think he's going to deny me, say he doesn't want to talk about it. But he sighs, and pours himself more of the wine. "My son was very troubled."

"Troubled how?"

"Not long after his wolf appeared, he began to suffer from what we call the red moon and the black. I think in modern medicine they would call it a bipolar disorder. It tracks to the phases of the moon. Mania when she is full and despair when she is empty."

"Oh, I think Abby has that."

"Steph!" I feel like she's betrayed a confidence.

Pere Claude pauses for a long time, studying my face. "Perhaps she does. But if she had the red moon as bad as my son, she would not find it so easy to sit here calmly and have dinner with us right now, on the day before the full moon."

"I don't think I have the red moon. Just the black. Does it work that way? Do you get the black and not the red?"

He nods. "That is somewhat more common than both."

"Well. That's probably what you have, then." Steph shrugs, responding to my stare. "What, you think I don't notice your mood swings?"

"Leon's problems went well beyond mood swings, Miss Steph. Most Varger with the red moon seek to control it. But he embraced it. Encouraged it. Chose to give in to the mania, as a wild ecstatic experience."

"Well, I guess that explains the illegitimate kids," I say.

He frowns. "We don't use that word. Illegitimate. You are one of our people. You are my granddaughter."

"Okay, fine. Not illegitimate." I take a deep breath. "Did he ever rape anyone?"

Steph and Pere Claude stare wide-eyed at me, as if I've said something very shocking. Pere Claude recovers first, holding out his hands in a kind of open-handed gesture. "I don't know that he did. I can't promise that he didn't. Did your mother tell you he did?"

"My mother never told me anything about Leon. It was what my father—my other father, Father Wisdom—what he said. And he lied about a lot of things, so I don't know whether he was lying about that too."

Pere Claude reaches out his hands to take mine, in a comforting gesture. His hands are big and too hot in the suddenly sweltering courtyard. "My dear. I cannot imagine how horrifying this must be for you. I'm sorry for everything—every bad choice made by every adult that led us to this place—but you are here now, and I'm glad you're here."

I squeeze my eyes shut, drip a few tears. He sounds so sincere. I want to believe him about everything. But just like when Viv talks about Leon, I sense a hole, a hidden thing, a thing not said. Deception. It probably isn't malicious. But without knowing what it is, I can't give him my trust.

I inhale, exhale very slowly. "All right. I'll be glad I'm here. What did Leon do during the black moons?"

"He tried to kill himself many times. But we are tough to kill."

"Oh my God," Steph says.

"He did succeed, eventually, right? Or died some other way? Vivienne told me he was dead."

Pere Claude nods, slowly. His stress ticks upward. "For several years, things had been escalating with him. After Evangeline was killed, especially. It was my fault. I thought I could use my strong personal dominance to compel him, but his will proved as strong as mine, and we ended up fighting constantly over every little thing.

"He left us during a full moon. He had partly mastered the trick of staying in human form, and he had his driver's license by then, so it wasn't hard for him to take a car. By the time the rest of us awoke to human form the next morning, he had already abandoned the car in Texas, and we lost his trail there. Years went by. Then one day I got a call from the Los Angeles coroner's office. They wanted me to identify a body."

"How did they know to call you?" I ask. There's something odd about this story. I don't get the impression Pere Claude is lying exactly, but I'm sure he's leaving out something important.

"Information that was found on his person."

"And how did he succeed in killing himself?"

He swallows. His distress seems absolutely sincere. "Gunshot to the head."

"Oh my God," Steph says.

"So that's a thing that actually can kill us?"

"Yes. A gunshot to the head can kill."

Steph bursts out with a little half-sob. She shakes her head. She stands up, begins to pace back and forth rapidly, waving her hands. "I'm sorry. I'm sorry. I'm just—what are we talking about here? People turning into wolves, people getting shot in the head? This whole thing is too surreal. Any moment I expect to see the TV cameras, and you finally tell me that you made it all up and of course there's no such thing as werewolves."

Pere Claude nods. Nothing seems to rock him. Well, except talking about Leon. "I believe I can help with that. Excuse me."

He pushes himself away from the table and converses briefly with one of the servers. The server brings out a folding screen, covered with a rich green satin. It looks like an antique. Pere Claude disappears behind it. His cowboy boots appear just to the side of the screen. His jeans appear draped over the top of the screen, belt still looped through. I notice the silver belt buckle, an engraved image of a wolf in profile with a single ruby eye. Then his shirt, all of this happening swiftly and smoothly, as if he's well-practiced, which I'm sure he is.

The atmosphere in the courtyard takes on a slippery electric feel. I sense a rising anticipation, as if something amazing is going to happen. There's a moment like a thunderclap, not a noise but a sensation, huge but gone so swiftly it's hard to be sure I felt it.

This is what it feels like to be on the outside, I think. To watch me transform, this is what people feel. My spine tingles.

An enormous white wolf pads out from behind the screen.

Steph yelps and jumps back, knocking one of the chairs to the ground. Her fear is a razor-wire of screaming yellow, but is she simply afraid of the wolf, or is she terrified by the supernatural dread of knowing that the wolf was human-shaped only two minutes ago?

The wolf sits, alert and calm, watching us steadily through pale blue eyes, jaw hanging open, pink tongue dangling on top of his teeth. At first glance he looks like any dog you'd see, until you start comparing his size to the things in the courtyard and realize few dogs are that big.

Then you notice the size of his jaws, the size of his teeth.

My, what big teeth you have.

I want to reassure Steph, so I kneel on the bricks in front of Pere Claude's wolf, putting us eye to eye. I dip my head, which I know he will interpret as a gesture of respect. I close my eyes and we nuzzle. I inhale the spicy black pepper scent of our kind, subtle when we're in human form, a knockout punch when we're in wolf.

"Abby no!" Steph exclaims behind me, the words ripped out of her in surprise. I can guess she's picturing those jaws closing around my throat, biting down.

"Steph, it's okay." I start rubbing behind his ears, like you'd do with a dog. His ears twist and his eyes lower, indicating pleasure. "We're kin. He won't hurt us."

"You're his kin. I'm not. What is he going to do to me?"

"You're kin," I reassure her, pretending more certainty than I really have. "You're my kin." I lock eyes with Pere Claude's wolf, feel my own eyes flash. "She is my kin and I will protect her with my life. I will kill to protect her."

His wolf dips his head, blinking—surrender? Then he licks my face. Definitely surrender. I think? I'm not sure what just happened.

Steph certainly doesn't know what just happened. She shrieks when his face gets close to mine, and then starts laughing, nervously, when she sees a licking tongue and not ripping teeth. It's the shrill laughter of a horror movie audience after a jump scare.

"Steph, it's really okay. You can pet him."

"I—I'm good, thanks." She drops into a chair suddenly, with an audible thud. "God. Okay. My God."

Pere Claude wolf and I exchange a look. Somehow I know he's asking my permission to approach Steph, and I indicate, through gestures, that he has it. He goes over to her and puts his head in her lap.

She jumps, but doesn't run away. After a while, cautiously, she strokes his head. "You're real," she says.

He pulls away from her, slowly, cautiously, and disappears behind the screen. The world goes slippery and shifts, then human hands grab his clothes. Pere Claude steps out from behind the screen.

He bows toward Steph. "I am sorry, Miss Steph, for the distress I caused you. But I believe things will be less traumatic for you if you can fully accept the reality of the wolf. Now you have touched him. You know he's real. And her wolf also is real." He nods at me.

Steph shakes her head, and reaches, half unconsciously, for the bottle of wine. I'm glad for her sake it's empty. "I guess so. I'm just—I saw it only a couple of minutes ago, and I'm already trying to turn it into—my brain skitters away from it. How could that be real? How could any of this be real?"

I try humor. "Come on, Steph, you like *The X-Files*, right?"

"THE X-FILES ARE FICTION!" For a second her outburst rings in the air, then she laughs. She keeps laughing. Laughing and laughing and laughing. Pere Claude starts laughing too, and then I'm laughing, and I'm not sure what we're laughing about, but it feels sort of good to all be laughing together, so we let that go on until we start to get tired of it.

"Pere Claude, did you understand the English words I said to your wolf?"

"In a way, yes. In a way, no. I understood the meaning behind them. You claimed Miss Steph as your kin and threatened me with destruction if I were ever to hurt her. I accepted that threat as your right."

"Well. Good." I try to keep things light, and laugh. "Not that I could make good on such a threat. I mean, look at us. You're probably two, maybe three of me."

"You might be surprised," he says, with a smile. "When Varger fight each other, it is not always physical strength that wins the day."

"How did you learn to do that, to transform at will?"

His brow knits as if at remembered trouble. "To begin, you must be a trauma morph. That means, you transform when badly injured, not only at the full moon."

My stress ticks upward. I know he can smell it. I try to calm down, ask very casually, "How common is that?"

He smiles. "Not common. But it does run in my family. Leon was a trauma morph and—" He stops, overwhelmed by emotion again. "He never mastered his wolf. It is an arduous discipline. It requires triggering the transformation many, many times. Over and over and over. More trauma than anyone expects." He sighs. "But by the time it is mastered, often the transformation has been bent entirely to the will. Summon him whenever you choose."

He takes my hand. "But even without the trauma morph, every young wolf needs to come to Bayou Galene and learn our ways. Vivienne tells me you do not wish to do this."

"Well, no." I squirm a little. He's making me feel bad, like I'm rejecting him personally by not wanting to go out there. "You know about the cult where I was raised." I hold up a hand, to stop him from jumping in the way Viv does. "Yes, I know the Varger aren't a cult. And I know you're not like Father Wisdom. He was a bad man. Power-hungry. I can tell you're not like that."

He smiles, inhales as if about to say something, but I put up my hand again. "Please, try to understand what you're asking me to do, from my point of view. I escaped one remote village in southern Louisiana ruled by a patriarchal authority figure. And now you want me to subject myself to a different one."

"Child, is that really how you see us?"

"I see through my own experience. You want my trust. Okay. Maybe you can earn it. But you can't demand it."

He inhales, a big, long, slow breath. I smell his stress going up and his eyes open wider, his nostrils flare. In Viv, this is the sign that she's about to fight me on something. But Pere Claude closes his eyes and exhales, just as long and slow and deep as the inhale.

"I understand," he says. And he gives me one of the saddest smiles I've ever seen. "You—challenge me, Abby. Much as your father once did. I made mistakes with him. I hope not to make the same ones with you."

"Thank you."

"But the full moon is just a day away. Surely you must join your people for that?"

I shrug. "Maybe."

"Maybe. That's your answer?"

"Yes. That's my answer."

Deep breath. Serious look. He nods. "As you say then." We all stand up, and it's time for a group hug, profuse thanks, and a ride home. But I think we all part feeling unsettled.

BACK AT THE HOUSE, BEFORE WE GO INSIDE, STEPH TAPS MY shoulder. "You want to go for a walk?" I nod. We start walking toward the river, aiming for the rust-colored footbridge that arches high over the railroad tracks to Crescent Park, a sliver of redeveloped waterfront that still wears the decayed remnants of its industrial past. The curve of the river puts downtown New Orleans across the water from us, seeming much farther away than it really is.

"Well, that was interesting," she says.

"Interesting for me too."

"Did you like your grandfather? You seemed to. But I don't think you fully trusted him."

"That's fair. I did like him. He's likable. But he's holding something back about Leon. I'm not sure what, but I felt it. There was a hole in what he was saying."

"You know, I felt it too. I got very sensitized to those holes, back when I was with George. Everything he said had holes in it." She gives me a one-armed hug. "I'm glad you don't have that trauma morph thing, though, that sounds horrible."

"Yes. That would, indeed, be horrible. If I had that thing. Very horrible."

Steph does a double take. "Wait. You do, don't you? You do have the trauma morph?"

We're passing a brick building Morgan has talked about, as an example of New Orleans' passion for preservation, and also of irritating post-Katrina hipsterism. Once a sugar warehouse, it was abandoned for decades before getting remodeled into pricy new condominiums. But they left all the graffiti painted on the bricks. The building tells me YOU ARE BEAUTIFUL.

"Uh. Yeah. I do. Luckily I found out it was a thing before I told any of them. And I guess my wolf killed George soon enough after the full moon, they didn't instantly realize what that meant."

"Wait." She frowns, stops walking. "You killed George? As a wolf, you mean?"

"Of course, Steph. What did you think happened?"

"They said it was a stray dog." She starts to get worked up. "That's what the coroner said! That's what the police said! That's what everybody said!" She's freaking out. I freak out in response.

"Well, it's not like the coroner is going to put 'werewolf' as cause of death!"

Is my stress because of guilt? But why? I don't think what the wolf did was wrong, not really. But here I am, voice getting shrill as I say, "I didn't have a choice, Steph! I already bit him, he was already an infected wolf, he already killed at least one person, and he was already threatening to come after you and Terry! Then he shot me with silver! He was trying to kill me!"

"I know, I know! I'm not upset!" she says, sounding very upset. "I mean, I'm not upset with you!" We're passed by a jogger and Steph clamps her lips shut, then seems slightly calmer after the jogger has passed. She half-whispers as she says, "I didn't know, okay? I mean, I could have known, I guess, but I didn't think about it. Maybe I didn't want to think about it."

I feel really stressed out and start walking again, needing the physical movement. "I know. It's a terrible thing. What do you do?" I realize I'm going too fast for Steph to keep up easily and double back around, start jogging in place. But that jostles thirty small courses of exquisite gourmet food and I slow back down to Steph's walking pace. "I'm sorry. I didn't mean to just spring everything on you like that. I guess I thought you knew."

"It really upsets you, doesn't it?"

"Shouldn't it?"

"I don't know." She squeezes my shoulders. "I don't know how upset you should be. I don't know how upset I should be. I did think sometimes about George ending up dead. I knew it was a possibility, the way things were going. But I always figured it was going to be my brother shooting him, you know? I thought about how I'd feel then. I really did think about it."

"And what did you think? When you imagined it happening that way? Were you mad at Morgan?"

She stops, frowns, looks off toward the New Orleans downtown skyline. "I was never sure. I guess I kept hoping it wouldn't go that way. I didn't want to wonder forever if my brother killed him because it really was the best option, or if it was because he was living out some vigilante fantasy. Morgan isn't as bad as some of his gun-toting buddies, but a lot of them, they want so badly to use violence to play the badass hero. They all want to be Dirty Harry or the Punisher or something."

We're near a coffee roasting plant, and I inhale deeply,

comforted by the smell. Coffee smells like optimism. "So what about me? Are you mad at me?"

"Oh, sweetie, no. No, of course not." She gathers me into a fierce hug. "He was trying to kill you. It was self defense. And you said he threatened me and Terry, too."

"Right. He said he was going to kill you, and bite his son."

"Ugh, really?" She looks a little sick, then laughs slightly. "That's really messed up."

"Yeah, it was. At the time I didn't know that wasn't what happened to me. That I got bit as a baby or something. I didn't know about the difference between the bitten and the born."

"Huh." She looks thoughtful. "That's funny, I never really thought about it. You started talking about your family here in the area and I guess—okay, I'll be honest. Until today I'm not sure I believed one hundred percent in the wolf."

"I know."

"I didn't think you were lying. I just, maybe, kept it in the same place I keep my Catholic faith. Where you can sort of believe something and think it's bullshit at the same time?" She laughs. "That doesn't make any sense, does it?"

"No, it does. I get it. You sort of believe the bullshit, but you mostly believe what's right in front of you. But then you get a fanatic like Wisdom, who had this burning need to believe in the bullshit more than he believed in what was right in front of him. He chose to do that. And I still don't know why. I don't know what makes a person—" My voice breaks. "I don't know what makes a person do the things he did. Ignore the suffering right in front of him, the pain of his own children, for the sake of a God nobody's ever seen."

I'm crying now and Steph hugs me. We stand in the remains of a warehouse, sheltered by a rusted roof, but no walls. Pigeons and crows scatter before us.

"It's okay," she says, stroking my hair. "He's gone. You know he's gone."

"Steph, I'm not really a violent person."

"No, of course not."

"I mean it. I don't want all this death and destruction in my life. I don't want to go live with the Varger and get tortured into submission. That already happened to me once, I'm not doing it again."

"No. No, you shouldn't have to do that."

"So you'll keep my secret?"

"Of course." She kisses the top of my head. "Of course."

14

STRIGOI

Steph and I are heading back to the house, when I pick up the scent of an idling car, and Opal. She must be running her car with the window rolled down so I can tell she's there. She probably wants to talk to me. Good, since I want to talk to her.

"Hey, Steph. I need to tell you something. I have a half sister named Opal. Not a werewolf. She's in the neighborhood right now and I think I need to go talk to her."

She frowns. "What, did she buzz you? I didn't see you look at your phone."

I laugh. "Scent trail. We don't always need phones."

"Huh." She looks thoughtful for a moment, then laughs. "Well. Okay." She hugs me. "Just keep me posted on your plans. With your friends or your sister or whoever."

I find Opal, hold my breath against the car fumes, lean in toward her window. "Opal. What do you want? Are you here to tell me about the other dead man?"

Her scent doesn't change when I ask the question. She's dressed in greasy coveralls again, face unreadable behind giant Audrey Hepburn sunglasses. "What are you talking about, hon?"

"At the abandoned Navy base. It looked like the same thing as before, a big party, a man ending up dead in what looks like a drunken accident. But you were in both places. And both dead men were in neighborhoods where I hang out. So I'd be sure to find them." I take a deep breath, choking on the fumes, nervous about where this speculation has suddenly led me. A bra in a trash can, that's one way to get my attention. But a dead man in an empty building, that's an even better way to get my attention. Would she have done it, just to fulfill a request from the Cachorros? Not killed a man exactly, but somehow arranged for him to be dead? I don't want to think she would have, but now that I've had this idea, it won't leave me alone. How hard would it be, to make something like that happen? To get a guy to a particular location and make sure he ended up dead?

She lowers her sunglasses enough to look at me over the top of them. One of her eyes looks dark, possibly bruised, and her face is pale. "Please get in the car, Abby. We need to talk about this."

My gut lurches in a moment of apprehension, but I get in the car anyway. After all, what can she do to me? She doesn't even have a wolf. She rolls up both windows, begins driving slowly through the neighborhood. "I'm a drug dealer. I'm not proud of it, but it's how I earn a living."

"Oh." I don't know what I was expecting her to say, but not that. Why not, though? I accidentally inhaled cocaine at the party site. Somebody had to put that cocaine there.

After a long pause she says, "Did you hear me?"

"I heard you. I don't know what to say."

"I know, it's a lot to deal with. I can hardly believe it myself sometimes. I wonder, how did I get here? Is this who I want to be? And it's not, really. I want to get out of this life. I try, but I keep getting sucked back in. Some new opportunity comes up, and there I am, putting together another wild party for men with more money than brains. I'm really ashamed of myself,

Abby. But I'm scared, too. These men I deal with, a lot of the time, they're not good people."

"But how do they keep ending up dead?"

"I don't know, Abby. I wasn't there when either of those men died. Usually what I do is get the party set up for my customers, then leave. I don't do drugs or alcohol myself. I would get terribly bored if I stuck around the whole time."

"So you have no idea how it happened?"

She seems agitated. "No! I don't! I didn't even know there was another dead man, how could I possibly know how he died? How did he die, anyway? Who was it?"

"He, uh, he bled out from a cut that looked like it could have been accidental. He was a big guy. White, tanned, dark hair. In a frat T-shirt, like the other one, but I don't think it was the same Greek letters."

She sighs. "So what do you want me to tell you? I mean, I know who it probably is, a guy named Andrew Jackson, and I'm not kidding about the name. He really wanted to party inside that abandoned Navy base. The site was more important to him than the hookers and blow. But once I got him set up there, I left. I told him if the cops busted the party, he was on his own. I really can't tell you what happened after that, I'm sorry." She sighs. "These guys, they make their own stupid decisions, you know? They decide to drink too much, they decide to do a whole pile of cocaine and not drink any water when it's August in New Orleans, they decide to party all night in an abandoned warehouse full of things you can hit your head on."

She pulls over to the side of the road, parks under a spreading, gnarled live oak. "I can't drive right now, I'm getting all stressed." She holds out her hands: white, trembling. "Because of what I do, I have friends—associates really—who are not very nice. You met one of them yesterday. And he's far from the worst. I'm scared of them, Abby. I really am."

She removes her sunglasses, displaying a bruise that's huge

and ugly and sick-looking. My gut churns with anger. "Who did that to you?"

"It doesn't matter. Nothing matters." Her eyes glitter with tears. "Damn it, Abby, I never set out to have this life. I had a plan for the future, and it involved a wolf who never showed up. After that, I didn't know what to do with myself. I fell into some bad things, and now I want out, but these men, they will not let me go. I think they're connected to the Russian mob. Part of a group that calls themselves the Strigoi?"

At the word I go cold. "Strigoi? Is that what you said?"

"Yes it is. Why, do you know about them?"

"I don't know. I've heard the word before. A man called me that."

"Was it here in New Orleans?"

"No, it was out near Las Vegas. He was driving by in a car and—um—you know—playing with himself? I yelled at him and I think my eyes flashed green, the first time I did that to anybody, and he got scared and said 'strigoi' and some other words I didn't understand. He might have been Russian."

"Well, my goodness. That word means something like witch or vampire, as far as I know."

"And these men you're dealing with, they call themselves that? Are they werewolves?"

"Well, I suppose some of them might be. Wolves of the bitten variety, anyway. I wouldn't always be able to tell, you know." She taps the side of her nose. "I suspect they're not, though. Criminals like to use folklore and magic to make themselves seem more terrifying than they really are. But after you've seen what a real rougarou can do—" She looks thoughtful for a moment, then pulls out her phone, taps it, and tosses it to me. "I think there's something you need to see."

It's a video. A little me, in motion, with sound. It's from yesterday—was that only yesterday? Yes. I met Opal yesterday. I had my confrontation with Dennis yesterday.

I see us together framed in the shot. Him, tall and thick and muscular, but a little fat too, like an off-season athlete who's been indulging in too much beer and pizza. And there I am, face turned away from the camera, with my floaty green dress and bare white legs, looking small and delicate and ready to play one of the fairies in a high school production of *A Midsummer Night's Dream*. He stares down at me with annoyed amusement, the way you'd watch a small yapping dog nip at your ankles.

From the speaker he says, "Bitch. I told you get gone, now."

"Leave my sister alone and I will."

"Sister? You say? Must come from ugly side of family."

It's bizarre to hear these words and remember hearing them at the same time. I feel displaced, disoriented. My life seems so unlikely, maybe none of this is really happening at all.

The knife comes out in a flash. The angle of the video changes and I see my own face. For a moment I look intense, frowning in concentration.

"Too ugly for rape, so—"

The wolf becomes enraged. My mouth stays closed but I unclench my teeth and the muscles in my neck start to jump and twitch as my nostrils flare. My eyes widen. Then my mouth opens up, showing teeth, at the same time my brows come down and my nose wrinkles up further. I've seen videos of wolves snarling at people, and this looks just like that. If I saw my own face, I would be scared. But his face stays laid back. My rage is funny to him, like the tiny helpless screaming of a mouse or a rabbit.

Then he's up against the wall, almost too fast to follow in the video. It looks comical, to see me, so much smaller than he is, holding him up above the sidewalk, while his legs kick helplessly. He drops. The second knife comes out. "Oh, you, you pay for that."

I hear the loud crack-crack-crack as my foot shoots out and slams into his knee, his crotch, his other knee.

As I grab the knife, my face moves from rage into a strange blankness. The cut on my hand looks worse on camera than I remember it feeling. Blood spurts out everywhere, but I don't appear to notice. When some of it hits my face, I smile. I don't remember it being the blood that made me smile, but that's what it looks like.

I look, not to be too delicate here, kind of psycho. It's not a human smile or a wolf smile. It's the smile of a killer.

I watch myself hit the man, with a meaty thud that sounds painful, damaging and cruel. He falls backwards, as I hit him again and again, with that disturbing meaty thud each time. All the expression has left my face other than that slight, crazed smile.

My nose crinkles in disgust—this must be the moment he pissed himself. The human feeling starts to come back into my face, and I watch a second or two of struggle there, before the video ends.

I'm torn between a horrified fascination, an urge to watch the video over and over, and a queasy impulse to throw my sister's phone right out the window of the car and watch it shatter. "I look like a psycho."

"Oh, sugar." Her voice is sympathetic. "That's not right. Don't you see what you are?"

I slump into the seat, sweating, but feeling cold. "I don't know what I am."

"You're my protector." She smiles, big and bright. "You want to protect the vulnerable. I'm your sister. It's okay to protect me."

I close my eyes. The video replays in my mind, fascinating and horrifying. "I have to protect Steph and Terry first. And after that my friends. I can't endanger any of them to protect you."

"Oh, I understand. If I had a friend who looked like your Edison, he'd be my number one priority too." She sees my face, and stops. "I'm sorry, it's just my nature to make jokes. But I do understand, really I do." She smiles brightly. "Anyway, it's my last night in New Orleans. I've got all my affairs settled and tomorrow I'll be leaving town with my brothers and sisters."

"That's your plan? Wait, that's their plan? To leave town before the full moon?"

"Well, of course, sugar. They don't want to be in Varger territory during the full moon. That can get ugly. The Cachorros came to meet you, and they did. But if you want to leave with us, I'm sure you can. Or just come out to say good-bye. You should say goodbye to Jaime and Reina, at least. Some-time before sunrise tomorrow, let me take you out there. Please say you'll come."

"Sure." This is all coming too fast and nothing seems quite real. When my phone buzzes with a text, I think at first it's a big insect that has somehow become trapped in my clothing, and slap at it. Maybe the lack of sleep is catching up with me.

It's from Deena.

> Hey, we're getting ready to do a thing, if you want to come by the hotel room

"My friends are getting ready to go out for the evening," I tell Opal. "If you could drop me off in the Quarter?"

"Oh, are you-all doing the tourist thing? Mind if I tag along? I'd love to say my goodbyes to this city before leaving."

> Okay if my sister Opal hangs around with us tonight?

> Sure! The bros would like that.

I turn to Opal. "Deena says it's okay."

"Fantastic, thank you. Tonight should be so much fun." She restores her sunglasses and begins driving again. "Well, it looks like I need to go get ready for the evening, so I'll drop you off near the hotel. Royal Sonesta, right?"

"Right." I nod, but I'm starting to feel nervous now, like everything in my life is about to collide all at once. Steph's family and my Seattle friends and the Varger and the Cachorros and the Strigoi. I picture them, all the groups of people I know, all coming from different parts of a huge urban stage set, each group with their color-coded outfits and signature theme music, and New Harmony is there too, and now that we're all together we're going to dance fight, which is a great relief to me. I think I can win a dance fight. I'm not sure about other kinds of fights.

"Abby?" Opal's voice startles me fully awake. "Abby, we're here." She's grinning at me.

"Thanks." I get out of the car. I feel nervous, for no reason I can put my finger on. Is it the red moon?

I hope not.

15

SEVEN DEADLY SINS

The hotel room is a day more stinky and strewn with detritus. Deena and Izzy sit on the couch holding hands, Edison next to them. Ward begins pouring Manhattans from a cocktail shaker, hands one of them to me.

"Abby, welcome. We've got a special thing planned for tonight."

"I'm going to take pictures." Deena holds up her phone, which is hanging around her neck with an extra camera lens attached to it. "I got some awesome swamp photos earlier. I know you're not here as a tourist, but you really should go out to the swamps sometime. I got to pet an alligator!"

"Has everybody got their drink?" Ward asks, and we all hold up our glasses. "All right, it's time to get dressed." Out of a bag, he pulls T-shirts in the same shade of maroon as the beer pong T-shirts and hands them to us. They're printed in glittery silver ink.

$$\Psi\ \Phi\ \Theta$$

Psi Phi Theta
Seattle Destroys New Orleans
with
Gluttony
Lust
Greed
Pride
Wrath
Vanity
Envy

"To sin!" Ward says, holding up his glass.

"To sin!" the rest of us answer. Then we all drink.

"This is good, matching shirts will help us keep track of everybody," Deena says.

"New Orleans excels at most of these," Izzy says.

"We're counting on it."

"Seven deadly sins." I stare at the T-shirts, feel a twinge at the back of my head, a nervous giddy feeling. I laugh and it comes out shrill. "You know, Father Wisdom used to speak about these deadly sins and how they would consign us to the eternal fires, and here we are using them as a checklist for a fun night on the town."

"You know it," Brad says, with a grin. Then he frowns. "Does that bother you or anything?"

"What? No, of course not. I just think it's funny." I force a big smile. "I don't believe any of that stuff anymore."

He nods and the conversation moves on, but I lose the thread. I was lying, of course. It does bother me. I don't want it to bother me, but it does. I don't even believe in hell, in sin, but I'm still a little afraid of it.

Maybe I always will be.

Opal knocks on the door, and I hop up to open it. She grins at me briefly then turns to the room. "Why, hello there everybody, how are you all doing?" She's heavily made up, covering the bruises and swelling around her eye with glitter and stick-on rhinestones. Her T-shirt is tight and her shorts are tiny and her hair is long and curly and bright lavender at the tips. She looks ready to party.

"Are you part of our posse?" Ward asks.

"I sure am, hon."

Ward holds up one of the deadly sins T-shirts. "I don't know if you'll want to put this on. I got way too many of them because of how the shop did the pricing, and to save money they're all the same size. Men's large. Which, by the way, if you have any need for dozens and dozens of shirts, I'm your man."

She laughs. "Sugar, believe me, I know how to improve the fit of a T-shirt." She winks at me. "And my sister over there is kind of an expert at it. Let's go into the bathroom, Abby, I've got a surprise for you."

In the bathroom she takes off the T-shirt she was wearing, appears in just a bra, then slips the maroon T-shirt over her head. "You want to do me up? I mean, make this thing look a little more exciting, you know?"

"Sure." I attack the fabric with my sewing kit, and soon it's been slit and tied and rendered tight and fringy and sleeveless and full of provocative holes.

"Bravo." She seems sincere. "And now for you." Out of her bag she takes a clothing item in pale silk and holds it up.

"White? I don't wear white. I'll get it all grubby."

"It's not white, it's ivory. And trust me, it is your color."

I study the fabric, then realize what it is and try to hand it back to her. "No. No way. I am not wearing a corset."

"Now, now, sis, I know you probably never wore a thing like this before. But you want to catch the eye of that Edison boy, and it's New Orleans in late August, and you're gonna have a lot of competition out there. So you gotta make the most of what you've got, darlin'. You don't wanna seem like a plain little thing he can just ignore, do you?"

"Okay, fine, I'll try it." I get out of the blue dress and let Opal fasten the corset around me. At first I find its firm restrictions almost comforting, reminiscent of the breast bindings I grew up with. Then she starts yanking on the strings.

"Too tight!"

"That's the idea, cutie. There now, you see?" She points me to the mirror. The ivory color looks all right, I suppose, but makes me feel weirdly naked. Although, naked, I would never have this perfect hourglass figure, all the pressure of the corset working to squeeze my waist into where my breasts should be, then push my breasts up practically to my chin. "Just a sec, I'm going to manhandle you a bit." She startles me by reaching down the front of the corset and lifting up the flesh of each one of my breasts in turn, a trick that mounds them up even higher.

I don't think another human being has ever touched the skin of my breasts before. And it's my weird semi-criminal sister.

"There. Raise your hands up like this." She slips another clothing item on me, a tiny bolero jacket in red velvet. "That'll cover your shoulder scars. Now, what do we do for a skirt?"

"I know." Quickly, I restructure a seven deadly sins T-shirt into a skirt with pockets. I am possibly now world-famous for this trick.

"Perfect, except—" Opal takes the scissors from me and gives the skirt a little side slit that shows an extra couple of inches of leg on the right side. "Now you're ready. Go get 'em!"

We emerge, to whistles and hoots and Edison saying, "Wow, you really do have boobs. I had no idea."

I blush and Opal grins at me. "Told you so."

We step out onto Bourbon Street into the thick, hot air. I realize the corset fails to breathe in other ways too, and I'm going to be way too hot in this thing. Still, women dressed like this during the 19th century, didn't they? They didn't have global warming back then, but they also didn't have air conditioning.

"Duuuuuuude," says Brad, appreciatively, as a woman in short-shorts walks by, cheap Mardi Gras beads bouncing and swinging over her breasts. "This place rocks so hard."

"Time for vanity," Deena says. "There's this place I want to go to, but it closes pretty soon. Fifi Mahony's."

It's on Royal and sells wigs, makeup, and accessories, all heading in the direction of super-fabulous drag queen, or French courtier right before the revolution. It would fit right in on Seattle's Capitol Hill, and this makes me feel at home, but also a little homesick. They have a few wigs on display that have been coiffed and sculpted so elaborately I'm not even sure how you would wear them: a three-foot lavender tower covered with glitter and flower petals, or a mermaid wig in shades of blue and green topped with an enormous tiara made of seashells and rhinestones.

"You like it?" asks one of the workers, batting his lashes at me.

"It's beautiful. But how would you wear something like that without toppling over?"

"Neck strength and posture, hon."

"Ooo, tiaras in black," Deena says. "My inner ten-year-old girl totally wants a black tiara suitable for wearing as goth queen of the universe." She puts it on her head and turns to Izzy. "What do you think?"

"Definitely."

"Oh, I want one," Edison says.

"The diamond color works better against dark hair," Deena says, placing one on his head.

"Look, it's my color," Izzy says, holding up glittery eye shadow in the yellow of a classic number two pencil.

"I'm not wearing any of this stuff," Brad mutters.

"You need this," Opal says to me, holding up an elaborate

choker, jet beads dangled and draped like something from a fancy chandelier.

"I don't have that much money."

"So. Let me buy it for you."

I think about objecting. I know where you get your money, and I don't want you spending it on me. But I don't say anything. I should never have agreed to her terms, why did I? She just made it easier to say yes. And she is my sister. I do need to protect her if I can, don't I?

She's right, the choker looks terrific.

Deena shows us her documentation on social media: #DeadlySinsNewOrleans #Vanity and there we are. Pictures of us, looking fabulous. Even me. Outside the sun is setting, and the moon, nearly full, rides high above us, bringing a rising giddy excitement.

The next thing we do is, we stroll down Bourbon Street, because of course that's what we do. Steph and Morgan are both scornful of Bourbon Street as the epitome of clueless New Orleans tourism, a cheesy frat party that stinks perpetually of vomit, exclusively for people who drink terrible booze, rock out to mediocre classic rock cover bands, and think flashing nipples for beads is a thing.

But I'm here with a bunch of fratty frat boys, and they're completely in their element, dazzled by the neon and the glittery crowd. All of my Seattle companions, Deena included, are looking around with dazed, happy fascination. Izzy wears a smirk, and makes knowing eye contact with me a couple of times, but doesn't have the heart to interfere with Deena's good time. Opal, meanwhile, acts exactly like you would expect a woman partying on Bourbon Street to act, flirting and laughing and woo-hooing on cue. I'm pretty sure it's an act, but a convincing one. If we're being shadowed by evil drug dealers, I can't tell.

"Oh my God, I can't believe I'm walking down the center of the street with no cars, this is awesome," Deena says. She snaps a picture. "Look at these iron lace balconies. Why don't we have these in Seattle? Just imagine Broadway if you could walk down the middle of it with a drink and it was full of balconies."

A disheveled woman veers toward Edison with a drunken smile, and hands him a daiquiri in a plastic cup, along with a string of silver Mardi Gras beads.

"You're cute," she says. "I think I need to go home. Taxi!" She lurches unsteadily, one sandal missing, toward a cross street where a yellow cab sits. Edison watches her with a huge smile, then takes a sip of the daiquiri. Fake fruit smell with the bite of alcohol tickles my nose.

"Why are you drinking that? She could have spit in it."

"I don't taste any spit."

"She could have the plague. She could be patient zero for the zombie apocalypse."

He laughs. "In that case, I want to die early while the electricity's still on." He holds out the cup. "Want some?"

I shouldn't, but I have a sip anyway. I taste ice, sugar, pretend fruit, and the chemical pop of alcohol.

"That's terrible." I hand it back. "How can you drink that stuff?"

He shrugs. "I've had worse."

"Dude, no," Ward says, taking the drink out of his hand. "Do not drink some gross second-hand daiquiri. Reed is going to get us all Brain Bombs."

Brain Bombs turn out to be a cocktail served in a cup of black, bomb-shaped plastic, lurid red lettering on the side advertising it as BOURBON STREET'S STRONGEST DRINK.

I scoff when I see it. "You know, there's probably five different drinks that all claim to be Bourbon Street's strongest drink."

Brad stares at me, obviously feeling challenged. "You've had stronger? You wanna test that?"

"Test it how?"

"We start chugging and see who gives up first."

"Fine. You're on."

Neither one of us gives up, which seems to impress the bros unduly.

"Now we both have to walk a straight line," Brad says.

I do an obviously better job, which shouldn't make me feel proud of myself, but it does.

We head down the street, toward Esplanade. The Brain Bomb simmers and stews in my gut, and I regret the corset, or the drink, or both. The Brain Bomb seems to have been engineered for frat boys who want to get messed up, not for people who care what things taste like.

Great, I've been a drinker for a day and I'm already getting snobby about it.

We pass one of those obnoxious men who carry big signs talking about how everybody is going to hell because of gay sex demons. He's got a megaphone, which he yells into, rendering his speech loud but so distorted as to be nearly meaningless. Some individual words emerge from the mush: Lord; sin; fornication; hell; demons.

Izzy and Deena laugh and make a point of taking a selfie of themselves kissing with his sign in the background, which seems to delight most people in the vicinity. Normally that would seem like enough punishment for such a man, but the horrible comments on the *Teen Mode* article have sensitized me, or maybe it's the moon. I feel a deep rage building up, that now-familiar sensation of something trying to claw its way into the back of my head.

"Hey, you," I snap at the guy.

"God loves you," he says, not through the megaphone.

"God is a fucking bastard."

He doesn't respond to my profanity. "God wants you to come home to Him."

I shrug off the bolero jacket and turn to show him my scars. "This is what your God did to me."

He winces, takes a step back. "Not God. Men. Men did that."

"Really? Because the man responsible told me God did it. He told me it was God's will. Are you saying he lied?" Every time I take a step forward, he takes a step back. It's probably very comical, like seeing a mouse chase around an elephant. We're getting a bit of a crowd, people attracted to the spectacle.

"Not everyone who claims to follow God really knows Him."

"No. So how do you know you're one of the good ones?" I take a step forward. He takes a step back. He's feeling a little afraid, I can smell it on him. This encourages the wolf. I let out the tiniest little growl, clench and unclench my fists. I catch his gaze, hold it, and he wilts. "I don't think you're good at all. In fact, I think you are very, very bad."

I could eat your face off.

I could rip your guts out.

I stop my hand, seconds from tearing the megaphone out of his grasp and shattering it against the grimy Bourbon Street sidewalk. Seconds away from taking him by the throat and pressing him up against the wall of a strip club.

I could.

But I won't.

I turn around, heart pounding, and address the crowd. "Hey, everybody! Do you know what's wrong with these sign carrier guys?"

"They're jerks."

"They're idiots."

"They don't like to see other people have fun."

"No!" I put on a little bit of the preaching intonation I remember from my father. I point at the man, as aggressive as I can make a pointing finger. "This man suffers from the sin of pride! He's out here praying on the street corner, for men to see! And I tell you, he's already had his reward! God does not know him! He is not a righteous man, humble before the Lord! He is a proud man! Showing off what he supposes to be his own virtue! He is proud!"

"Good call, Abby," Deena says. She snaps a picture while Ward holds up a spare deadly sins T-shirt in front of the man. She sends it out, #SinOfPride. Everyone laughs, and Ward hands a few spare T-shirts to people in the audience. The sign carrier melts into the crowd, seeming subdued, possibly by my glare. We move on.

I want to feel pleased. We humiliated one of those sign-carrying preacher guys. But instead I just feel stressed out and unsettled, not rid of that sensation of something clawing at the back of my head trying to get in, disturbed by how close I was to doing something violent that I would probably regret.

Probably.

WARD SAYS, "TIME FOR GLUTTONY," AND STEERS US DOWN A side street and into a huge dinner buffet.

"It smells fantastic," Deena says. She starts taking pictures.

The smell is fantastic, yes. But it also smells like a lot of meat. I know I'm the only vegetarian in our group. Sometimes I think I'm the only one in the whole city. It's only been a few hours since our meal with Pere Claude, so I'm not really hungry yet. Anyway, I'm not sure the corset leaves much room for food. I order a grilled cheese sandwich from the kid's menu.

"That's not gluttony," Deena says, looking to my sandwich from her plate piled high with shrimp and crawfish in the shell.

"That's barely even dinner," Izzy says.

"It's a pretty good sandwich though."

"You could just drink more," Ward says. "That counts as gluttony."

Reed looks thoughtful for a moment, then disappears and comes back with a drink for me. "Bourbon milk punch." It might be the first words he's said to me while sober. I still can't tell if he likes me. But the milk punch is delicious.

It's not a huge drink, though, and I finish it quickly. Reed gets me another drink without asking. I think he's running down the restaurant's list of specialty cocktails, because he gets me a different one each time. Sazerac. Hurricane. Swamp water. Pimm's Cup. Ramos Gin Fizz. Just about every time anybody gets a plate of food, Reed gets me a new drink.

I watch my friends eat. I watch strangers eat. I watch crisply-attired restaurant staff haul out new chafing dishes piled high with every kind of meat you could think of. This really is an ode to gluttony. There's just so much food everywhere. Plates over-flowing, big, fleshy people, tall young bros who shovel it in like they're stoking a massive internal furnace.

I have an odd flashback to New Harmony, one of the times things were getting really bad there and we didn't have enough food to go around. I remember watching my older brothers get first pick of what was already not enough. That was the way of it. The girls starved first. Why? There was some scriptural justification I'm sure, but I no longer remember what it was.

I'd forgotten about that, until just now. I'd forgotten the pain of hunger. When I left New Harmony, it had become so constant that I barely thought about it anymore. It was a hard gnawing sensation in my core, dulling my thoughts, weakening my limbs and my control, until the horrible moment when the smell of my own sister's flesh, searing on a funeral pyre, trig-gered a moment of stomach-gurgling hunger.

Meat bothers me because I'm scared of it.

I'm scared it's not okay to want it.

I'm scared it's not okay to want anything.

"Dude, why aren't you drunk?" Brad says to me. "You've been sucking 'em back like a sorority pledge."

"Maybe they're not that strong here?"

"Wrong! These things are fucking hammers, believe me."

He gestures with his drink, sloshing it at me, seeming pretty drunk already.

"I've never been drunk before, maybe it's some kind of beginner's luck."

Brad drains his glass, slams it down on the table, and points at me. "Oh. Dude. It's on. I will see you lip-walking by the end of the evening."

Deena snaps a picture. "Wrath," she says.

"I'd call it pride, myself," Izzy says.

We leave the buffet and end up back on Bourbon Street. Deena wants to buy a cigar, then the bros and Edison all have to buy cigars, then they have to head down to the river to smoke their cigars. Opal buys me and Izzy drinks. We stand upwind of the smoke, and watch them.

"My new girlfriend is such a freak," Izzy says, with a smile, as she watches Deena gesture with the cigar.

Opal says to me, "The quiet one likes you."

"He keeps buying me drinks, I guess. Last night he told me that he didn't think I was hot. But then he asked if I wanted to make out. It was weird."

"Oh, my, yes, if he did that, he certainly does like you." She glares at the bros, a coldness in her eyes I haven't seen there before. "In fact, I would say what you describe is fairly typical behavior for one of these frat boy types. If you keep on spending time with them, you'll learn all about that. As a young and reasonably attractive female you are not a person to them. You're an object. Like a trophy. He does not look at you and think, do I like the look of this girl? Do I want to spend time with this girl? No. He thinks, will this girl impress the other frat boys? That's all he cares about. And you are nothing to them. Nothing."

We stand in awkward silence for a moment, then Izzy takes a loud slurp of her drink, holds it up toward Deena as if in a toast. "Well, thank the good Lord I don't date boys of any kind."

Opal laughs, flutters her eyelashes, goes back into her usual Southern belle mode. "Oh, now, never mind me. I can be a bit cynical at times. I don't mean anything by it, y'all. I love men."

She's watching Edison while she says this. I try not to think about it.

Cigars finished, the others join us and we start walking down Bourbon Street again.

"You all just crossed the rainbow line," Izzy says. "Welcome to Gay New Orleans."

A cluster of middle-aged male tourists lean out over one of the iron lace balconies, watching the crowd pass, tossing Mardi Gras beads. They spot Edison and start waving to him, the crushed-grass smell of their sexual interest wafting down. Apparently his charms are universally recognized. "Oh, honey, you want some beads?" one of them croons.

With a huge grin, Edison stops and lifts his shirt to flash his chest. For a moment everyone is stunned by his lean athletic perfection. Then all the men throw beads at him. He catches the strands easily, including one massive necklace where the largest beads are three inches in diameter. Deena takes pictures.

"Magnificent!" One of the men kisses his fingers and makes a little bowing motion.

"Oh, sweetie, can I take you home to Nashville with me? Pretty, pretty please?"

The men laugh, and Edison laughs, and we walk on. But I feel weird and hot and kind of angry. Jealousy again. But it's ridiculous. Edison wasn't interested in those guys and they knew it. Everybody was just clowning around. But my stomach is churning, and I feel like maybe I want to hit something.

I fold my arms and glare instead. "It's cheesy to flash for beads. It's not even Mardi Gras. It makes you look like a dumb tourist."

"Well, I am a dumb tourist." He shrugs, and drapes the super-sized beads around his neck.

"Okay, that's envy for Abby," Deena says. "Lust and pride for Edison. The rest of you need to step up your sinning game."

"Let's go to a strip club," Brad says. "I want to do some lust."

I inhale, exhale, try to calm down. I thought I could handle my jealousy. But I'm not any more in control of myself than I was last night.

It's okay. I can feel a thing. I don't have to act.

16

SCARS MEANS YOU SURVIVED

As we wander the city, our attempted forays into both lust and greed keep meeting a particular dead end: only Reed and Opal are twenty-one, and strip clubs, adult novelty shops, and casinos all have strictly enforced age requirements.

My fresh ID does me no good. I should have made myself twenty-one.

"Why don't we try something like a burlesque club?" Opal says. "I know a place a few blocks away, come on."

The building has a shabby-chic outside, reminiscent of the Preservation Hall exterior. A painted sign identifies it as Wicked's Dungeon.

At the entrance, a paper sign: 18+ only.

"Hooray, I get to use my new ID!"

But I don't. In spite of the sign, nobody's checking ID at the door, maybe because it's still too early in the evening. Heavy, gloomy music pulsates over a big dark space, lit with flickering candles, populated by scattered clumps of people dressed in black leather and polished steel. In our maroon T-shirts and casual shorts we look completely out of place, but nobody seems to care. In spite of the indoor smoking ban, a few people have lit cigarettes of clove-infused tobacco.

"Oh, it's a goth club!" Deena says. "That must be some kind of a deadly sin, right?"

"Despair," I say. "On some older lists, despair is one of the seven."

"Fantastic." She snaps a few pictures.

Reed buys drinks, while we seat ourselves at a corner table, easy to find in this mostly empty club.

We drink and talk for a while, but I'm distracted by two things: a sensation of music thumping through the wall and the floorboards, which fights with the music playing in this room, and a creeping smell of—well, I can't quite figure it out. There's violence, pain, blood, but also pleasure and sexual desire.

"Excuse me," I tell the others, and follow the smell, like a tattered ribbon of dark blue velvet. I probably look like I'm searching for a bathroom, ducking around mysterious corners and up narrow stairways and pushing through doors that look like they should be locked, but aren't.

Finally I push aside some red velvet curtains, and find myself in hell.

It's hot, red-lit, and full of people writhing gasping, groaning. Their flesh is being sliced, deformed, rearranged, pulled into other shapes. Tortured.

Except everyone is happy. People are groaning in pleasure—well, pain too—both at the same time, is that possible? I swallow, mouth drying out, head thumping. I exhale slowly, acutely conscious of how tight the corset is, how shallow my breathing as it rasps in my ears. I know what this is. I live on Capitol Hill. I know people do these things for fun. I've seen the equipment for sale. I've joked about some of it being similar to what Wisdom used for our chastisements, did he know he was being kinky, ha-ha.

But until I was surrounded by people using these things in earnest, I didn't know how familiar it would feel, how much like the tortures of my childhood. A sick, cynical laughter starts burbling up at the back of my throat. As a child, my sense of smell wasn't acute enough, and my experience wasn't broad enough, for me to know certain things that I now wonder. I wouldn't have known if Wisdom got off sexually on whipping us. I wouldn't have known if my older siblings got off on it. I wouldn't even have known if I did.

My whole body is tingling now and I'm rooted to the spot. Staring at a skinny, pale young man suspended from the ceiling entirely by fish hooks. Watching a busty woman in a tight waist cincher that squeezes her brown flesh to spill out on either side, as she snaps a whip across the glistening and tightly muscled back of a young woman. It causes more noise than pain. She's trying not to leave scars, right now. But scars aren't forbidden. Over in the corner, an older, heavily tattooed man is using a knife to cut designs into his thighs. The shallow cuts bleed little, and he rubs charcoal into them, which stops the bleeding and leaves vivid black marks showing the path of the knife. My nose tickles with ozone, as a man wrapped entirely in plastic applies a mild electrical current to a man wearing nothing but a sweaty loincloth. Backs arch, muscles tense, teeth grit. Some of the people in this room have an orgasm. I can't spot them visually, but I can smell it, a deep green wet smell that I've never encountered before, but somehow know exactly what it is.

I don't know how long I could go on standing here, inhaling, exhaling, terrified, confused, and, in spite of everything, turned on. The last part is the bit I'm not sure about. I want to be here, but at the same time, I want to be anywhere else.

"Your first time?" A woman—transgender, I think—in a green leather corset and matching top hat comes toward me, sympathy in her eyes. "It can be a little overwhelming."

I nod, throat too dry to speak. "I—uh—" She's not trying to kick me out, but I still feel like I need to explain my presence, so I shrug out of the bolero shirt, show her my scars. "I think I'm processing some—uh—"

"Past trauma." She nods. "A lot of people are. And if you're just not ready to play with anyone else, that's fine. Everything you do here is up to you. I'm Juniper." She shakes my hand very delicately.

"Abby." Suddenly I want to cry, and I don't even know what emotion is causing it. Gratitude or lust, despair or relief, love for this kind stranger right in front of me or hatred for Wisdom? Is there a word for feeling all of those things at exactly the same time?

Juniper notices me crying, and squeezes my hands gently. Her hands are very soft. I'm trying to think about what I want, and even if I figure out what I want, how to ask for it.

Then my companions stumble through the red velvet curtains, like puppies invading a dinner party.

The room, as one, glances at them, and I feel the waves of disruption and disapproval. Juniper drops my hands and frowns slightly. "Are you kids lost?"

"I'm sorry, we're going to move on, so we had to find Abby." Deena smiles at me. "I'm really sorry. We didn't mean to just barge in here. Are you ready to go?"

"I am." I tell Juniper, "Thank you. Thank you so much." I take her hand again.

We make eye contact and she nods. "Do whatever you need to do to heal yourself," she says. "A scar is a good thing. It means you survived."

"Dude, is that guy actually hanging from a bunch of fish-hooks?" Brad says, jaw dropped, eyes goggling. We hustle the boys out of the room as fast as we can.

"WHOA, THAT PLACE," WARD SAYS, WHEN WE'RE OUT ON THE sidewalk again. He wipes his forehead. "I think that was all the deadly sins plus a few that haven't been invented yet." He's making a joke, but is genuinely shaken up.

"I need a drink, now," Brad says. "I need to kill the brain cells that remember what it looks like to see a guy hanging from a million fishhooks."

"You guys are wimps," Deena says.

Izzy smiles and squeezes her waist. "Baby, if you like that stuff, I know some places we can go later on."

Reed gets new frozen daiquiris for everybody.

"What were you doing in there, Abby?" Edison asks. "Were you thinking about getting cattle-prodded?"

"Not really." I think about Juniper's first words to me. Not "Are you lost?" but "Is this your first time?" She knew I belonged there, even before I showed my scars. "Why, are you thinking about getting cattle-prodded?"

He grins. "Only if you do it. While wearing that corset."

My guts rearrange themselves the way they do when he grins at me like that, and I laugh, It comes out fluttering and nervous. "We can do that tomorrow. I need to get a cattle prod first. Where do you buy one of those?"

Edison frowns for a minute. "I don't know. Someplace they have cattle?"

"Maybe not tomorrow then."

"I want to do some lust," Brad calls out. "Regular lust, not fishook lust."

Opal says, "I know a club where the strippers like to go when they're off duty, come on y'all."

It proves to be a regular bar, like the other bars we've seen tonight, but more crowded.

Unable to find a table, we cluster in a corner while Reed goes to get drinks. Edison strikes up a conversation with a woman who may or may not be a stripper, although she's certainly wearing the shoes for it. My jealousy is tempered by amazement at the way she can walk around like a normal person in those spike heels. I can crawl around on the ceiling of a gym, but I couldn't manage those shoes.

Deena leans over to whisper in my ear. "You can't be jealous about Edison," she says.

"Was it that obvious?"

"He's been my friend ever since we were dorky little kids. I was there when he was a spindly nerd who got picked on all the time and I was there when some kind of puberty thing kicked in and all of a sudden he turned into mister super athletic hot stuff. And I've been there when his lovers turned jealous. They start dating him knowing he's not strictly monogamous and then they get jealous anyway."

"I know. Jealousy is my problem, not his. I totally get that."

"Okay." She smiles, gives me a one-armed hug. "Good. As long as you remember that, and don't start blaming him for the way you feel." She sighs. "I know, I'm probably too protective of him. But he's a lot more vulnerable than he seems. And I guess you are too. I read that *Teen Mode* article."

"Did you like it?"

"It made me want to burn down the patriarchy even more than usual." She grins, before turning serious again. "It also made me understand you a little better, I guess. You do a pretty good job of acting like a normal, shy teenager most of the time, so I sort of took you that way. But you're more like a really adaptable space alien who arrived here from another planet six months ago." She brightens. "Oh my God! You're just like David Bowie in *The Man Who Fell to Earth!*"

This last statement is delivered loudly, into a conversational lull, between songs.

"Dude," Brad says. "You think everybody's David Bowie."

"Not you, Brad, don't worry." She grins at him. "I think I need a restroom."

"Me too. I think they're that way." Izzy steers her toward the opposite corner of the bar, and I follow.

There's a line for the restroom, and by the time we come out, we've gotten separated. The first person from the rest of our party I spot is Opal, talking to a huge beefy chunk of a man who towers over both of us. One of the Strigoi? I do smell a lot of tension on both of them. I tap her shoulder. "Opal. Hey."

"Abby." She gives me a tight smile.

"Who you, bitch?" the man demands, in a thick accent reminiscent of Dennis. Another Strigoi, probably. He folds his arms awkwardly over bulging muscles. Not natural-looking muscles, to my eyes. They look like the product of steroids and gym addiction, bulky and inefficient.

"It's all right, Ivan, she's just my sister." Opal puts a hand on my arm, as if claiming ownership. "Let's get going, Abby." She steers me through the crowd.

"He just called me a bitch."

"Technically true, hon. You don't want to get into it with him, trust me on that. We should all get on out of here right now."

But as we push through the crowd, somehow Ivan maneuvers around to block us. He has the same bruisy smell about his sweat as Dennis, heart rate and breathing elevated, stress chemicals high. I stare right into his eyes, but he doesn't wilt the way most people do. Instead he bristles, staring back, taking it as a challenge, making an obvious point of how far down he has to look in order to meet my eyes.

"Leave Opal to me, bitch." His Russian accent is thick. "Get back to faggot friends."

"Excuse me, what did you say?"

A tiny smile plays about his lips. He puts his hands on my shoulders, heavy, resting them there as if I'm a piece of furniture. He leans in close, hot stinking breath exhaled right into my face. He presses down, making a point about how big he is, making it seem like he's ready to crush me. "I said, go away. Go see disgusting faggots."

"That's what I thought you said." And I punch him.

At first it feels good to release all that emotional energy into a moment of violence against a target that richly deserves it, to feel the power of my own body as it forces him through space.

It's a solid hit, and he reels, spraying blood and spittle. But he doesn't go down, and I can tell the pain of the damage isn't registering as strongly as it should. Maybe that's the drug? He rallies instantly, shaking himself and crouching low, muscles flexing.

He knows what he's doing. A professional. I should have listened to Opal. I might have just made a very big mistake. Except, the thought that I might be in real danger seems oddly thrilling.

Something grabs both of my arms. Two men, as big as the first, one on either side of me.

I wasn't expecting it, and they get a firm hold that I can't break instantly. I wonder if the bouncers have arrived and two other big men will shortly be grabbing Ivan's arms, but no such luck. These guys are Ivan's buddies, as I see from the flickering looks they give each other, the half smiles and nods as they coordinate their attack. They hold me for a few seconds, long enough for me to feel like I'm going to explode with frustration. The first goon gets in a really hard punch to my abdomen that makes me glad I'm wearing the corset.

He notices my armor and adjusts his aim, to hit me in the face this time. He pulls back, readying for another punch, and his expression goes blank.

It's the same look I saw on my own face in that video. I know what he's thinking. He's picturing himself pummeling me, delivering blow after blow until I collapse to the floor, groaning, broken, helpless, afraid. He's done this before. He thinks he knows how it's going to go.

Anger surges, and I use the men gripping my arms as leverage, lift up my feet and kick them out into Ivan's gut. He's not expecting either the move or how much power is behind my kick. He staggers backward so hard that he crashes into a table and sends glasses and cups of cheap beer flying.

I don't pause to gloat. Instead I drive my feet backward into the knees of the goons holding my arms. It throws off their balance enough that I feel their grip weaken just a touch.

Now the bouncers are starting to close in. Instead of pressing my advantage, I do something that galls the wolf: turn my anger into a pretense of fear. At New Harmony this was an instinctive reaction, done without thought. Rage and fear have a lot in common. Both involve ramped-up adrenaline, shaking, shouting, maybe crying. Another wolf could probably tell the difference, but not a human.

I arch my back as if struggling helplessly against their grip, let loose with a gurgling high-pitched wail that turns into a sob. I hope I sound at least as convincing as a horror-movie star. I start to babble, keeping my voice high-pitched. "No, please, no—"

The goons are a bit slow on the uptake, and they regard me for a second with confusion. Then they notice what's happening and let go of my arms. I collapse to the floor, curling around my gut, which really does hurt quite a bit, in spite of the corset's protection. I see bruises on my arms, shaped like massive goonish hands. They hurt too. But they're already starting to fade.

"Hey, now, what's going on over here?" one of the bouncers booms out, in a voice like James Earl Jones.

"She start fight." Ivan, doubled over his own gut, stares at me sullenly.

The bouncer gives him a "you have got to be kidding me" look. Then he says it. "You have got to be kidding me. Get on out of here before I call the cops." Arms folded, he and two other bouncers watch the three goons slink away. Then the first bouncer kneels to talk to me. "Sorry, kid, I know you don't want to think about this right now, but are you twenty-one?" I shake my head. "Okay. I can just let you go, or I can call an ambulance if you're hurt."

"No, I'm fine. Just scared." I rise to my feet, smiling at him. "We're going. It's okay." He nods, but does not take his eyes off me until I've collected the others and we're back on the street.

17

DEATH SHOTS

I start walking rapidly, with no direction in mind, just trying to deal with the adrenaline still rioting through my blood. The others scurry to catch up with me. Deena asks, "Abby, was that my imagination, or were you just at the center of a big bar brawl?

"Not your imagination."

"That was some quality wrath, dude," Brad says. "I've never been in a real bar brawl before."

"But how was there suddenly a bar brawl and you were at the center of it?"

"I met some jerks. Things escalated."

"You're okay, though?"

"I'm okay." Am I okay? I seem to be. I shake myself, observe that the bruises are gone and my stomach doesn't hurt anymore. All better. Like it never happened, except that I'm soaked with beer. "But the corset smells like beer now. Can you wash a corset?"

Opal laughs. "Ah, sugar, it'll smell like beer forever, as a reminder of—" she stops, brings out her phone. "Excuse me a minute." She answers a phone call, turning away from us and muttering tensely. "Really? I'm kinda busy—are you sure? Okay, fine. Fine. I'll take care of it." She sighs heavily and turns to the rest of us. "I'm sorry, y'all, I have something I really have to do right now. Abby? Will you keep me posted about where you go? I do want to join up with you all later."

"Oh, sure. Sure, I can do that."

She kisses my cheek. "Talk to you later, hon. It's been quite the evening."

I follow the others through a series of grungy dive bars, until we find one where the gritty, urine-scented interior opens up to a nice outdoor courtyard. It's after midnight now and the air has cooled off to the point where it's just about perfect. We seat ourselves around a big, round iron table. There's a chalkboard with a long list of all the shots they sell, identified by gimmicky names: Brain Hemorrhage, Screaming Orgasm, Sex on the Beach, Four Horsemen of the Apocalypse, Cement Mixer, Prairie Oyster, Liquid Steak. Tonight, their special is "all shots five dollars."

Brad laughs loudly when he sees it. "Yes! It's a sign! Death shots! The time has come, my friends." He makes blurry eye contact with me. "We are still in it, brah."

"Death shots? What are those made out of?"

"It's like a drinking game," Deena explains. "You go around in a circle counterclockwise. You propose a type of shot—you know, like, tequila—and everybody has to drink one of those, or drop out. Then the next person names a shot, and so on, until the last person still drinking wins."

"Wins what?"

"You know. Wins. Hey, let's put money on the table so we can get a little greed in. I think that'll take care of all the sins."

Ward says, "Perfect way to finish things off. I propose one dollar per person per shot."

Izzy folds her arms. "I'm from New Orleans, y'all, I do not play drinking games."

"Oh." Deena looks unhappy for a moment.

Izzy kisses her cheek. "It's okay, baby. You can party with your friends. I'll just be right over here at the next table, sobering up and making fun of y'all."

Deena brightens. "Okay. I call a Brain Hemorrhage!" Everyone makes groaning noises and I look at her curiously. She grins. "I should warn you. Part of the game is to propose shots that are kind of weird or disgusting. You'll get it."

A Brain Hemorrhage turns out to be peach schnapps, grenadine, and Irish cream. The grenadine sinks to the bottom and the cream floats on top, curdling. It smells and tastes extremely sweet, but looks disgusting and feels gross on the tongue.

Nobody drops out. We do a few rounds that continue the theme of being mostly sugar with a disgusting texture, then Deena says, "Bros, I hate to admit this, but it's getting late and I am getting into the passing-out zone."

She pushes her chair away and goes to join Izzy. They lean in and have a low, intimate conversation that involves a lot of laughter and blushing.

Meanwhile, the shots get stronger and more disgusting. Mayonnaise instead of cream, hot sauce and more hot sauce.

Edison burps sour alcohol, coughs and says, "That's it, I'm getting out while it's still fun." He joins Deena and Izzy.

"Well," Brad says, smug. "Wimps dropping out and it's still on. I call a Mexican Shotgun Wedding."

This turns out to be tequila, Tabasco, and a smoked bacon salt that I guess is supposed to be a little bit reminiscent of gunpowder? It's sulfurous, anyway. Since I don't eat bacon, I don't know if it tastes like bacon, but it does taste a bit like bacon smells.

We go with the heat theme for a while, escalating until we reach a Raging Inferno—pepper vodka, cinnamon schnapps, Tabasco habanero, and black pepper.

Ward drops out, after the Raging Inferno starts fighting to

come back up. He runs to the bathroom, body language unmistakable.

Brad makes eye contact with me again. "You still in, girly?"

"Of course I'm still in. Boy-ey."

"It's your turn. What's your shot?"

"Little Death in the Afternoon."

"Absinthe? Heavy duty," says Reed. He goes up to the bar and comes back with only two shots. "This thing is obviously between you two. And word of advice, bro—you've seen *Raiders of the Lost Ark*, right? The chick wins."

Brad scoffs, and we down our Little Deaths in the Afternoon. Or is that Little Death in the Afternoons? We go back to curdled shots for a couple of rounds, only these are stronger and less sweet than the first few. I think the idea is that if you focus on the texture it's likely to make you throw up. But I'm fine. Sure, I'm kinda cheating by being a werewolf and all, but he totally asked for it.

Then he suggests oyster shots, and I pause.

"Oysters? I'm a vegetarian."

He grins, obviously thinking he's got me now. "Ha! It doesn't matter why you won't do the round."

I sigh. I know I told Pere Claude no seafood, but an oyster really is more like eating a sea bug, right? Not an animal-animal. It doesn't even have eyes. "Okay. Oysters it is."

The oyster shooters come in a tall shot glass: brownish-gray oyster, shot of lemon vodka, topper of cocktail sauce.

I down it. The oyster isn't bad, actually. It tastes like the ocean smells. I inhale as it goes down my throat and think of Seattle.

Brad downs his. He smiles, but there's a queasy look behind his eyes. I inhale deeply. I've got him. His breath has changed, and has that whiff of Bourbon Street about it. Vomit. He's ready to lose it.

I move in for the kill. "Let's do another oyster round. And

somebody get a bucket and a damp towel, because he's going to need it very soon."

"Don't count your… " he trails off, obviously having trouble finding the word. His eyelids droop, then he forces them open with a burst of determination. "Chickens. Chickety chicken chick."

It takes two more rounds of oyster shooters to put him under. He has a way of rousing himself every time Reed slams a new shot down on the table. But finally, on the third oyster, he can't get it down, and I was right about the bucket and the damp towel.

Ward helps clean him up, back from his own unpleasant adventure and seeming much more focused. I stand. I feel a little unsteady, like the alcohol finally did whatever it's supposed to do. I gather up my winnings, roll them, hand the roll to Reed. "For the drinks," I say, and he nods. I know it's not enough to pay for everything I've had tonight, but it still makes me feel better.

The rest of us start moving to go, except Brad, who remains slumped in his chair. He seems overly still and doesn't smell quite right.

"Is Brad okay?" I ask out loud.

"He should be, he pumped his own stomach pretty hard," Ward says.

"Brad. Hey, Brad." I look into his eyes. "I beat you, Brad, doesn't that piss you off? Hey, Brad. It's Abby. The little girly chick. Hey! The tiny chick beat you, girly girl. Come on, aren't you pissed off?"

He doesn't respond. His breathing and body temperature seem alarmingly subdued.

I sigh, guilt beginning to claw at the back of my throat. Guilt, and probably oysters and vodka. "Guys, I think this is dangerous. I think we have to get him to the emergency room."

"What? No way. He's been drunker than this lots of times." The bros seem unconvinced, but my words have attracted the notice of one of the workers, cleaning up the empty glasses at a different table.

He's stern. "Look, you kids. If you need to call 911 for your friend, go out to the street right now, and do not tell them the last bar you were at."

"Yeah, okay." I nod. "We've got it. Come on, dudes."

Thanks to my extra-human strength we get a non-responsive Brad out onto the street fairly quickly and prop him against one of those distinctive French Quarter light poles. I hold him upright, waiting for the ambulance, not sure what I'll do if he actually stops breathing. But I'm certain that somehow my presence can save him. The guilt gnaws at me. I didn't make him do anything, not really. He chose to put every last ounce of alcohol down his own gullet. It's his problem that he kept going when he shouldn't have. Maybe it was a game, maybe I cheated. But everyone else knew enough to drop out when their bodies told them to. It's not my fault. I didn't make him do anything.

I think about what Opal told me, about the dead men, about how she didn't make them do anything. Maybe I understand a little better now. Brad made all his own choices, and maybe I didn't help, but it isn't my fault either.

No matter how guilty I feel, it isn't my fault.

Is it?

The ambulance arrives and takes Brad away. The bros hail a taxi, and Ward, Reed, and Edison climb in.

"I sent for a Lyft, it should be here soon," Deena says.

I check my phone and realize that, while I wasn't paying attention, Opal was texting me a lot, telling me she was done with her business, and were we still out, and where were we?

I text Opal:

> Sorry, got distracted.
> One of the bros is going to the hospital.
> Alcohol poisoning

Oh no! Do you want a ride out there?

Sure.
I'm at Dauphine & Governor Nicholls

"My sister is getting me," I tell Deena and Izzy. "I'll see you guys at the hospital."

18

RAMPAGE

O pal arrives, seeming tense. Her car is packed full, reminding me of Steph's car when she first picked me up, the car of somebody who's leaving town in a hurry.

"Abby, thanks for getting back to me. Which hospital are we going to?"

"I didn't ask. Shoot. Where would you take a frat bro with alcohol poisoning?"

"Probably Touro Infirmary." She taps something into her phone and then places it in a rack on the dashboard where a computer voice starts giving directions. "Did you have a good time with your friends after I left?"

"I did. Up to the point where I got in a drinking contest with one of the bros and put him in the hospital."

"Oh, sugar, you're a menace. But don't you worry. This is New Orleans, some frat boy nearly dies from alcohol poisoning every night. They've got it down, I'm sure he'll be fine."

I rub my temples, which are beginning to throb. "I hope you're right."

"Headache?" I nod and her smile turns to a smirk. "How much did you have to drink, anyway?"

"I don't know, I had frat boys buying me booze all night." I think back, try to count, lose track quickly. "A lot, I guess. Even by frat boy standards."

"Oh, my, you're in for quite the treat."

"What? That sounded sarcastic."

"It was, I'm so sorry. You see, the wolf makes you resistant to alcohol, which means it takes a lot to get you drunk. But the hangover is a side effect of how much alcohol your body had to process. So it doesn't matter whether you ever got properly drunk or not, later on, you suffer. More than a human would, to tell you the truth, since you can drink more in the first place."

I groan in answer. Of course, what did I think was going to happen?

"You'll be fine. You might think you're going to die, but you won't." She smiles. "How about after the hospital, you go out to the den with me, see if Reina has a potion or something she can give you? Then you can talk to Jaime about whether you're taking off with the Cachorros."

"Okay. Sure." My head is thumping pretty bad. I would probably do anything anybody suggested at this point.

"I think the den is going to—" She pauses, frowning. We're stopped at a traffic light on an empty street. She taps the phone. "That car behind us —"

SLAM!

We get rammed from behind, hard enough that the trunk pops open.

"Damn it!" Opal fumes. "What the hell—" She seems about to open the door, then stops, turns back to me, her face pale. "Lock your door. Don't get out of the car."

She's afraid, I think, or maybe just excited. Then I see what she sees: the car behind us is full of goons, the three from the club plus one. The three from the club get out of the car, carrying guns.

Opal stomps on the accelerator, but has to slam on the brake right away as a second car pulls in front to block us. She reverses and tries to pull around the forward car, but the original car pulls around to ram us from the driver's side. The door dents and we go skidding. Opal, frantic, tries to pull to the right, but she revs the engine and nothing happens.

"Those fucking assholes wrecked my car!"

"Opal, what's going on?"

"I don't know. Don't get out of the car. They want us out of the car. They can't get us if we stay in here."

A bullet whizzes through the driver side door, lodging in the seat cushion. "GOD DAMN IT!" Opal shouts. "That went right through the door! Right through it! Damn it! Fuck!"

The man Ivan gestures with his gun. "Get out, girls," he says. "Or we keep shooting car."

"Fuck shit," Opal mutters, low. If she had a wolf it would be a growl. She gets out of the car and glares at Ivan. "I told you fucking Strigoi, I'm out of it, okay? I don't know where the coke is. Just leave me alone. You already wrecked my car, just—"

"Your 'sister' needs out, too." He glares at me. "Hands up. We keep eyes on you."

I comply. Four goons surround me. Two cars, seven men? Yes, seven. The four holding me, plus Ivan and two guys flanking him. Damn. I'm starting to be afraid of what I'm going to have to do to get out of this. Breathe. Stay focused. Try to figure out what's going on. Try to ignore the thunder in my head.

"I wasn't lying. She is my sister."

He shrugs. "Whatever. Also your muscle. Clever. She look like little nothing, but we know rougs here in this town. We take her first."

One of the four men shoots me in the back.

Sʜᴇ's sᴜʀʀᴏᴜɴᴅᴇᴅ ʙʏ ᴇɴᴇᴍɪᴇs ᴀɴᴅ ʀᴇᴀᴅʏ ᴛᴏ ꜰɪɢʜᴛ.

But first, she has to get rid of that annoying thing around her body. She drops to her back and rolls, trying to rub it off, biting helplessly at it. It's at her exact midsection and no matter how much she contorts and stretches she can't seem to get at it with her teeth or claws.

God damn look at that.

One of her enemies makes human noises, laughter, and she focuses her rage on its proper target again. She puts the annoying thing out of her mind and attacks, leaping right at his throat, bringing him down with a quick bite.

The other enemies have GUNS and keep firing bolts of pain into her body, which send her into a rage stronger than any she's felt before. She doesn't stop to savor any of her kills, to consume their guts or howl her victory. Efficient, she leaps from one throat to the next.

One enemy, the one she thinks of as first enemy, is running. Finally, a little pleasure for her as she chases after him, pounces, brings him down. He is the last and she can finally stop to rip out his guts.

But as she's chewing into this well-earned victory feast, her stomach warbles. She's ill. She ate something bad. This enemy has poison in him.

She howls her distress and runs, runs to find a safe place to sleep and allow herself to heal.

"Dᴀᴍɴ ɪᴛ, Aʙʙʏ! Dᴀᴍɴ ɪᴛ! Yᴏᴜ'ʀᴇ ᴀ ᴛʀᴀᴜᴍᴀ ᴍᴏʀᴘʜ!"

Viv and Nic are yelling at me. Well, Viv is yelling. Nic is standing there holding a black cloth. I seem to be human again. It's still night. For a split second I have no idea what's going on, except everything smells like vomit and that annoying thing is still tight around my midsection.

The smell of vomit reminds me of the taste of—the taste of—

Dry heaves. Viv is still yelling at me. "Five! You went to wolf form and killed five men! How could you let that happen?"

Five? Damn it. Wolves can't count, I guess. But it makes sense now that I think about it. She killed the four men immediately around her, and brought down one who was running, so where did the other two go? Into one of the cars, maybe? It would make sense. Automobiles really are like kryptonite for us. So where are they now? "I was attacked, Viv. Shot. They were going to kill us. He even called me a roug."

The black cloth turns out to be a robe, which Nicolas drapes around my shoulders. Vivienne continues to rage. "Fuck, what have you been doing that five men tried to kill you?"

"Seven men tried to kill me. Two of them got away, I guess."

"All that, and you let two of them get away?" Her rage is incandescent.

"They probably got into one of the cars. How many cars were at the scene? Can I take a look?"

"No, you cannot go take a look, what the hell is wrong with you? Régnault is at the scene now, cleaning things up for us. Making it look like a drug deal gone wrong."

That's what it was, more or less. But she doesn't need to know that, so I don't say anything.

"Silver." Nic uses a plastic bag to pick up a smashed bullet out of a puddle of vomit. "That silver bullet legend has saved us so many times. I always wondered if it was one of our own who started the myth, but nobody seems to know for sure."

Viv takes a deep breath, as if she's about to begin yelling at me again, but we get interrupted by the arrival of a police car, lights spinning, but no siren. I scramble to my feet, tying the robe more securely. They're going to try to take me out of here right now, force me to Bayou Galene. How can I get away? Where's Opal?

Régnault gets out of the car. "It's done. Five very bad men, criminals, killed each other in a shoot-out. No innocent people were harmed."

"Thank you for doing this, Reg. I know it hurts you to tell all these lies for our sake."

He smiles, displaying a flicker of that sexual interest he has in her. "I tell them for you, chérie. But I serve the people of this city. If the truth would serve them better, I would tell that." Then he seems to notice me for the first time and his face takes on a mixture of awe and fear. "And your niece here is the little girl who did it, hey?"

"Yes," Viv hisses out, folding her arms and narrowing her eyes at me. "This is the very bad little girl with a trauma morph she didn't tell us about, who let her wolf kill five men."

"So small," he murmurs, looking at me. "I forget sometimes the power of your kind." Then, louder, he says, "These men who are dead, they were very bad men. Criminals. Murderers. Not even their mothers will mourn them, hey? You have done the people of this city a great service." Then he looks me right in the eyes, and makes his voice quiet, but stern. "Do not do it again."

"No, it will not happen again, because you're coming back to Bayou Galene with me right now," Viv says.

I don't say anything. I just fold my arms around the robe and stare back at her. "What if I say no?"

Régnault looks between us and clears his throat. "I'll move on, chérie, if that would be all right? Death always brings so much paperwork."

"Wait," I call out. "Mr. Régnault, there were two men who got away from the scene."

He nods. "We could see from the evidence that one or more men escaped."

"Those men—what's going to happen with them? They saw me transform. And they know silver doesn't do anything."

He smiles. "This has happened many times before. They will try to forget. Such an unbelievable thing, no? It becomes easy to doubt the memory. To think you must have imagined it, or been mistaken. Nothing for you to worry about." He nods to us and drives away.

The instant he's in the car Viv explodes at me again. "How can you even think about not coming home with me after what's happened? This is exactly why we don't allow uncontrolled trauma morphs to live in the outside world."

"Those men were going to kill us, Viv, what was I supposed to do? If I stayed human to kill them, how would that have helped?"

If I stayed human it would have been murder.

I can't think about this. My head hurts.

"You didn't have to kill them! If you knew how to handle yourself, if you were trained, you could have disabled them without killing. There were dozens of things you could have done. But you refuse our training. So stubborn—"

"You're the ones who refuse to train me here in town! Until three weeks ago I didn't even know any of you existed, and once you introduced yourselves, all you could do was try to tell me how I was living my life wrong and I had to live it your way in order to be right. But I was raised in crazy torture cult, I've heard all of that before. Exactly all of that. You lie to me, but expect me to tell you the truth. You don't trust me, but you want me to trust you. You expect my obedience just because you're the senior wolves in some pack hierarchy I never agreed to follow. And I don't agree now. I'll tell you the same thing I told Pere Claude. My loyalty, my trust, you can earn it, but you cannot demand it."

She inhales like she's about to retort, but I shut her down with a green glare. "You yelled at me for killing five men who were trying to kill me, but how many bitten wolves have you killed?"

Her stress spikes way up and she spits back, "I don't count them, Abby! I do what I have to do. You have no idea how much destruction and death an uncontrolled bitten wolf epidemic can cause! It's our job to prevent that!"

"But do you always have to kill them? Aren't there any alternatives? Treatments? Adjustment periods?"

"Why are you asking me this? Did you bite one of those men who escaped?"

Behind me, Nic is doing something. I don't consciously identify it as "firing a gun" but somewhere in the back of my mind I must have figured it out, because I whirl out of his line of fire and the tranquilizer dart—I assume that's what it is, with that big red tassel—fires harmlessly into the grass.

"Fuck you." I spit out the words and I'm gone.

If I actually had to fight both of them, I'd probably lose. But I make this a chase instead, and I am faster.

I trace my own trail back to the crime scene, hoping to find Opal from there. And then? I'm not sure. Maybe she can take me out to the Cachorros, or somewhere else entirely. I don't want to plan too far ahead. The Varger know about my trauma morph now and that probably changes everything.

I'm getting near the crash site when I spot Opal's car, running, not quite as smoothly as before. She spots me and pushes open the passenger side door. "Thank God, I thought the Varger were going to nab you as a trauma morph for sure. Get in, close the door."

I do. She gives me a smile, her face pale and smudged with grease, then hands me a plastic bag. We drive off. I examine the bag, find all my things, battered and soaked with blood. Most of the blood is mine. "Where are we going?"

She grins. "We're going to meet our father."

19

CHOKE COLLAR

For a moment I can't process the actual literal words she just said to me. "Meet our father." I imagine Father Wisdom, rising from the grave and stumbling around as a zombie. But that can't be what she means. "Leon, you mean? Leon is alive?"

"Indeed he is."

"Does Pere Claude know? Wait, he has to know. He's the original source on Leon being dead. Why would he lie about that?" I fold my arms, feeling sick with betrayal, and also just sick. I've got a hangover and I'm full of bullets. "Opal. Before we get too sucked into talking about Leon, I have to tell you something. The wolf didn't kill all the men. Two of them got away. I don't know where they are now. This could be bad."

She nods. "I know. It's okay, the Cachorros have got this. As for why Leon's dad would lie to you, I don't know. What I do know is that after Leon tried to kill himself, he spent a long time in a coma, and even longer in what they call a semi-catatonic state. But a few years ago Leon woke up again, and he's been contacting his children ever since. It's possible his father doesn't even know he's awake. The Varger don't know as much as they think they do."

A sharp, sizzling pain in my gut and I double over, groaning, curled around the shredded, bloody corset. That feeling, I think that's a bullet traveling through my muscles. Bullets, or anything else embedded in my body, tend to work their way through me until they hit empty space. A lot of the time they end up in my digestive tract to get expelled from one end or the other, or pop right out of my skin like bizarre pimples. While they do this, sometimes they hurt. Sometimes they hurt a lot.

I've been shot before, but never so many times. I remember at least six bullets going in, and there were probably more I didn't make note of. Waves and waves of cramps roll through me. I take off the seatbelt and thrash, trying to find some position that brings relief, without success.

"Abby? What's wrong with you?"

"Bullets." I groan, gagging and coughing and manage to spit one of them out.

"Whoa, okay." She laughs a little bit. "I never thought about that. You don't have any open wounds, but the bullets are in your body right now, aren't they?"

"Uh-huh." I take off the corset, flinging it to the floor of the car, and a bullet pops out of my side, creating a small wound that heals rapidly.

"I've got a painkiller for you, if you want. An herbal concoction that works on y'all. It's in the back in a mason jar."

I lean over the seat and grab a mason jar full of brown liquid. It contains alcohol, herbs and sugar. It's not the worst-tasting thing I've had to drink tonight.

My stomach roils around unpleasantly, but I feel slightly better. As the liquid works its way through my body, my head clears and I start to feel detached from the aches, pains, twitchy muscles and nausea.

"What's in this thing?" Then I notice there's a sticker on it with a skull and crossbones. "Damn it, Opal, are you trying to poison me?"

"Oh, please, I wouldn't have the faintest idea how to poison one of you wolves. That sticker is there because it's poisonous to me. Otherwise I might drink it by mistake. Those compounds Reina makes all look the same, and I don't have your sense of smell to know the difference."

"Huh." I stare at it, feeling suspicious. But also feeling so much better that I keep sipping. I feel weird. Not bad. Just weird. I open the window and inhale deeply of the outside air, notice something with my peripheral vision. "Hey, Opal, does it look to you like that car might be following us?"

"I'm counting on it, sugar, don't stare. We're luring them out to the amusement park, where Jaime and the others are going to take care of them for us."

"Oh. Okay." I lean into the corner between seat and door, where the breeze hits me full in the face. Cool air from the dashboard air conditioning collides on my skin with the warm, moist air from outside and I shiver. I turn my head to look at the passing scenery and see the car without appearing to look at it.

She tosses me her phone. "Call Jaime, tell him it's showtime. Ask how he wants to play it. Use speaker phone so I can hear."

He answers. "Opal?"

"Abby and Opal both. We're on our way. What's the plan?"

"Strigoi following you?"

"Yeah."

"Get them on site and keep them busy until we've got you surrounded."

"Busy how?"

"Busy thinking about something other than getting surrounded by wolves. Don't let on that you have resources. Act scared and weaker than you are. Don't start the fight until you absolutely have to. We want to make sure we get all of them this time."

"That wasn't my fault!" I say, because I feel like it was my fault.

"I know. You were acting alone, no backup. We're fixing that. We're your backup now."

"Thank you, Jaime."

"De nada."

We park the car at the outside entrance to the park, where the boar's head continues to rot. The car that was obviously following us drives on.

"Look, they think they're being clever," Opal says. We start walking toward the center of the park. The sky is beginning to lighten with the approaching dawn. A bird sing-songs its call: whee-woo, whee-woo. The setting moon looks full, but I know it's not quite, not until the next time it rises.

The Strigoi come up from behind, with guns. Do they know I can smell them? I turn my head and make eye contact with Opal. Are we surrounded yet? I would smell that, I think, and I don't. A flicker of worry. If I follow Jaime's plan, it means making myself incredibly vulnerable in the short term.

"Hold," one of the goons shouts out with authority. "Hands up. Turn around."

We obey. The goons on site are the two who escaped earlier, plus two more. Only four men. They already know four men couldn't hold me before. What are they thinking?

Two of the men have axes. Maybe they think they can lop off my head. Which would, I have to admit, kill me. I tingle with a nervous anticipation that isn't exactly fear. We've got this. Right?

"Hello girls," says the man who seems to be the lead goon, one of the two who escaped.

"Hello, gentlemen," Opal says. "Obviously you've followed me out here because you believe I'm going to lead you to this buried treasure you're after."

"That is idea, yes." He smiles. He gestures toward me with his gun. "First we take care of this roug."

I put up my hands. "Please. He shot me with silver, I couldn't help myself."

"Well, roug, you turn wolf, we chopping off your head. But you play nice, two little girls live, yes?" Two of the men step forward, handcuff my arms behind my back, slip a muzzle around my face and a choke collar around my neck. So that's why they think only four men can hold me this time. Equipment.

"Very nice, gentlemen, you've given my sister the Hannibal Lecter treatment. So what do y'all want? You think I'm just gonna to lead you to the stash?"

"Yes. We think yes."

"And why would I do that?"

"Because you don't, we kill you." He smiles broadly. "We know is just two, no team."

"But I do have a team, darling. I have a whole pack of rougarou just like her, tracking me right now." She delivers this completely true bit of information as if it's a lie, and they laugh.

"Yeah? And where these other rougs are, hey?"

She gestures vaguely. "Around. They hide. You know, like wolves do? When they're stalking prey?"

"So we can see these rougs now?"

"I have to summon them. Just a minute." She throws back her head and howls, an entirely human sound. They laugh.

"Get going." The lead goon nudges her with his gun. She starts heading toward the center of the park. We move cautiously, slowly, the fourth man's axe right at the back of my head, metal shockingly cold against my neck in the swampy air.

Birds begin to chirp in earnest, air filling up with their sharp, musical chorus. I smell the other wolves around us, but I don't think they're close enough to be in position. I close my eyes, seem to see the dark, spicy ribbons of the Cachorros as they drift through the air, entwining, almost meeting to form a circle.

But not quite yet.

I stumble on a pit in the ruined pavement, deliberately go to my knees, test the strength of the men holding me, the power of the choke collar.

It's more effective than I might have guessed. The muscles of my neck are strong, but I don't know how to tense those muscles to protect arteries or windpipe. I might be just as vulnerable as any normal human to passing out because I got the blood supply to my head cut off.

This could be bad.

This could be very bad.

They laugh, and yank me to my feet again with the power of the collar. They speak to each other in a language I don't know. They use the word "strigoi" but I'm not sure if they mean themselves or me.

The Cachorros are drawing closer.

Now they're revealed in the morning twilight: tense, feral, dark shapes with glowing eyes. The Strigoi notice them now and exude a bit of fear. In the distance, gunshots. Birds shriek and scatter. I sense a wolf has transformed, which means one of the Cachorros must be a trauma morph.

The man with the axe swings at my neck, but I was prepared for that and drop my head out of his range. But that means I'm pulling hard against the choke collar.

My vision goes blurry and dim. Nothing seems quite real. I watch a wolf, fur so white it seems to glow, chase down two men. There's already blood around her muzzle, stark against the pale fur. Why is she chasing them? She's much faster than they are, she could easily have caught them already. Is she chasing them here for some strategic reason, or just having fun?

She brings down one, first nipping at his ankle so that he stumbles, then pouncing on him fully, ripping open the flesh of his throat while blood sprays everywhere, staining her white coat. It looks just like a nature program Morgan and I watched together once, one that came with a "parental guidance" warning. Most nature programs are more sanitized. They show the chase, but not the blood and death that happens at the end.

She brings down the second man. Then, she takes the time

to enjoy herself, gnawing into his abdominal cavity. She throws back her head and howls, gore smeared around her nose and mouth. The howl means, I am victorious, my enemies are nothing but meat.

In the end, what are we, Abnegation?

Meat, sir. Meat or monsters.

And which will you be, child?

I think I'm a monster, sir.

Wait, I'm passing out. Time to start the fight.

It's an awkward hands-free struggle that involves a lot of head-butting and flailing and dodging. I do a fair bit of damage to the men I'm fighting, but without hands or teeth, I'm having a hard time figuring out how to fully break free of them. If I take the time to focus my strength on busting through the hand-cuffs, they take advantage and come at me with the axe again.

Then Jaime appears, a swift shadow darting through, neatly snapping three necks.

Without the pressure of fighting the axe, I focus my strength and break the handcuffs, then rip off the collar and the muzzle.

"Thank you."

"De nada."

I glance over to the white wolf, and she's Andrea again, naked and pale in the pre-dawn light. She picks Strigoi guts out of her teeth and comes over to us. "Those two were from a second group." She gestures toward the dead men. "These Strigoi mofos might send even more. I think we need to stay on high guard for a while."

Jaime nods. "That was my thought as well." He calls out to the rest of the Cachorros. "Prepare the bodies for disposal but don't take them out to the swamps yet. Right now, everyone on guard for more Strigoi. Tight formation."

The others howl briefly to mean "heard and understood" and begin to roll the bodies into blue tarps, drag them into a pile.

"That's what you do? Dump them in the swamps?" I ask.

He nods. "They get devoured by alligators."

"Oh. Okay. Uh, good. That's good."

"You should have me go wolf and chew on them a little bit," Andrea says, inspecting one of the men as she helps Jaime roll him into a tarp. "Make sure it doesn't look like murder even if one of them is found."

"Good idea. You do that, Andrea." He turns to me with a smile. "Abby, it's time to take you to meet our father." The rising sun lights the sky on fire.

○ ⚜ ○

MY FATHER WAITS IN ONE OF THE RUINED BUILDINGS. JAIME leads me through the maze of destruction and neglect, into a space of candles and draperies and hushed voices and soft music. It feels like a sanctum, something sacred and secret. My father's scent is all over, a heavy dark smell like Pere Claude, but sharper and redder. Does my father really smell dangerous, or is that just my imagination? I start to feel tense.

Jaime draws back a red curtain to reveal a small room within a room, a tent of velvet, a nest of pillows.

And there's my father. Sitting on an elaborately painted bench that might have once been part of one of the rides.

"Go in alone," Jaime tells me. I do. The curtain drops behind me.

"Leon," I say. Confirming.

"Abby," he says. Also confirming.

I think he would be tall, if he were standing up, maybe Nic's height. He wears a wide-brimmed black hat, and doesn't appear to have any hair underneath it. The stubble of his beard looks like it was once a deep auburn, but now is mostly gray, thin and patchy. His skin is pale, drained, but with a smattering of washed-out freckles. Eyes, sunken, in my own shade of green. Gaunt cheeks, shaped much like mine when I first left New

Harmony. Large, square hands, nearly skeletal, resting on an elaborately carved cane in ebony and silver.

He really does look like me. Like me if I were old, sick, male, and much taller.

A wave of pity washes through me. I realize that part of me was thinking, if that jerk really is still alive, I'm gonna kick his ass. But now that I see him, I can't think that. His sunken eyes and stick arms evoke too much pity in me, remind me too much of Ash when she was dying.

"What's wrong with you?" It comes out sounding more cruel than I meant.

"Cancer," he says.

Oh no, he's missing a bunch of teeth, I see it when he opens his mouth. *He's missing his teeth.*

I have a moment of sick, visceral horror, unable to stop staring at the black void where his teeth should be. My heart thunders in my ears.

"Do werewolves get cancer?"

"Not unless the wolf dies."

"I don't understand."

"Have you heard of Arda's Wound?" I shake my head. He continues, "It is caused by certain very severe head injuries. The body survives, but the wolf does not. Without the transformation, gradually, all the gifts of the wolf are lost. We become as vulnerable as anyone to disease and injury. I have brain cancer. It is not treatable by human means."

"I'm sorry to hear that. I wanted to hate you, but I'm finding it hard."

"I spent many years hating myself, if that's any comfort to you."

"Hating yourself for what?" I ask. He doesn't answer immediately, and a sense of urgency gives me boldness. I ask the question I really want to know. "Did you rape my mother?"

He inhales, deeply. Then he exhales in a sigh. "I'm sorry. I can't say for sure."

"What? You can't say? Why not?" Pure rage washes over me for a moment, and I'm seconds, I think, from taking him by the throat. No. Not like that. I curl my hands into fists, hold myself steady. "How in the ever-loving what the fuck could you not be sure about a thing like that?"

"Please." He makes a sit-down gesture. "Let me explain."

20

LEON

I pull an overturned milk crate forward and sit, which puts us at more or less eye level.

"When my mother Leah Evangeline was killed, I didn't handle it well. I wanted vengeance. I needed to make those men pay for what they had done."

"What men? Who killed her?"

"Hunters," he says, with a hint of a growl. He's probably been twenty years without a wolf, and looks like a scarecrow, but he still sounds like he could rip out the throat of anybody who might be called 'hunter.'

"Was it an accident?" For Morgan's sake, I feel a need to defend the concept of "hunter." He shot me when I was in wolf form, and might have killed me, but he didn't know it was me.

"No." His voice is cold, flat. "It was not an accident."

He lets that sit there until I ask, "But how do you know?"

"They drove onto our land and shot her from their truck. They took her body away as a trophy. She had brilliant red fur, a color other wolves don't have, only the rougarou. It was not an accident. It was murder."

I shudder, chills down my spine as I feel his outrage. Didn't I see it as murder, when Father Wisdom killed Ash? And didn't I go back to New Harmony for my own vengeance? Sure, I didn't consciously plan to kill him. But when he ended up dead, was I surprised? Was I upset? No. I was glad.

"So you took revenge. Okay. I get that part of it. And your father didn't want you to do that. I understand that too. But how does that mean you don't know whether or not you raped my mother? Because if rape was your idea of revenge, I have to kill you right now."

He smiles with surprising warmth, the effect undone by the gaunt cheeks, the missing teeth. "And that would be entirely within your right. No wolf would tolerate such a thing. We consider sexual domination to be very low and weak, and take rape seriously as a crime."

"Then why would you do it?"

"As I plotted my vengeance, I used notes from the historic Pere Diaries to try to recreate the traditional berserker drugs of our people. Have you heard of those?"

"You mentioned them in your diary. What do they do?"

"They help bring about a pure killing frenzy. But sometimes they cause memory loss."

"So that's your excuse? You were hopped up on berserker drugs and you don't remember everything?"

He closes his eyes, shakes his head. "It's not an excuse. You asked me how it's possible I could not be sure, and that's your answer."

"Well, it's a shit answer." Overwhelmed by anger and frustration, I stand up and start pacing around the little room. "You chose to take the berserker drugs, knowing what they might do. So I'm just going to treat you like you've done the worst, okay? How would that be?"

I lean in close to snarl at him, and smell the intimate sickness of his breath and body, the rot and decay. I recoil, disgusted, but also burdened by pity in spite of myself.

He looks up, meets my gaze, then looks away. A gesture of submission. "That rage is your right."

"Damn it!" I don't know what else to punch, so I pound my fists into an unforgiving rusty metal bar. My hands sizzle with pain as the fingers break, then tingle as the breaks heal instantly. "I came here to kick your ass! Then it turns out you have cancer! What the fuck am I supposed to do about that? How am I supposed to hate you the way you deserve to be hated?"

His mouth quirks into a smile. "You would prefer that I be more purely evil in your eyes?"

"Well, Father Wisdom was pure evil, it's not like I don't have experience!"

He stares up at me. I stare down at him. He frowns, concerned. "Do you have the red moon? You seem very agitated, but I'm not sure."

I fling myself back onto the overturned milk crate, stare into his eyes. "I'm not sure either. I've been really stressed out and haven't slept much the last couple of days. But there's been a lot going on." As if on cue, I feel a bullet work its way into my throat and I gag it up, hold it out. "See?"

"Oh, my. I did hear that earlier tonight you demonstrated the power of your trauma morph. Killed five men." He sounds proud. Like a proud dad.

I grimace. "Yeah. Well. They were planning to kill me."

"Of course they were. Of course." He rests his forehead, briefly, on his hands where they cradle the silver top of the cane. The silver is worked to resemble the head of a wolf with emerald eyes. "If I did this crime, I'm sorry. And if I didn't do it, I'm sorry that I can't tell you with any confidence that I didn't. But I did get better. I stopped abusing the berserker drugs. I had to blow out half my brains and spend years recovering from that, but I'm sober now."

"And dying of untreatable cancer."

I smell the fear on him, as I say the words. He's been so long without the wolf that he doesn't smell much like one of us anymore, the pepper of his sweat faded to almost nothing. "Yes. Dying of untreatable cancer."

"So why are you here now? Just saying goodbye to all your kids?"

A brittle green flash in his eyes. He still has an echo of the stare. "Is there something wrong with that?"

"I guess not. So, here we are. Meeting. For the first and maybe the last time. What do we talk about?"

A small smile, mouth closed, sparing me the horrors of his toothless state. "Anything you like."

"Okay. Why did you leave Bayou Galene? Was it just because you wimped out on trauma morph training?"

On the phrase "wimped out" he glares at me, eyes flashing briefly. It's a little disconcerting. Am I always doing that to people? A green-eyed flash of intensity that makes you feel like the world is slipping out from under you? "I didn't wimp out, child. I wanted my freedom. It's something you ought to understand. Better than most of my children." He gestures, as if taking in the entirety of the Cachorros. "They have always been free. They never had to fight for it. You did." A gentle smile. Fatherly. "And you're still fighting now. There's a reason you aren't out at Bayou Galene this very minute."

I shrug. "You got me. So, is that what you're offering? Freedom?"

His eyes flash. "Yes. Freedom. Why do trauma morphs have to be controlled, or imprisoned? To maintain the secrecy of the wolf-shifters. But we're facing a time, sooner than anyone thinks, when secrecy will become impossible. You're young, you know what the world is now. Everything that happens is captured electronically and broadcast around the globe in an instant. No matter what we do, at some point in the next twenty years, we're going to be exposed. The world will know we exist."

His passion makes his voice stronger, and he has a little of the presence, the force of personality, that he must have had when young. It's compelling. He has a good voice, not quite as deep and resonant as Pere Claude's, but low, smooth, easy to listen to. And he's right. I've had all these same thoughts, listening to Vivienne and Nicolas and Pere Claude try to convince me to give up my freedom for the sake of their secrecy. I've thought, what does it matter anyway? Somebody is going to put up a transformation video any day now, no matter what I do.

I add a thought: "Not to mention, Varger secrecy is based on keeping nearly all of our people in the same little town that could be totally wiped out by another Katrina, and is probably going to be underwater in twenty years anyway."

His eyes light up and he reaches out to seize my hand, an eager smile on his face. His hand trembles, stronger than such a skeletal hand seems like it should be, as if I'm grasped by a tree root. "You do understand. You do know what I'm fighting for."

"I do?"

"An end to the lie, and the only possible future for our people. We must make ourselves known to the world. But it has to happen on our terms. Not an accident. Not something that allows us to be cast as monsters."

I nod, although I'm a little unnerved by his passion. I'm not sure I like him holding my hand like that, but it would seem awkward to shake myself free of it. "Okay, so, what do you think? Should we be caught on camera using our super-strength to do heroic things in public? I would be good with that."

He removes his hand, places it back on top of the one resting on the cane. "Your imagination is noble. But heroics can be dangerous. They have a tendency to backfire. Strength draws challenge. Your power starts to seem to the rest of the world like a curse, not a blessing. A world of superheroes becomes a world of supervillains."

"So, no playing Batman, okay. What do you think we should do?"

"Be as normal as possible. I have children, and will soon have grandchildren, all over this country. They live their lives in the world. They have jobs and families. Average Americans, who happen to make a point of going camping once a month."

"That's your big plan? Demographics? Well it's not going to work."

He frowns at me, with a fierce eye flash. "You say it's not going to work? How do you know that?"

"I know that because of the math. I mean, maybe I don't get algebra, but I do know it takes more than twenty years and twenty kids to totally change the face of the whole country. That's what Father Wisdom thought *he* was doing. All those guys who follow the Christian patriarchy, that's what they're planning to do, take over through demographics. But it's not going to work."

His anger turns thoughtful. "Demographics won't work, you say. But what about converts? Bitten wolves?"

"With wolves, I have no idea. The church is dying. Nobody my age goes to church. But they don't need converts either, because they're trying to take over through political influence. They have these, like, clubs and prayer breakfasts and secret organizations that provide ready-made legislation and get-out-the-vote efforts that specifically round up people to vote for certain religious candidates, and that's what works. You don't need, like, suburban werewolves taking the kids to daycare, you need werewolves in congress. And why am I telling you all this, anyway? I'm babbling."

"You want to save your people, just like I do." He smiles. He looks like a proud dad again. "My father wants that, too. But I'm not like him. I will give your ideas a fair consideration, even when I don't agree."

"Well. Great. That's great."

He studies my face for a long time, and I have nothing to say, so I study his face back. The warm light of the candles is flattering to his ruined visage. In low light he could be a tough, lean old wolf, not a shambling zombie ready to die. What is he staring at? Our family resemblance? Some clue to my character? That zit on my chin that's starting to itch?

"I've been told I look like you," I say, finally. "Vivienne in particular tells me this. When I irritate her."

"Vivienne, is it? Oh, that takes me back." He laughs. "When I was young, before I had fully come into my manhood—perhaps you look a bit like I did then."

"But a lot shorter, right?"

"Does that bother you?"

"Of course it bothers me! Most of my half siblings are tall and I'm pretty sure I'd be tall just like that if I hadn't been starved while growing up. That's a thing that was done to me, like these scars on my shoulder. I was warped. Damaged. I never had the chance—" I stop. I'm not sure what I'm trying to say. "I'll never know what I could have been."

"None of us know that. But it might comfort you to know that my mother was fairly short, only a couple of inches taller than you are now. You look like you take after her. The wolf usually comes only after full adult height is reached."

"Huh. Okay. I don't know if that makes me feel better. I guess I did get a little taller after I left New Harmony. I didn't kill him." I wasn't expecting myself to say that. We both look at me, confused.

"Didn't kill who?"

"Father Wisdom. The man who raised me. The man who broke me. I wanted to kill him and I didn't and I thought it was me being moral but now I think maybe I was just being a coward. I was glad when he was dead. I wanted to look at his face. I wanted to see for myself that he died in pain. When I saw his dead twisted-up grimace it was just about the best thing I ever saw. I have dreams where I kill him, over and over, and they're not nightmares."

Why am I telling him all this? I feel weird. Disconnected. Unfocused. As if this is a dream. Is that the fatigue catching up with me?

He smiles, lips closed. "You are conflicted. You aren't comfortable with the spirit of vengeance that rides you."

"I guess."

"You would rather be the hero."

"I don't think that's possible. I don't think the hero gets to kill people. I just don't want to be the villain."

He looks at me, eyes shining with a kind of hungry pride. It's the way Wisdom used to look at Justice, his most perfect and beautiful child, the one who took his lessons most to heart, who followed in his footsteps most closely. When Wisdom looked at Justice like that, sometimes I felt envy. But now that I'm enduring the force of that gaze, I'm not sure I like it. Maybe it's better not to have a parent look at you like that.

He says, "I say you are a hero. You destroy your enemies when you have to, but you would rather save the people you love. I know you don't love me. But would you save me?"

21

THE BITE

I blink. None of this can be real. "I can't save you from cancer. That's ridiculous."

Leon uses the cane to push himself to his feet. He is tall, with a frame that would be impressive if well-muscled, but right now his broad shoulders just make him look even more gaunt. From a leather pouch on his belt he removes an odd curved knife, blackened and discolored, but sharp.

He holds it out toward me, handle first, as if he wants me to take it. "This is the agnara. A traditional knife used for trauma morph training. If a transformed wolf bites one with Arda's Wound, sometimes the wolf is restored in the one who is bitten."

"No shit? Wait. You're asking me to stab myself into wolf form and then bite you?"

He nods. "I have known about this cure for some time. But until the cancer, I didn't seek a restoration of my wolf. I feared his return would also bring the red and black moons, the turmoil and suffering." He closes his eyes for a moment. "But now I find, in spite of everything, that I would prefer not to die."

"Yeah, I get that. But why me? You have dozens of children, or so I've been told."

He nods. "I do have many children. And many of them love me, strange as that might seem to you. Some have even performed this service for me. But not every bite brings the cure. And the bite, in wolf form, is harder to engineer than you might think. A moon-transformed wolf thinks like a wolf, has no reason to bite someone who is not an enemy. But a trauma morph is different. If the human has a strong purpose before the transformation, the wolf carries it out. That's why your wolf kills your enemies for you."

I shudder at the memory. Not long ago she killed five enemies. Five men. Not good men. Maybe the world is better off without them. But still. Five men is a lot of people to kill. I imagine them behind me in a line, following me like shambling zombies, all my dead. The dead I loved, like my mother and sister, and the dead I killed, like George and the Strigoi. Wisdom is there, in that line. Their faces are rotting and their eyes are empty.

I shake my head. The fatigue really is catching up with me. It felt like I was falling asleep, right into a nightmare.

I don't want to stab myself, but I can't let him die, when I could save him. Can I? I can't add another zombie to that line.

I stand up. I accept the blade. He sinks back to his bench with obvious relief. I test the edge of the blade with my finger, find it sharp, cutting. Not too much pressure would be needed to send it deep into my flesh.

But I can't. I look into his eyes. How can he ask me to do this? "You know, if you want me to bite you, maybe you should be the one to stab me. Then the wolf will be angry at you."

He laughs softly. "If I make her too angry, she might kill me."

"I suppose she might." I stare at the knife. I stare at him. "You really need me to do this? What about Jaime?"

"Jaime does not have the trauma morph. His natural wolf adores me. I have never been able to taunt him into a bite."

"Hmm. Figures." I pace around the room a little bit, playing with the edge of the blade. I punched a steel girder because I was feeling angry and it broke my hand, why is this different? But it is. A wound, to trigger the trauma morph, has to be deeply traumatic. Something that would kill me if I didn't have the wolf. I can feel this, the same way I feel the wolf right there, ready to do my bidding.

"What about Andrea? She's a trauma morph."

"Bitten. The bitten cannot restore the wolf of the born."

"Huh. Makes sense I guess."

"This is something only you can do."

"Uh-huh." I know what he's trying to do here. Flatter me into it. You're so special, you're so great, even your awesome brother Jaime who's better than you at everything else can't do this thing. I play around with the knife, thrusting it into the air away from me, pressing it against my own stomach, just under the ribs. The pressure makes me belch, a taste like bourbon and oysters. I start coughing violently, kneel, bring up another bullet. How many times was I shot anyway?

"Are you all right?" he asks.

I hold out the bullet. "This is really getting ridiculous. Is there some kind of record for how many times one of us can get shot?"

His eyes glitter with a sympathy that seems genuine. "I don't know of any upper limit, I'm afraid. My personal record is twenty-three. And it took four days for the last one to be expelled."

"Hmm. This might end up being sort of close to that." I remain kneeling on the floor, rub my forehead, where the inde-cision, or maybe the hangover, makes itself felt as an aching tightness.

"I have a painkiller," he says. "One moment." He uses the cane to brace himself as he bends down to grab a small jar full of sticky-looking brown liquid. He offers it to me, then sits down again.

I take the jar. It smells like the one Opal gave me, but stronger, sugar-free. Only four ounces, I down it in one gulp. It tastes sharp and medicinal and churns in my guts for a while, before spreading out from my center, hot and dark, like a black sun, radiating. My fingertips tingle with heat and emptiness. I feel strong, but hollow and restless.

I want to.

I want to do violence.

I'm ready.

I stand up. I press the knife against my gut, thinking I'm going to press harder, send the blade into my flesh, but nothing happens. It's like my arms won't obey me.

I look at my father's face, eager and hungry.

"Why," I say to him. I didn't mean to say anything, but now that I'm speaking out loud, my anger surges in his direction. I imagine it like a red hand reaching out to take him by the neck. I point at him with the agnara. "Why should I do this for you? After all your deception? Your crimes? What you might have done to my mother? Maybe I'm the only one who can save you. But do you deserve to be saved?"

His eyes flash green and he pushes himself to his feet again. He looms over me, tall but fragile, like a damaged tree. "Do I deserve it? Deserve?" His annoyance shows in his voice and for a second, just a second, I think we're going to fight after all. Right now I'd win. I tense up, wiggle my fingers. Maybe I will kick his ass.

But he sighs, shaking his head, letting it all go, sinking back down, resting his hands on the cane, his head on his hands. "I don't know. Do I deserve anything? Probably not. Maybe this really is my judgment, my punishment from the gods. It's all up to you."

All up to me.

That thought brings a strange thrill. The power is mine. My choice. I can tell him to piss off and there's nothing he can do.

"Let me think about it," I say. Tormenting him because I can. I push my way out through the red curtains and Jaime is right there, eager, worried.

"Did you do it?" he asks. "I didn't feel the transformation."

"Not yet," I say. Now that I see the timid hope in my brother's face, I feel oddly shamed. Jaime wants this. He wants me to save our father. "I, uh. I'm finding it difficult to do the—the thing." I gesture with the agnara.

He nods, understanding. "The trauma morph is a hard gift. So much power, when you call the wolf, but so much pain to get there." He gives me a little half smile. "It's a funny thing. When we fought? If you had gone to wolf form, you would have kicked my ass."

"What do you mean?"

"Just as the born are more powerful than the bitten, the wolf is more powerful than the human. That's part of why my father's people honor a mastered wolf so much. I can't call the wolf, but you can." He squeezes my shoulder, then releases me quickly when he feels the ridges of my scars. "I'm sorry, I forgot, does it hurt when I touch them?"

"It doesn't." I smile at him. "Thank you. I think I need some fresh air."

I leave the ruined building, head out into the early morning quiet. The day already feels heavy, warm and moist, the sky white and low. Several of the Cachorros are asleep, all curled up around each other like puppies. It's cute until you notice the bloodstains.

I spot Reina and Andrea, awake and talking. Andrea has a cigarette, both of them hold bottles of beer. I go up to them. Reina smiles at me. "Have you bitten him?"

"Not yet. I'm finding it hard to summon the wolf in cold blood. Andrea, how do you do it?"

She sucks on the cigarette, flame bright in the shrouded

morning. "Well, it gets easier with practice. You've never done it before?"

"No. Before this, it was always my enemies trying to kill me. This feels too much like trying to kill myself. It feels wrong."

Reina gathers me into a hug. "And if it feels wrong to you, then you should not do it. Leon has lived his life. Jaime can lead the Cachorros. I have told him this for years. I fear his devotion to his father is misplaced. Given to a selfish man who does not deserve it."

"Yes. That's it exactly. Does he deserve for me to do this?"

"Does anybody deserve anything, really?" Andrea says. "I mean, we're all killers here, aren't we? Some people would say we all deserve to die."

"Andrea," Reina says, her voice a warning. She hugs me tighter. "Abby has only killed in self-defense."

"Dead is dead." Andrea shrugs, tosses the cigarette to the broken pavement, grinds it out with her foot. "Good luck, kid. The trauma morph is an awesome power, but not everybody has the guts to use it."

She walks away, and I feel shamed again. "I have the guts. I grew up in a fucking torture cult, okay? I'm not afraid of pain."

"Of course not. You're not afraid of anything, I know. Andrea is a jerk, don't worry about it."

"No, I'm afraid of a lot of things. Myself, mostly. My wolf. I'm afraid of doing the wrong thing. I'm afraid this is wrong. But I'm also afraid not doing this is wrong. I guess that's why I'm out here. If I were sure of myself—but I'm never that sure of myself."

"I understand. It's all right. You don't have to be sure."

"But Jaime really wants it, doesn't he?"

"He does. But that doesn't have to be your concern. Other people always want something from you, no? You're young, you're healthy, you're powerful. Those things belong to you, nobody else."

She strokes my hair. Steph does that. Hair-stroking. When I

was little, it was my favorite thing in the world to have my mother stroke my hair, comb it, braid it. But that soft rush of pleasure always felt a little shameful, too. Surely it must be wicked to enjoy such a fleshly thing, when our only joy is supposed to be in the Lord.

I close my eyes. A memory flashes into my head, a memory of New Harmony. "I used to imagine these different ways of dying, when I was young. Sometimes I would test them out. See what happened if I cut myself with a rusty nail, or ate something that was supposed to be poisonous. I got sick but I never died. Now I think maybe that was the wolf. All along, the wolf was always there to save me."

"I'm so sorry. No child should have to go through that. No child should want to die."

"I don't know if I wanted to die, really. I was never very serious about it. If I were serious, I would have broken into the big house and taken Wisdom's shotgun."

"No child should want to die," she says, more firmly. "This is wrong. What was done to you in that cult, it was wrong. And this is wrong too. It's wrong of Leon to do this. To ask you to do this. Jaime too. The wolf is yours, she doesn't belong to them. They should know better."

"But they don't really have a choice, do they? This is just how it works. This is how you summon the wolf. It's kind of funny, in a way. You'd think being tortured all the time growing up would make this easier, but it doesn't."

"You don't have to do this."

"No, I know I don't have to. But maybe I want to. Maybe I want to know what it's like to save a life other than my own."

"But you have saved many lives. Everyone at New Harmony who was saved, was saved by you."

"But I'm also the reason they were in danger in the first place. That was just me trying to fix my own mistake. This is different."

I pull away from her embrace. "I'm going to do it."

She meets my gaze with a golden flash. "Are you certain of this?"

"Right now I am. But let's not wait."

REINA TAKES MY HAND AND LEADS ME BACK TO JAIME. THEN SHE takes his hand and both of them watch, tense, as I push my way into the small red nest again. My father is still there, waiting. Patiently. What else is he going to do? I have all the power.

"Have you decided? I have more painkiller, if that will help you."

He holds out a jar. I take it from him and swallow it down, caught up in a surge of feeling I can't name. A fierce joy with a hint of rage to it, like the feeling when I threw Jaime across the room, but bigger somehow.

I can call the wolf. So close, it almost feels like I should be able to summon her at will, without sliding the knife into my flesh, but the knife goes in anyway, the pain red and sharp and somehow exactly right, and I think of the fishhooks and the whips and a low soft voice telling me, scars are good, scars mean you survived.

I throw back my head and

She howls, rends her father's bitter, starved flesh, and then—

I WAKE UP, WITH THE SENSE OF A RED VEIL LIFTING.

Morgan is pointing a gun at me. It swivels up to point at the sky while he says, "Oh, my God, Abby?"

I'm naked, as per usual it seems, in the courtyard of CharliQ's. Morgan, Izzy, Deena and Edison are all gathered around. Izzy has the presence of mind to throw me another one of those giant yellow Frere Jack's T-shirts. I put it on and stand up, hands in a gesture of surrender, even though Morgan's gun is no longer pointing at me.

"You're a real loup-garou," Izzy says, seeming more delighted than scared. "Just like Grammy talked about. You turn into a God-damned, no-fooling, furry-ass wolf."

That's when I notice Edison's arm is bandaged over a fresh wound. I don't have to ask. I can smell that I'm the one who bit him.

22

BERSERKER

"I don't remember a thing." I keep saying this. I have a headache, different from the one after the hangover. That was a dull, pounding thud. This is more like being stabbed repeatedly from the inside, as if a swarm of bees is trapped inside my head and trying to get out. Coffee drops into my gut like an acid bomb, but I drink it anyway.

"We came back here after Brad got out of the hospital and were just having some breakfast when we caught you—wolf you —trying to get into one of the smokers," Izzy says.

"I tried to chase you off," Edison says. "I don't know, I probably did it wrong. Made you feel cornered. That's why you bit me." He smiles, although he looks pale, maybe a bit feverish. Stress, or the effect of my bite?

"I don't remember," I say.

"I tried to shoot you," Izzy says. "I thought that's what you do, when you get bitten by a strange animal, you have to kill it and take it to the hospital so they can find out if it has rabies. But apparently I'm a terrible shot."

"We decided to call your uncle Morgan," Deena says. "But by the time he got here, you had run away again. He took us to the hospital to get Edison bandaged up, then we came back here and decided to try to find the animal, because apparently if they don't know that the animal didn't have rabies, they have to assume it did, and give you all those shots. Rabies is really bad. Apparently Stephen King was not lying when he wrote *Cujo*."

"I set out that big dish of yesterday's soup bones," Izzy says. "I figured if you smelled it, you might come back for it. And you did."

Morgan cradles the gun, a haunted look on his face. "I nearly shot you," he says.

"Morgan, you already did shoot me a couple of months ago in the kitchen of the Seattle house. Don't worry about it. You wouldn't have killed me without a head shot."

"What's going to happen to me?" Edison asks. "It's the full moon again tonight, isn't it? So do I get to——" he makes a very human-sounding *aroooo* noise.

"You seem pretty cheerful about it."

"I'll become like you, right?" He grins. "That's not so scary."

I hug him. "Not quite. I'm a born wolf. You would be bitten. It's different."

His mood dims. "Different how?"

"There's a transition period. Sometimes successful, sometimes not. I have to contact my brother Jaime, he's helped people through it. He can help us." I picture my phone with its shattered screen. I think it's in a bloody plastic bag out at the den. I look at Morgan. "You have a truck, will you drive us out to the ruined amusement park?"

His face stays dazed, blank. Then he nods. "I'll do it."

At the truck, Morgan pauses, gets something out of the second row of seats. "Here, you'll want these." He hands me a pair of his old sweatpants, which I wriggle into and roll up at the cuffs. "Thanks." Edison sits in back and I direct us to the park. We drive mostly in tense silence until I spot the rotting boar's head. It's fallen off its pike and I have a feeling of apprehension that I can't fully explain.

"You guys, go ahead and stay in the car, okay? I'll go on foot. Keep the doors locked. Don't open to anybody other than me. Human me. Okay?"

"What are you worried about?" Edison asks.

"I'm not sure. Something here doesn't feel right."

But as soon as I get out of the car, I know the answer: the Cachorros have already gone.

I take some time exploring, to be sure. I find boar bones, discarded clothing, red plastic cups that used to hold beer. Smells of sex and violence. In the nest my father left behind, I find the plastic bag of my things, placed neatly, as if anticipating me coming back for it. The contents are intact, and include the black silk robe, now as thrashed as everything else I was carrying last night. The agnara, in its leather wrappings, is placed neatly, next to my father's wolf-head cane.

It seems pretty clear what happened. My father knew my bite worked. He could feel it. So they all took off as soon as possible. And these are, what, lovely parting gifts? Consolation prizes?

Or, maybe they're a little kinder than I thought. The agnara, so I can begin trauma morph training on my own. And the cane because it hurts like hell and you spend a lot of your time hobbling around.

Either way, I take them.

I inhale deeply, as if I could read intention in the scent memories left behind. And the big inhale reveals something that shouldn't surprise me at all: a dead body.

I find a beefy young man in one of the maroon Deadly Sins T-shirts. He must be one of the Strigoi goons. I don't remember this one from last night, and I thought they all got rolled off to the swamps to get eaten by alligators. So maybe this one came after us later? And why is he wearing the Deadly Sins T-shirt? That must have come from Opal, right? Where else would he get it?

My scent is all over the dead man, and his throat was ripped out.

My wolf must have killed him. But I don't remember it.

I drop to my knees and throw back my head, let loose a howl of rage and frustration. I feel used, dirty. Whatever they gave me as a painkiller, it wasn't just a painkiller. It made me violent. It made me forget what I did. I killed a man and don't remember. I bit my friend and don't remember.

They don't care. They got what they wanted from me and just left. My father, my siblings. They never cared about me as a person, not even Jaime. When we fought each other as equals, that was a lie. Everything was a lie.

I howl, and howl, and howl.

In the distance I hear police sirens, as if in answer. I shouldn't stick around.

Back to the truck. I tap on the door. Edison and Morgan both jump, seeming terrified for a moment, before opening the door and letting me back in.

"What the hell, was that you?" Morgan says. "Or is there actually a pack of wolves out there?"

"Uh, no, it was me. I was kind of upset. Sorry."

On the broken screen, I text Jaime.

> `Bit a friend last night. Can you help?`

He answers right away.

`Heard you sister. Meet us nearby @ the break-`
`fast club come alone.`

Morgan drops me off at The Breakfast Club, a diner, with instructions to call Steph when I'm ready to get picked up. I get a vegetarian omelette and pick at it. I should be hungry, after everything that's happened. I can tell the wolf didn't eat anything last night, not even the bones that Izzy put out as bait. But my stomach feels all wrong, incapable of digestion,

Jaime and Reina enter the diner, slide into the seat across from me. Reina wears lightly tinted sunglasses and a knit cap that hides the tips of her ears, while Jaime wears a troubled smile. "Hello, Abby."

"Hi, Jaime, Reina. You said you heard me. Howling, you mean?" He nods. My curiosity sidetracks me for a moment. "How far away can you hear one of us howling, anyway?"

He shrugs. "Farther than you might think, but beyond that, it's hard to say, since it depends so much on weather conditions. But we weren't as far away as we intended to be. We had a bit of a delay leaving town. Engine trouble."

"All right. So, if you heard me, you know I'm pissed off at you."

"Of course you are," Reina says. She folds her arms, seeming pissed off herself.

He grimaces and puts a hand on her arm, as if to calm her down. "I'm sorry, Abby. You ran off. We didn't know where you'd gone. But we couldn't change our plans to wait for you to return to us. We really do need to be out of Varger territory before moonrise. This engine delay puts us far behind schedule."

"You could have tracked me if you wanted," I point out.

He frowns. "Maybe. But your wolf was very hostile earlier. She didn't seem to want anything to do with the pack. We thought it best to let you go."

"Well that's because she was all drugged up! Whatever Leon gave me, he said it was a painkiller, but it caused me to black out an awful lot of time. Time during which the wolf killed someone. And, hey, do you want to maybe tell me about that? About me killing someone and I don't even remember doing it?"

He tries to make his smile reassuring. "Another of the criminals. No need to worry."

"Fine. So what the hell was in that so-called painkiller my father gave me?"

"Berserker drugs," Jaime says.

I hiss, so angry I can barely form words. "You. Gave me. Fucking. Berserker drugs. The. Hell."

Reina jumps in. "Painkillers are hard for the wolves, yes? Born and bitten both. We process traditional human drugs too fast, or the pathways don't work in our brains, with our body chemistry." She taps her head. "A small dose of the berserker drugs usually works as a painkiller, without being enough to cause the berserking effect. Usually." She looks at Jaime. "This is what I mean, when I tell you our sample sizes are too small." She looks back at me. "I was a research chemist, before, although nothing I'm doing now would pass in a scientific setting."

Jaime closes his eyes and dips his head, an apology. "I'm sorry. We thought the dose was too small, and the berserking effect isn't supposed to take hold in women anyway. We didn't know."

I sigh, harsh, a bit of a growl. "So. You gave me an experimental dose of an experimental drug and it had an effect you weren't expecting. And you're shocked by that. Fine. Moving on, how can we help my friend who I bit?"

Reina brings out a mason jar full of brownish liquid. At a glance it might be the berserker drugs again. "This is a cure for the bite. Your friend should drink it slowly over the next several hours, but must finish it all before moonrise."

"More drugs? What the hell?" I open the jar and sniff. Not the same herbs as the berserker drugs, but I have no idea what they do. "Why should I trust that this is intended to help him, and not kill him?"

Reina sighs. "I can't give you any reason to trust me, if you don't. So it is up to you."

I stare at her, shake my head. "That's the problem, though. I do trust you. Instinctively. But now I know how easily my trust can be betrayed." I look at Jaime, who hangs his head, like a dog being chastised.

"We didn't know," he says again. "Are you here to ask to travel with the Cachorros? Now that we know your hostility was caused by the drug effect, Reina and I can take you to join the others, if you want."

"No. No, I really don't think so." I glare at them.

Reina nods. "It's all right. But please understand, no matter how you feel about us, we have the same goals. We want more bitten wolves to be successfully socialized. And I want everyone bitten to have a choice." She holds up the jar. "I chose Jaime. I gave up my old life to be with him. I have no regrets. But your friend, they should make an informed choice. So offer the cure. If they choose the wolf, you must help them. And if they choose the cure, you must still be there for them, because the cure may not work."

"An informed choice." I stare at the mason jar. "How informed? What do I tell him? What is it like to be one of the bitten?"

"Just like being one of the born," Jaime says, squeezing Reina's hand. "Only a little less so. The gifts of the wolf are not as powerful."

"No," Reina says firmly, shaking her head, kissing his hand. "You know that is not true, love. There are many risks. Some do not survive the berserker moon, in spite of our best efforts to help them through it. And afterward, even if everything goes well, your friend will not be the same. I am not the same. Better in some ways, perhaps. But different forever." She taps Jaime's head, then her own. "Your brain, it was always made to be a wolf brain, yes? My brain, not so much. Sometimes it's hard to feel like myself, to know who I am. Your friend needs to know all this, before they choose."

"So, how do I restrain my friend, in case the cure doesn't work? How do you restrain a bitten wolf during the berserker moon? Especially when I'm probably going to be a wolf myself?"

"Probably?" Jaime looks puzzled. "There is some doubt?"

"Well, I stayed human last moon. It was hard, but I did it."

Now he looks impressed. "So you have partial mastery of the wolf already? Amazing."

Reina nods thoughtfully. "That would be the ideal situation, for you to be in human form with all the gifts of the wolf. Your transformation earlier today should help you to suppress her later. But it sounds as if you're not sure you can manage it tonight?"

"Right. A month ago everything was a lot less stressful. I have no idea what's going to happen tonight."

"Your preparation is the same either way. Take your friend away from human habitation, and restrain them physically before the moon comes. Wrap them very tightly. Ropes all over. Think of how a spider wraps her prey. For yourself, set the intention of not fighting your friend even if they escape their bonds and challenge you. Chase them all over, but your wolf might kill them if you fight."

I inhale. Of course that's true, but I hadn't thought of it before. That stupid wolf could kill him. "This cure better work," I say.

"I hope it does. And whatever you do, don't let the Varger know about your friend. You cannot trust them to take care of the bitten."

"I know. Thank you."

"De nada." She squeezes my hands. We rise, and they both hug me, then go.

I CALL STEPH. "I'M DONE."

"Hi, kiddo. I guess the wolf is out of the bag, huh? How are you doing?"

"I'm okay. I got a cure for Edison from one of my brothers. We hope it will stop him from transforming."

"Your brother? You mean Nic?"

"No, a different brother. I have a lot of them, apparently."

"Well, my brother is having some kind of a big paranoid freak-out over here, worrying that every animal he's ever shot was a human in disguise." Pause. "It's not like that, is it? There's really only the wolf shape-shifters, right?"

"As far as I know."

"So, do you want me to pick you up and take you back into town?"

"No! Not town." New Orleans, which will be swarming with Varger, many of them hunting for me, all of them ready to kill Edison if they find out what happened to him. "Please, have Morgan and Edison pick me up here. Tell Morgan to get camping equipment ready. Edison and I need to spend the whole night out in the woods." I have a thought. "Remember that book I got from the used bookstore, the one with the leather cover? I didn't really get it from the bookstore. It's a diary that belonged to my father Leon. Could you bring it? I think it's just sitting on a table in the living room."

"Sure, of course."

"And, this is going to sound kind of nuts, but bring a lot of rope, okay? Like, enough rope to completely mummy-wrap somebody Edison's size. Maybe twice over."

"Ah. Okay. I think I get it." Pause. "Are you two really going to be okay?"

"I hope so.

I pace around for a while, then pull out my phone, notice I'm almost out of battery, notice I have a text message from Opal.

U ok?

Yes

You with the Cachorros?

No

Where you facing the moon?

Out in the woods I guess. Barataria?

How's Edison?

What? Does she know I bit him? How would she know that?

Why?

But before she answers, my phone gives me a low power warning and the screen shuts off. Shoot. I pace around, every minute seeming to last forever. Finally, at last, I spot Morgan's truck.

I was expecting the truck to contain just Morgan and Edison, but instead it's completely full of people: Steph and Terry and Deena and Isobelle. It's a big truck. I end up riding in a weird little half seat in the rear, where I can make faces at Terry in his little backward-facing baby carrier, and he laughs.

"It's nice to see everyone," I say.

"We have so many questions about werewolfing," Deena says. "First of all, is it awesome? Because it seems kind of awesome. Are we sure Edison wants to be cured?"

"You want to be cured," I say, although I entertain a brief fantasy of Jaime carrying Reina off in a swirl of lust. No. Too dangerous. "The transformation can be deadly. It doesn't always go well. And the entire rest of your life would be different. Your brain, not just your body. Oh, and a lot of the bitten end up looking kinda weird too, permanently half-shifted to wolf form? I mean, most of the time you can still walk down the street without attracting a torch-wielding mob, but people will notice."

"Huh." Edison looks thoughtful, but not entirely convinced.

Izzy speaks up. "She's right, you want the cure. I've been hearing tales of the loup-garou all my life, and even knowing that a lot of those stories were probably bullshit, believe me, you want the cure."

"Here." I hand him the jar. "Start drinking it now."

"You know it's not technically legal for people to be drinking alcohol right here in the car while I'm driving, not even in Louisiana," Morgan says.

"But in Louisiana nobody's going to bust us," Steph says. "Probably."

Morgan says, "Steph tells me there aren't other kinds of shape-shifters, just the wolves. Is that true?"

"As far as I know. I'm pretty sure if there are, they have to be somewhere far away from here, or the Varger would know about them."

"Good." He nods, relieved. "I've never killed a wolf. I know other hunters who do. Trophy kills mostly. Sometimes they're doing a favor for a rancher that sees the wolf as a threat. Sometimes it's almost like they see the wolves as competition. But I respect your kind." He pauses. "I mean, wolves. Your kind as wolves." His stress chemicals spike upward, his sweat a kind of rusty orange. "I really could have killed you, you know."

"Head shot, I told you. Only a head shot would have killed me. And even then, it would have to be just the right head shot. We survive bullets to the head all the time."

"According to Grammy, if you gots to kill you one o' them loup-garous, use an axe on the new moon, take off they head," Izzy says, imitating her grandma's accent.

"That is actually one hundred percent correct. No silver, no bullets, no wolfsbane, no frogs, no throwing rice. But we are more vulnerable on the new moon, and we can't survive having our head removed from the rest of our body." I pause. "I'm pretty sure we can't survive that."

"What about other parts?" Deena asks. "I'm sorry if that's

gross. But I mean, what if you lost an arm or a leg? Would you grow it back?"

"I don't know. Probably? Maybe not right away. I don't know."

"I could have made a head shot," Morgan says. "I have really good aim. Damn it, Abby. How could any of this be real?"

"I don't know. How is anything real?"

"I'm not sure it is." He takes a deep, shuddering breath. "I keep feeling like this is some weird-ass nightmare I'm having, and I'm gonna to wake up soon."

Edison sips the cure. "I feel the same, but I kind of like it? I mean, yesterday, I lived in a regular boring world where my worst problem was how to tell everybody that I was quitting the Huskies football team. And today my big problem is that I might be a werewolf. I dunno, I kind of like this world better."

"You're quitting football? Why?" Deena asks. "I can't believe this is the first I'm hearing about that."

"It's just too much, you know? All the pressure. All the expectations. And it's not like I'm going to join the NFL when I graduate or anything like that. So it started to feel like a waste of time." He sips the cure. "I don't know if you know this, but football players are just like frat boys. They can be real assholes. I mean, I already knew that, but since Deena started to come out as gay, it seems more relevant."

"You're a lesbian?" Morgan asks, frowning, glancing at Deena. "Why didn't I know this?"

"Because you've always been a little blind to that sort of thing, dear brother," Steph says. "Did you miss the part where Izzy and Deena are dating?"

"What? Izzy, you're a lesbian too? How long has that been going on? Does your grandma know?"

"Of course her grandma knows. Grandma Charli knows everything," I say.

"Yeah." Izzy laughs. "I thought she didn't know. But this

morning she came in to work while Deena was still there and we were holding hands and she just looked at us and nodded."

We continue to talk, bantering, teasing, and I have a powerful sense of love and fear: these are my pack, these people in the car right now. These are the people I have to protect.

No matter what it takes.

23

THE SNAKE AND THE WOLF

Morgan picks a campsite for us and helps us set up. He gets the fire going, points out the cooler he's packed with several pounds of fresh venison. "We'll be back here tomorrow at sunrise to get you," Morgan says. "And I hope to God you're okay, but I guess it's out of my hands now. Watch out for alligators." He pauses. "Who wins, in a werewolf-alligator fight?"

"The werewolf," I declare, with confidence.

"Do you eat alligators?"

"I can't imagine the wolf going to the trouble of eating an alligator when there are so many fuzzy little nutria about."

"So… all that time you claimed to be a vegetarian, that was just denial?" Morgan asks, with a grin.

"Not exactly. It's more complicated than that. But call it denial if you want."

He takes a deep breath. "I have something. For you and the boy both. I don't know if you'll be willing to wear them."

He pulls out a couple of dog collars and I burst out laughing. "You really are determined not to shoot me accidentally, aren't you?"

"They've got these chips in 'em, see?" He presses the dangly metal bit, engraved to identify me as "Abby" and give the Marchandes' address and his phone number. "They're elastic, so you won't choke." He demonstrates. "That way, tomorrow, if you're not right here, we'll still be able to use the chip tracker to figure out where to pick you up. And—" His voice wavers a little. "Hunters know to look for a collar. A tag. With this you're not a wolf. You're somebody's pet."

"Okay." I slip it over my head. It's comfortable enough, I suppose, although it makes me feel like an idiot. "For you I'll wear it."

Edison puts his on, and poses. "How do I look?"

Gorgeous. I laugh. "Like you're ready to go out clubbing."

Big group hug and Morgan leaves us alone with our camping supplies and our sexual tension. Edison grins at me. "So, we've got hours until sunset, what do we do?"

We make out! part of my brain screams. But another part feels like that would be a very bad idea. I swallow. Hard. Work the saliva back into my mouth. "I need to be kinda zen here tonight, Edison. I'm hoping if I stay calm enough I can suppress the wolf, stay human."

He nods, but looks disappointed. "Somehow I knew wild sex orgy wasn't going to be on the list."

"We'll be exploring bondage a little later, does that do it for you?"

He laughs. Sips the cure. "Honestly? Kinda it does. I mean, I would have stayed at that club you found if we weren't with the bros. And that time you flipped me? Deena was mad, but I wasn't. I thought it was hot. I always daydreamed about dating a woman who could toss me across the room. Like Wonder Woman or something. I didn't know she would be a foot shorter than me and also a literal werewolf, but, yeah. I'm going to enjoy getting tied up by you."

"Edison, could we please talk about something less provocative?"

He gives me a knowing look. "You're turned on, aren't you?

I can smell it. Is that a werewolf thing?"

"It would be." Oh, no, is the cure not working? Maybe it's just not working yet. "It's annoying, in a way. I can tell what's on everybody's mind all the time because I smell it in their sweat."

He nods. "People think about sex a lot more than they admit."

"They sure do. Hey, I know what! Let's play a game. Tell me about the least sexy thing you've ever seen."

"The Republican National Convention."

I laugh. "Okay, you had that one ready to go."

"I had to watch it for a civics class. Everybody there seemed kind of old and mean and constipated, you know? Even the young people. It was impossible to imagine any of them having sex, even the ones with a zillion kids. Deena claimed she has fantasies about hate-sex with one of those hatchet-faced blond fascist ladies they always seem to have around, but I think she was just trying to be funny."

"See, you started out talking about the least sexy thing ever, and somehow you steered it back around to talking about Deena's possibly satirical sex fantasies." I take a sip from my own bottle, a giant container of blue Gatorade.

"We need to change the game, then. Because if you say 'least sexy thing ever' that forces me to think about what would be the most sexy thing, then imagine the opposite of that."

"Good point. How about the most boring thing you've ever seen?"

"The Republican National Convention."

I laugh helplessly for a while. "You set me up, you dog."

"I didn't, I swear. I was just being honest both times. All right, let's see. I did watch part of an Andy Warhol movie once. One he made, not one that was about him. That was pretty boring. It was a guy who was asleep."

"Just that? A guy who was asleep?"

"Yeah. It was part of an art exhibit Deena took me to. She thought the movie was boring but she was more excited about it.

Like, 'wow, this is so boring, it's amazing!'" He sips the cure, smiles. "She's kind of a hipster, you know?"

"Yeah. I always worry she's too cool for me."

"Me too."

"You? How could anybody be cooler than you?" Whoa, that just blurted right out of my mouth, didn't it?

"Because I've known her since we were in first grade. I was, like, this shy gawky little kid who didn't know how to talk to people, and Deena was this popular funny loudmouth who was always getting in trouble. She was a year younger than everybody else because she got moved up a grade, but she still fit in better than I did."

"You were shy?"

"I'm still shy. That's why I do things like play football or be in a band or whatever. It's like, it makes it so I can seem like I'm interacting, but I don't really have to talk to people."

He sips the cure. "I think I'm the most boring thing I know of."

"You are not boring."

"You say that. But, like, here we are, just the two of us, and we're already running out of things to say. That doesn't happen with you and Deena, does it?"

"What makes you think you're the boring one? Maybe I'm the boring one." I stand up. "It's less boring if we go for a walk. Also, it can't hurt to check out the territory."

"Hey, yeah!" He springs to his feet, excited to have a purpose.

WE WALK AROUND UNTIL THE SUN BEGINS TO HANG LOW AND RED in the sky. "It's getting close. Finish the cure and let's get you tied up."

I know how to tie knots, and I did get that very brief glimpse of the BDSM world last night—was it just last night? I wish I had Juniper here to consult, I bet she'd have all sorts of helpful tips. The tricky part is imagining what's going to happen to these ropes if he changes shape. The corset stayed around my midsection, but that corset would have to be chained to something very strong in order to hold me back. I need something that restrains his limbs, and I'm nervous that I'm getting it completely wrong.

"I feel like Houdini," he says, shaking the ropes.

"Houdini was the escape artist?" I'm still not a hundred percent on pop culture references.

"Yeah, he was the escape artist. But don't worry. I have no idea how you get out of these ropes."

"But you're not wolf-shaped yet."

"Neither are you." He makes eye contact with me, his own eyes brown and deep, but not flashing. Not yet. "If I stay human, you'll stay human, right?"

"That's the plan." I smile, try to be reassuring. But I'm not sure of myself.

I roast some of the venison, as my last act before stomping the fire out. Sure, it's swampy around here, but it's also late August. If anything is going to catch on fire, it's now.

"That smells so good," Edison says, and I feed him a strip of the meat. "Oh my God, it tastes even better."

"It was marinated in alcohol and spices."

"I can smell that."

"Regular sense of smell, or super-duper-wolfy sense of smell?"

Through the ropes, he manages a full-body shrug. "I can't tell, I'm sorry. Are you hoping I won't go on a rampage if I'm already full of meat?"

"That is the idea, yeah."

I consider the venison. I hear Pere Claude telling me, *you don't want the wolf to be hungry.* If the wolf is hungry, is she more likely to show up? I can't deny that possibility. I can't deny the meat smells good to me. And really I have bigger things to worry about than whether it's ethically defensible for me to eat a deer while I'm still human. After all, wolf me might eat a deer or two, but she's also killed five drug dealers and a murderous ex-husband. Wait, six. Six drug dealers.

That reminds me of something—no, it's gone.

I inhale deeply of the charred flesh and my stomach lurches in hunger, for the first time today. But still I hesitate, a strip of venison halfway to my mouth. I told Edison I'm not sure if I ever really believed in God, and maybe that's true, but I know I believed it when Wisdom told us that it was wrong to kill an innocent animal just so you could eat it. That was a sincere and true belief that lingers in my heart even now, as I am, stuck sharing a body with a vicious predator.

Maybe there is a God after all. A God who likes to play cruel jokes.

The venison does taste amazing.

We wash it down with cans of beer from Nola Brewing and Abita Springs.

"Morgan really did think of everything," Edison says, as I tilt the beer into his mouth. "Although this is weird. I think maybe I always had a fantasy of a woman tying me up and feeding me beer and venison, but I didn't know that until right this moment."

"Edison, no. No fantasies. We're trying to stay cool here. Why don't I read to you while the sun is still up ?"

I pull out Leon's book. I flip through it until I find something that looks easy to read out loud.

"Check it out, Edison, this is from my father's diary. I think it's like a werewolf folktale."

"'THE SNAKE AND THE WOLF.'

"In the morning of the world, the Bon Dieu made all the animals and he loved them all very much. But in time he felt lonely, and wanted a man to talk to, a creature more like himself. So he said to all the animals, make me a man. And the animals did as the Bon Dieu asked. Every animal in the green earth came forward to present his man to the Bon Dieu. And every animal had made a man that was much like himself.

"There were rabbit men and skunk men. There were lizard men and lion men. There were fish men and dragonfly men, crab men and eagle men, rat men and horse men, spider men and sheep men. And all of these men were very good, each after his own fashion.

"But the animal that made the very best man for the Bon Dieu was the wolf. Because the wolf is as strong as the bear and as clever as the monkey, as beautiful as the lion and as fast as the cheetah. He has the far-seeing eyes of the raven, and no creature is wiser save the Bon Dieu himself.

"The Bon Dieu was so pleased with the wolf man that he gave him a special boon: that the wolf man and all his descendants might share in the gifts of the wolf and take on his shape when the moon is full.

"For a long time the wolf man was the leader of all the new men, and there was harmony throughout the land, because the wolf man was kind as well as wise. Because he was strong he had no fear, and because he had no fear, he had no evil in his heart.

"But the snake man was the most hated of all the new men, for he was selfish and dishonest. Yet he was also very clever and ambitious and, just like the wolf, he had no fear. But unlike the wolf he had no love either.

"He believed that he should be the one to lead the men. And so he began to sow discord among the other men, and every time, he sought to blame it on the wolf man.

"Finally, when he saw the beautiful daughter of the gazelle man walking alone by the river, and the wolf man sleeping under a tree nearby, he saw his chance.

"Now, the men did not eat each other as the animals who

made them did. The lion man did not eat the gazelle man. The eagle man did not eat the rabbit man. The panther man did not eat the rat man. This is because men were very few in those days, so the Bon Dieu declared it should be so. A man might eat another kind of animal, but never another man. And so it is to this day, although men are now very great in number.

"The snake man was swift, and had poison in his mouth, and murdered the gazelle man's daughter. This was the first murder in all the world. It was silent, and did not wake the wolf man. And the snake man smeared blood around the mouth of the sleeping wolf man and went running through the town crying out that the wolf man had eaten the gazelle man's daughter.

"The townspeople saw this: the wolf man with blood on his mouth and the gazelle man's daughter lying dead. And so they believed the snake man, and they drove the wolf man and all his family away from their town and out into the wilderness. Then they made the snake man their leader.

"And so it has been ever since. Men are led by snakes, and they hate wolves beyond all reason."

"I like it," Edison says. "Regular European fairytales are so anti-wolf. Which is weird because wolves and dogs aren't that far apart. Deena and I were watching this program, and I guess all you really have to do to get a dog is start breeding wolves for lack of aggression. In just a few generations you start to get dogs. So your best friend and your worst enemy are pretty much the same thing." He pauses. "Whoa. I feel kinda stoned, is that the moon or the cure?"

"Or the beer. I have no idea." I look back to the book for more reading material, and notice something, like a postscript, on the snake and the wolf story. I start reading.

"What is it?" Edison asks.

"Oh, sorry. Let me read it out loud.

"This is a traditional story of our people, one every child grows up hearing. The wolf is the wronged hero, naturally. But what if there's another way to look at it? The wolf man fails. His own honest, straightforward nature blinds him to the treachery in the nature of others. The snake man succeeds, and why? Because he does what has to be done to accomplish his goals. Why are we not the masters of this world?

"Why do we fear the hunter and the real estate developer when all men should fear us? We have so much power, and what do we use it for? Hunting deer. Protecting our own narrow kingdom. We speak of the gifts of the wolf, but the wolf brings curses as well. We are loyal and passionate, but I say we are too loyal, too passionate. Our emotions rule us, even when those emotions are a weakness.

"Love and remorse, the snake man is not held back by these things, why should we be? This is the secret of the berserkers, the olvhetnar. They were unchained by their emotions. They acted. And they could not be defeated. Why did we ever give up that power? We were shamed into it. A true Olvhetnar would take revenge against these men who slaughtered my mother like a sheep. He would be their nightmare. And so will I. I will follow that path. And in the end my father loves me and will forgive me, because that's his nature. But I will have no regrets. No remorse."

I pause. "Wow, that got dark. Sorry."

"Dude. Your dad wrote that?"

"I guess."

"He sounds kinda messed up."

"He was, I guess. His mother, my grandmother, was killed by hunters. That's what messed him up. But, I don't know, maybe he was even more messed up than I thought." I stare at the book in my hands, wondering. How honest has Leon been, at any point? Was he honest with me this morning? Honest when he wrote this diary? Honest when he told me that he didn't remember whether or not he raped my mother? Honest when he killed the men he held responsible for his mother's death?

I rub the surface of the book, fingers picking out the stamped initials. Opal said, we're werewolves, a little deception is baked into the pie. She included herself. Deception. Wolves who pretend to be human, humans who pretend to be wolves?

Something is nagging at the back of my brain, some connection struggling to be made. Like the bright moon about to rise, something is coming. Something I missed. Maybe something that happened during the empty space in my memory?

I hear a little electronic buzz, which must be Edison's phone. I didn't realize he had it with him, but of course he does. I left mine, broken and dead, in Morgan's truck, but I didn't say anything to Edison about his phone. He says, "Oh, get that for me, would you? I'm a little tied up."

"Those jokes are going to get old pretty fast," I grumble, pushing the ropes around so I can fish the device out of his pocket, then re-fastening the ropes.

I expect to see a message from Morgan or Steph. But the text is from Opal.

I can't get Abby on the phone do you know where she is?

I call her back. "Opal? You wanted to talk to me?"

"Oh, Abby! Thank the Lord I got you. It's all falling apart, sugar, the Varger know about Edison."

"Know what?"

"They know you bit him. He went to the hospital for a dog bite, and you had a known trauma morph in the same twenty-four-hour period? The Varger can put two and two together."

"Oh no, I wasn't thinking about that. Of course they know everything that happens in a New Orleans hospital."

"Right. And that place you said you were going, Baritaria? They know to look for you there."

My stomach drops and rolls in a panic. "They're coming here?"

"I think so, yes."

"Well, where can we go now? They'll track us!"

"I've got a car. Send me your exact location and I can take you somewhere safer."

"Okay. Sure. You can get us here." I send her our location.

"See you soon, hon. I'm so sorry about this. The Varger truly are evil, and they own this town. There's just no getting away from it."

We hang up. "Opal's getting us. Hopefully before the Varger figure out where we are."

Edison frowns. "And the Varger are?"

"Sorry, I forgot you wouldn't know. They're the wolves, the pack I guess, led by my grandfather Pere Claude. Then there's also the Cachorros led by my father Leon. The two groups are kind of at odds. Or, they would be if the Varger knew the Cachorros existed. Or maybe not, maybe it would be a big happy family reunion. I really don't know. People on both sides have been lying to me, but I'm not sure who's been lying about what." Nervous, I start pacing around.

Edison says, "You don't trust her, do you?"

"What? Opal? I guess not. But I don't trust anybody. so I'm not sure it's important that I don't trust Opal."

"Opal's not a very honest person, though. I mean, you can tell that just from hanging out with her."

"You can?"

He shrugs, in his wrappings, embarrassed. "Deena and Izzy and I were talking about her. I'm sorry if that's rude. It was at breakfast before wolf you showed up."

"And you thought she wasn't trustworthy?"

"Well, none of us knew about all this wolf stuff yet, so we were just, like, 'Abby's sister, what did you think?' Deena thought she seemed a little—you know, like she was always hustling for an angle?"

"I guess that fits. But I don't know what else to do now. A car is basically the only way to avoid getting scent-tracked at this point."

"What about Morgan? He might be able to get out here and take us to a new location."

"Before sunset? I'm not sure of that. And, if the cure fails and you do have a berserker moon tonight, I don't want Morgan to be right there."

"But it's okay if Opal is?"

"Yeah." I nod, feeling a little more sure of myself. "She's part of all this, he's not. Anyway, it's kind of her fault I bit you, so if you eat her I'll feel bad, but not like if you ate Morgan."

He smiles, responding to my light tone, but it turns to a frown. "Am I really going to eat a person if the cure doesn't work?"

"I sure hope not."

"But I might."

"Uh. Yeah. Kinda. You might."

"Shit. This whole thing is a lot, you know, a lot heavier than what I was thinking."

"I'm sorry." I give him a hug through the ropes. "I never meant to deceive you. It definitely is a blood and guts and death sort of situation here."

"It's still hard to believe any of this is really happening. I've seen you as a wolf and you actually bit me and it hurt and I got bandages and everything, but I still can't fully wrap my brain around it. I keep feeling like I'm going to wake up from a dream."

"I'm sorry. I guess maybe you get used to it eventually."

Opal drives up in her car. She must have been close. She gets out, smiling.

"Abby. Edison. Let's go."

She claps me on the shoulder and I feel a tiny sliver of pain and then—

24

THIBODAUX TAXIDERMY

PAIN
  Jaws of a monster around her ankle, she lashes out, snarling and snapping, unable to reach her enemy. Kill—

I shake my head and the fog clears a little. My right leg is held by a trap, the springy kind, like a jaw full of razor teeth. But it's been modified, teeth sharpened so that it's digging deeper into my flesh, tearing skin. The smell of my own blood is sharp and tinny in my nostrils, warm tendrils trickling down my ankle. I'm hurt, but not severely enough to trigger the trauma morph, not yet.

My own jaws are human. It's daylight, barely. I'm in a big open space that smells of neglected wood and toxic chemicals, machine oil and hot metal. I try to focus my eyes. Some kind of warehouse or manufacturing plant? Whatever was made here, it left behind a lot of animal parts: teeth and fur and bone, many bones, like an animal graveyard.

I spot a bin full of glass eyeballs, and it clicks: this was a taxidermy shop. Father Wisdom took us to a taxidermy shop once. For all I know, he took us to this one. It was the same reason he took us to a butcher shop, to demonstrate the macabre cruelty of dismembering animals and using them for things like food or clothes or decoration. The space currently shows signs of being used as an auto shop, with a motorcycle in one corner and engine parts scattered around. It smells heavily of Opal.

I spot Edison, still cocooned, propped against a wall on a mezzanine level and guarded by two big men wearing maroon Seven Deadly Sins T-Shirts. They look like Strigoi. In fact, I think I smell—Dennis? The guy I beat up on Sunday? What is he doing here?

"What's going on?" I ask out loud.

Opal giggles and moves into my field of vision. "Oh, good, you're awake. I wasn't sure how long the knockout drugs would work on you. My plan doesn't require you to be awake, but it's more interesting if you are." She stands just beyond where I can reach and uses her phone to take a video selfie. "Hey, Daddy, how you doing tonight? Feeling wolfy? I bet you are. Check it out, the little girl who brought your wolf back, she's in a trap. Just like in the *Saw* movies, you ever see those?" She swings the phone around to film me. "I rigged it up myself, special for one of the rougarou, but she's my first live test case, so who knows how it'll work?" She looks into the camera again. "I should also mention that I'm the reason you had car trouble leaving town. You wolfy types always did underestimate the importance of simple mechanical skills. I could've been a real asset to the team, you know? Well, too late. Now, you'll never believe what's going to happen next!"

Dennis limps into the room, leering at me, Deadly Sins T-shirt straining across bulky muscles. "Hey, Red. Not so tough now, eh?"

"No gloating," Opal says. "This is my show, honey, I'm the only one who gets to gloat."

"You set me up? This guy really is your friend?" I want to vomit, but that might be the drugs.

"Friend? No, not that. But, in exchange for some cocaine, of the highest quality if I do say so myself, he did agree to let you beat him up. I wanted a way for you and me to bond quickly, sis." She grins. "Of course, I might have been just the teensiest bit deceptive, letting him see your itty little self but not telling him you're one of those deadly rougarou he's maybe heard about. Then again, I don't know if he would've believed me until he saw you in action."

Dennis grunts. "You pay for this, Red. I limp maybe whole life."

Opal shrugs. "Yes, of course, darling, that's why you're so motivated to turn her into a rug, we do get it." She turns her attention back to the phone. "You hear that, Daddy? See the gun he's got pointed at her head? She goes wolf, that gun goes off. Blam! Right into the base of her skull at very close range. Just like how Grandma got killed, isn't it? And then we're going to make her into a rug. Juuuust like grandma. She even has the same beautiful red pelt as grandma. Isn't that precious?" She steps away from me and Dennis, sweeps her phone around to capture a panorama of the warehouse. "You remember this place, Daddy, I know you do. Thibodeaux Taxidermy. Used to be the largest taxidermy shop and tannery in the entire southeast. Your people even liked to shop here once upon a time, I do believe. There was a cobbler right there in the corner who made those red boots your mother liked so much, remember when you told me about those? Anyway, it's been pretty much abandoned since you slaughtered everybody all those years ago. Good job on the slaughter, by the way. People think this place is haunted."

She turns the phone to show herself again. "Well, that's it, Daddy. I just wanted you to know what I'm up to, since you didn't want me traveling with your pack. Wolves only, isn't that right?" She makes a kissy face and then shuts off the phone, turns toward me with a smile. "He should be seeing that fairly soon, I reckon. I don't know if he'll come to save your life, but he'll surely come to prevent the gross indignity of your wolf getting made into a rug.

"He really likes your wolf, you know. He wasn't too impressed with your human self, at least, not when he first told me about you, asked me to help engineer a bite. 'Only child I sired in wolf form and she turned out to be a runt.' Those were his words. But this morning? After I showed him the video of your trauma morph, and then after you bit him? He could not stop gushing about your wolf. He thought she was magnificent. Which reminds me, you need to see this before you die."

She turns her phone toward me and plays a video. Half a second of static, then a big, red wolf rolling around on the ground, snapping in obvious frustration at the pale corset that binds her waist, while four men watch.

That's me. That's what I look like in wolf form. As a wolf I look huge, not as large as Pere Claude, but still bigger than almost any dog I've ever seen. My teeth are enormous. Do normal wolves have teeth that size? No wonder people are afraid of them.

And yet, to see those giant teeth biting helplessly at the corset, like a dog trying to get out of one of those neck cones, it's—

Comical.

The men are laughing.

"God damn look at that," one of them says.

The wolf looks pissed off, forgets about the corset, and bites their throats out.

Just like that.

"Let's have the slow-motion replay," Opal says. The clip goes back to the beginning and jerks forward frame by frame. The helpless rolling around seems to take forever. Yet, the slaughter is still almost too fast to see. The wolf snarls. She launches herself into the air. Her teeth flash. Blood explodes from the man's neck. He reacts. He falls. And already the blood is spraying from another neck.

"Such an efficient killer," Opal says, with approval. "Leon was exactly right about that. I wish I'd gotten the rest of it but I had my own skin to worry about."

Something she said is nagging at me. "What did you say? About him siring me in wolf form?"

"Oh, yes. It's a funny thing about Leon. It's not in the diary I gave you, but it is in one of the ones I've seen, he kept track of absolutely everything when it came to fathering his children. Who, when, how. And of course, the results. My wolfless state was just data to him." Her rage ticks up. "But once he was sure of it, he had no further use for me at all. I thought things had changed. When he asked me for this service? To get you out there to bite him? I thought he'd decided that I belonged in his pack after all. I really did. I was such a fool."

"That snake lied to me. He does remember."

"Lied? Oh, yes, he's quite the liar."

"So are you." I simmer at her, helplessly.

She barks out a short laugh. "Well, there is that. We have a lot in common, Leon and I. Mostly our less savory characteristics. All right, enough chitchat, time to get Leon's doom out here."

She starts filming again, smiling into her phone. "Mr. Claude Verreaux? Hey, how you doin' tonight? I'm one of your many, many grandchildren by Leon. My name is Opal." She swings the phone around to show me. "And that is your grandchild Abby, I know you're familiar with her. I'm wolfless, but she's not. And I don't know if you know this, but Leon is awake, and active, and he's moving forward on that idea he always had to force you all out of the closet? He had me kidnap your granddaughter in order to broadcast her transformation at the full moon, live across the Internet." She points the phone at Edison. "And then we're going to film her eating that boy right there." She turns the phone back to herself. "Anyway, Leon just wanted me to let you know what he's planning tonight so you can prepare. Lovely talking to you."

She clicks off and smiles at me. "The Varger should be able to figure out my location from that, and Leon's father will be on his way here soon. With any luck they'll arrive at exactly the same time but it's hard to engineer something like that."

"I don't understand."

She laughs. "Of course you don't. Because my plan really is that convoluted. That's part of the fun, though, don't you think?"

"I understand you're mad at Leon for ditching you, but just getting some Cachorros and Varger in the same place at the full moon? It'll be awkward, but they're not going to kill each other. Pere Claude and most of the Cachorros are family."

Her smile twinkles with pure mischief. "Oh, but there's something I haven't shown you yet." She taps on her phone, and a minute later, big, beefy men start filling the room, all wearing Deadly Sins T-shirts, some holding what appear to be guns full of tranquilizer darts, some carrying axes. They must have emerged from automobiles, since they pop instantly from can't-smell-them into surrounding me. How many are there? A dozen? Two dozen? Shit, New Orleans really does have a Strigoi problem.

"Not tranquilizer drugs," she says, seemingly in answer to my thought. "Berserker drugs. I've told them—through Dennis, I don't speak Russian myself— that the rougs are coming, and if they shoot the rougs full of these drugs, that the rougs might bite them and give them the same power that you all have."

"But—will that even work?"

"I don't know. But the drugs got you to bite your boy over there, didn't they?" She glances up at Edison with a big smile. "And I have given them some very useful pointers on how to fight y'all, so they will hold their own better than most." She grins. "Which, let's be honest, basically means it'll take them a little longer to end up dead, and they might take one or two of you with them. Probably not, though. If any of you wolves end up dead, it'll be because you killed each other. And they know that. Every one of these men knows that most of them are simply going to get killed by a bunch of angry rougs. But also, every single one of them assumes that he's the special one who's going to survive, and it's all the other poor saps who're gonna get it."

She pops open a tiny bottle of champagne and swigs from it. "Anyway, I'm hoping to start an absolute werewolf massacre but it's possible I've miscalculated terribly and the only person who will get killed is me, and honestly, the longer I stay here talking to you, the more likely that is. But it's thrilling! Now I know why serial killers start writing letters to the cops." She pauses. "Oh, now that's an idea. Assuming I survive this, I'm gonna send a letter to the Times-Picayune. What do you think, should I be the Frat Boy Killer? Or the Cocaine Killer? Or the Party Killer? I don't know, those all seem a little cheesy."

"The Frat Boy Killer? Shit. I was right. You were causing those deaths."

"Of course I was, sweetie." She sips champagne, lights up a cigarette. "Although the first one really was an accident, more or less. He was every inch the frat boy, twice used his daddy's money to weasel out of a rape charge. But he paid well. He'd partied with us before. But that particular night he just kept asking for more and more and more, and I thought, 'he's gonna kill himself if he keeps this up.' But I didn't say a word. I gave him everything he asked for. Then he died, just like I thought he would.

"It's not hard to kill a frat boy type. They're not afraid of anything. But they're not like me, where I just don't feel fear, or like you, where you're not afraid because you're the most dangerous thing in the room. No, they're fearless because they're so incredibly stupid. They don't think anything bad can ever happen to them. They strut around like kings, thinking they're protected by some divine inherent specialness. But if you took away everything in this world that props them up, why, they couldn't even make a sandwich for themselves."

She glances up at Edison with a big smile. "Last night was so much fun for me, you know? The bros were absolutely perfect. I really enjoyed hanging around with them all night, knowing how much I wanted to kill them in my usual fashion, but choosing not to." She puts out her cigarette in the empty bottle, drops both to the floor. "I suppose it's time I get on out of here." She turns to Dennis. "You remember the plan, right?"

Dennis gives her a thickly evil grin. "Wolf rug."

"Close enough, hon. Well, it's been quite a time. See you in the next life, sugar."

She walks out, leaving me caught in a vicious trap and surrounded by Strigoi.

25

GRANDMOTHER WOLF

D ennis leers at me and I look away. I have to think this through. I wish I were better at thinking. I wish I were somebody really smart, like Izzy or Deena. What would they be thinking, if they were here? What would they notice?

I glance up at Edison. Only two Strigoi guarding him, that's barely a thing. But they do have axes. There's a window near where Edison is, so if I got to him, I could probably get him out of here easily.

If I could get to him. What about this trap? It hasn't triggered my trauma morph yet, but it's painful, distracting, making it hard to think. And we're so close to the full moon, I feel the wolf nagging at me, longing to emerge and deal with these many enemies that surround us. Except I'm pretty sure that in wolf form I would never be able to figure out how to release the trap, I'd just lose the foot.

That's probably Opal's intent. She mentioned the *Saw* movies for a reason.

I glance down at the sharp, rusty mechanism, shiny with silver at the places where she filed it down or put in new welds, and realize I don't know much about how traps work in general. I need to get a closer look.

I plop down to my butt, which Dennis notices, but he doesn't shoot me yet, just grins. "Tired, Red?"

"Dizzy." I shake my head, like I'm trying to clear cobwebs out of it. I keep my eyes half closed, watching him closely through my eyelashes until he looks away. He says something in Russian to one of the other Strigoi, laughs. I take my chance, press something that looks like it might be a lever.

PAIN

A bullet just went right through my hand.

"Knock it off, Red. Make too much trouble, fool around with trap, I just kill you now, forget rug."

Damn. My hand hurts, even though it's already mostly healed.

I hear a car pull up outside. The Strigoi tense. Reina, Jaime, Andrea, Tammy and Leon appear in the warehouse, moving almost too fast to see, although Leon is still obviously slower than the others, pausing for a moment in the doorway to assess the situation, steadying himself against the wall.

Then everything goes wild. Music blares out, intensely loud, hard-driving and fast. Strobe lights flash at irregular intervals, catching Cochorros and gangsters in some stunning freeze-frame moments as they fight, but also making it hard to focus visually. Worst of all, a loud engine of some kind starts running, clanking and whirring and spitting out a foul smog of the worst-smelling black smoke I've ever encountered. Opal obviously engineered all of this to help nullify rougarou advantages, but is it working?

Only one of the Strigoi is dead, so, probably. Under normal circumstances I think they'd all be dead already.

Leon gets shot with a bullet.

That ozone, electric feeling sweeps through the room, bigger and wilder than any time I've felt it before, as if the air in the room is howling. With the born, usually the change happens too fast to see, but with Leon, there's a shimmer in the air, a shuddering, a moment where it feels as if the reality where he's wolf-shaped and the reality where he's human-shaped fight each other for dominance and then—

With a sensation like a thunderclap—

The wolf wins.

Like his father, Leon has a wolf that is large and pure white. He shakes his head. Rougarou wolves all have a ruff, but his is unusually full, like a lion, befitting his name. The strobing catches him as he stretches luxuriously, like a dog waking up from a nap, and gazes around with sharp, brilliant green eyes full of wonder and intelligence. He's such a beautiful animal that for a moment, almost, I want to love him. I want to believe he's good. I want to think that everything bad I suspect about him is just Opal lying to me, trying to get all of us to fight each other.

A berserker dart goes into his flank and he begins to rage and snarl.

Dennis is watching all of this, more interested for the moment in the details of my father's transformation than in me. I press what I think are the release levers on the trap, only to find they work in reverse and the teeth of the trap bite more strongly, digging deeper into my flesh, intensely painful, down right to the bone. I clench my jaw to keep from crying out. In a single strobed moment I see that Dennis noticed what I was doing. He's maybe a strobe away from shooting me again, probably in the head this time.

The quickest way out of this trap is to help it take off my foot. I position my hands on either side of the wicked jaws, ready to use the wolf's strength to push them together. One. Two.

SLAM!
OH GOD OH GOD OH GOD DON'T THINK ABOUT IT DON'T
THINK ON THREE LEGS SCRAMBLE UP THE RAMP TO
EDISON DON'T THINK GRAB HIM DON'T THINK DON'T
THINK DRAG DRAG DRAG DON'T THINK DON'T THINK,
OUT THE WINDOW, FALL, HE FALLS ON TOP OF ME, DRAG
DRAG DRAG

I let go of Edison. I got shot a couple of times with bullets and one of the berserker darts. The drugs are making me feel a little weird, but I don't think I got a large enough dose to trigger the berserking effect. My foot (not a foot the absence of a foot) is tingling and aching, blood already clotted, and I have a moment of morbid fascination wondering if it's regrowing itself already and would I be able to watch it happen? Would it start out as a tiny baby foot or what?

Wait I got shot and lost a foot and I'm still human.

Why?

Because I had a stronger purpose, getting Edison out of the warehouse as quickly as possible, and the wolf bent to my will.

I'd probably feel really great about myself if I weren't in incredible pain and also MISSING MY DAMNED FOOT.

The Varger pull up in a single truck. Pere Claude, Vivienne, Nicolas, and a male I don't know all get out and stand, at high tension. The moon is probably less than five minutes away at this point and their body language is extremely wolfy. Pere Claude's eyes flash red and his voice is heavy, growling, full of rage when he asks "Where. Is. My. Son?"

"In the warehouse, but don't go inside, it's a trap. There's a bunch of Strigoi in there planning to shoot you with berserker drugs. It's like a rave, strobe lights and heavy metal and stinky engines and things, all designed to put the wolves at a disadvantage."

My grandfather and I stare at each other for a moment, a hard stare, eyes flashing. Then he growls and shakes his head.

"My son is fighting an enemy, and I must help or I'm not his Hunt Leader."

He rushes in and the others follow. Damn it, they're all going to kill each other. Why doesn't anybody ever listen to me? I check on Edison. I was hoping to get one of the others to guard him, but they all rushed into the building like idiots. He seems okay. Breathing, anyway. He's really drunk, though. He'd have to be, to stay passed out during me dragging him out a window and all the way here. I wonder how much alcohol she dosed him up with? How many "frat boys" has she killed that way? Overdosing them on alcohol, knowing they could end up dead and also knowing that nobody in New Orleans is ever going to question whether such a death is foul play?

The moon rises, her force sweeping through all of us. Inside the building, grunts and shouts turn to howling and snarling. Inside me, Fluffy asserts herself again, trying to insist it's her time.

No, I tell her. I have to think human style right now. There's something—

A smell of oil. Old, rancid. And a phone buzzing from a place where I'm not expecting the sound of a phone.

I crawl toward it rapidly, make a vague note that the stump of my leg doesn't hurt anymore, although it tingles and itches. Around the corner, I find an area full of junk and discarded scraps of wood, rusty waste barrels of noxious chemicals. In the middle of this is a phone, in a nest of wires and plugs, and it has to be a bomb, right? What else would it be? The screen shows a countdown. Sixty seconds. That buzzing I heard must have been the countdown starting, timed with the moonrise. Because a bunch of wolves won't know how to deal with a bomb.

Shit.

How do you defuse a bomb in sixty seconds when you don't know how bombs work?

I can't. I just have to try to get all the wolves out of there before it goes off.

Fluffy nags at me again. If I let her take over, I'll have four limbs instead of three, and she's faster. She knows how to lead them.

She's right. Time to give up. It's your show now, Fluff, don't let me down.

I close my eyes for a moment of focus, let go of something. It feels like opening a fist I was holding closed. There's a moment of intense feeling, not pain exactly, but almost like pain, intolerable and torturous, focused around my—her—our —

FOOT. SHE SHAKES HERSELF ALL OVER, TESTS THE FOOT FOR strength, howls. She feels hungry and weak from the effort of restoring herself, but she has priorities stronger than hunting.

She rushes into the building, howling, *FIRE FIRE FIRE FOLLOW ME OUT FOLLOW ME.* Inside is chaos. Loud noises, flashing lights, bullets flying, wolves snarling and fighting each other like badly behaved cubs, not focusing on their true ENEMIES, the men with the GUNS. Their fighting technique is bad. One of the ENEMIES lies on the ground, arm savaged, but still alive.

(*Opal was right it does work for that huh*)

The white wolves, the hunt leaders, her kin, fight each other, setting the tone for the others. They are strangely well matched. GRANDFATHER is much larger, FATHER is much younger. GRANDFATHER has been very healthy but also very comfortable, without hunger, and FATHER has been sick, wolfless, for so long that his newly returned wolf is starving with need, ferocious with it. But they are kin, they should not be fighting like this.

She snarls at them, meaning, knock it off you two, be leaders, get your people out of here. But they ignore her, too deep into the spirit of rage and combat.

She needs help. She reaches out for it and feels something

come over her in that moment, a spirit which is not quite her own, but which belongs to her. It feels both new and familiar, something she has never had, something she has always had, and she thinks maybe that spirit means GRANDMOTHER and now she howls with two voices, her own and one that is older, deeper, borrowed, and together they howl so loud, above all the din and chaos, and say

FOLLOW ME NOW TO LIVE FOLLOW ME FOLLOW ME

All the wolves pause for a moment to flick their ears and eyes toward her. She chomps at the noses of the two white wolves, as if they're cubs who need to leave off their squabbling and pay attention to something more important.

They stop fighting, shocked into stillness for a moment.

I AM GRANDMOTHER WOLF FOLLOW ME she howls at them and they know she tells the truth. *FOLLOW ME* she howls.

FIRE IS COMING

They follow her now and she leads from behind, barking and snarling and howling and nipping to keep them moving in the right direction in spite of all the distractions.

BIG NOISE!!!!

Her people react with confusion and fear, not understanding the new bad smells, the damage, the flame. They turn dumb like skittish horses.

She roars at them with the other voice *GRANDMOTHER WOLF IS SPEAKING GET OUT GET OUT GET OUT* and they obey, they get out, and finally she is the only one inside and she can leave.

Thank you GRANDMOTHER she says as the spirit fades.

(wait was that really the spirit of my grandmother because that would be absolutely the weirdest)

Hey, Red

One of the enemies speaks in human words and she turns, ready to kill him, but her head —

26

HARVEST MOON

Dear humans of New Orleans:

For two years now, I have taken a life whenever the full moon draws nigh. My victims were strapping young men of wealth and privilege, "frat boys" you might say, or young men of a similar disposition. They appear to have killed themselves through their own stupidity of excess: choking on vomit, falling down stairs, cocaine-induced heart failure. But believe you me, every single time, I was there to lead them down that path that ends in death.

Each one of these men deserved exactly what he got.

I am a spirit of vengeance.

As a token of my good faith, you will find one of my victims today: a man at the ruined amusement park who will appear to have been killed by a wild animal.

Let all frat boys beware.

Yours, The Frat Boy Killer

"Sorry, we haven't found anything yet," Barney tells me, pointing at the screen where Opal's official serial killer letter is on display. I'm in the Bayou Galene media den, staffed with the wolfless, which the Varger call immue. We've become friends over the last month, as I mentally prepare for my possible new role as one of them. They're helping me with my current project, which is feeding information to the NOPD and the FBI in the hope of getting my serial killer sister nabbed by law enforcement.

So far, no luck.

I spent three days unconscious after the full moon, and when I woke, my new foot was there in its foot shape. But it was weak, and still isn't a hundred percent. I've been hobbling around on my father's cane, which I find grimly amusing. My brain appears to function as well as it ever did. I remember the same Bible verses and still fail to comprehend algebra. But I get tired easily.

I have new scars. A thin, zig-zagged white line around my ankle, a knot at the back of my head. These may disappear in time. Nobody seems to know.

Healing injuries so severe took almost everything out of me, including my will to fight the Varger. They have nursed people like me through damage like this for hundreds of years. They know what they're doing. For the last month I have done exactly everything Pere Claude and Vivienne and Nicolas told me to do. I exercised when they told me to exercise. I rested when they told me to rest. And I ate dead animals when they told me to do that.

"You'll never get enough protein to heal injuries of that magnitude from a vegetarian diet," they told me, and I believed them because of how fragile I felt, like I was starving. That good old survival instinct kicked in, the way it does. I sat on a porch swing with my father's cane in my lap, and accepted it as a kind of tribute when my people brought me what seemed like a never-ending parade of animal flesh: smoked, broiled, grilled, jerked, skewered, pickled, sausaged, smashed into paste and smeared on toast, boiled in a big pot with seafood and corn on the cob.

I would like to believe that I hated every minute of it, but I would be lying to myself. In a visceral, instinctive, animal way, I loved every bite. And it wasn't just because my people are uniformly terrific cooks. It was because I needed it so much.

And that, I think, is probably the end of that. I'll never be a vegetarian again. I feel like I lost an argument. Maybe all the arguments.

"Does that help us find her?" I ask.

"Not so far."

"And what about the Cachorros, do we know where they are?"

He looks slightly embarrassed. "I don't know. Pere Claude told us not to pursue them."

"Really? We're just going to let them go?"

"I guess. His reasoning, as he explained it, is that unless they make trouble, we have no reason to pursue them. We simply look for trouble as usual."

I nod. I'm not satisfied with that answer. I doubt Pere Claude will be satisfied with it either, in the long run. He and his son not only met up again after so many years, they kinda sorta tried to kill each other. But nobody except me remembers that night very well, and I don't remember anything after I got shot, although I was relieved to find out they don't think any of the Strigoi escaped. But I can't get a clear answer on the thing that's been bugging me ever since: was I really possessed by the spirit of my grandmother? Is that a thing that happens to us? All Pere Claude could tell me is that some of the Pere Diaries talk about being "ridden" by the spirit of a departed wolf, usually a former Pere, but the typical modern interpretation is that they weren't being literal.

My phone buzzes. It's my new phone, a Varger special,

expertly hacked and set up with custom apps and extra security. It's also much bigger and fancier than my old phone.

It's Steph, wanting to talk. "Hi, sweetie, I wanted to catch you before the big moment."

"Hi, Steph."

"I wanted to tell you that I love you no matter what."

"Thanks. You too."

"Do you know what you want? Wolf or no wolf?"

"I don't know. Not for sure. I guess I'll just take what comes."

"I'll come out to see you soon either way."

"Thank you. Oh, I have another call."

"Bye. Love you."

"You too."

It's Deena, wanting to video chat.

"Hey, how are you guys doing?" I ask her.

"We're good here. School's about to start. Izzy and Edison and I got that place together in the U District we talked about. We're calling it Chez Lunatic. What about you? You have a head, but you're obviously not wolfy."

"I wouldn't be wolfy yet anyway. Moonrise is still a few minutes away."

"Oh. Okay. I guess I wasn't sure of the timing. What do you think? Do you think you're going to be wolfy?"

No. I don't. I don't feel the wolf at all. And that feels unexpectedly bad, empty, puts a squeeze of dread on my heart. "I just don't know."

"Well, bonus, if you're not, you can come out for a visit sooner."

"That is definitely true."

"Good luck, either way."

I disconnect. Barney is giving me a sympathetic look. "That was your loufrer in Seattle?"

"Yeah. I got a whole pack of 'em out there."

Etienne, director of the track and chase teams, comes into

the room to hand Barney a piece of paper. "We don't have a permanent maison in Seattle. Historically it's a low incidence area, so we send people up from San Francisco when needed."

I nod. He's been giving me little tidbits like that all month. He's had Arda's Wound for about five years, and he says that people like us, who still retain some gifts of the wolf, are extremely valuable during the full moon. We stay human, but we can track people by smell. It could be an exciting life, I guess. Get sent all over, investigating. Just like *The X-Files*, if the only thing they ever looked for was werewolves.

A wave of weakness pulls me down and I collapse onto a chair, rest my forehead on my hands, hands on the cane. I remember watching my father make this exact gesture. He was dying. I don't think I'm dying. Not just yet, anyway.

"Opal got me to give my father back his wolf, then she took mine," I say.

"No, you don't know that," Etienne tells me. "Injuries like what you've had can take several full moons to heal. Don't get impatient. You have to pace yourself."

Deena pings me again:

Hey look what I found.

It's an edited portion of the clip of wolf me struggling to get out of the corset. No static, no slaughter, no men standing around, just thirteen seconds of a big red canine going nuts because she can't fully reach her own waist with teeth or claws.

I hold it up toward Barney. "I thought you tech people scrubbed all of Opal's videos?"

He's embarrassed. "Uh. We determined that particular portion was harmless, and provided, uh, good cover on the viral rumors that were already going around, you know, people talking about the dog in a corset video—"

"You thought it was funny."

His ears turn red. "We thought it was funny."

Deena writes:

> You're famous, dude. Everybody's using
> this gif.

> If my wolf is gone forever, at least she had
> one true moment of glory.

She sends me a smile. I send her a smile. In a text message nobody can tell how conflicted I really am.

OUT IN THE BIG FIELD, UNDER THE LIVE OAKS FESTOONED WITH Spanish moss, the rougarou are having their big fais-do-do. They spend the whole day eating barbecue and playing music and dancing and sometimes tossing each other around just for the fun of it.

When the moon rises, they're going to chuck off their human skins and put on their wolf skins, and roam the countryside raising a big old ruckus, terrorizing all the folks who are out there in the swamp, the ones who don't say their prayers, who don't go home when their mama calls.

Maybe they'll bite you, make you one of them.

The first howl goes up.

ACKNOWLEDGMENTS

A big thank you to everyone who helped make this book a reality:

- Jim Kling, who knew how it needed to start.
- Carol Otte, who knew how it needed to end.
- Bridget Coila, my New Orleans native guide.
- Shannon Page, who agreed once more to be my editor.
- C.S. Inman, who knew what Abby looks like.
- My parents, Pat & Fred McGalliard, who helped out with emergency electronics equipment when I didn't have a computer capable of running Photoshop.
- My husband, Paul Carpentier, who actually kind of hates it when I try to bounce plot and story ideas off of him, but he lets me do it anyway.

ABOUT THE AUTHOR

Julie McGalliard is a writer, data scientist, and occasional cartoonist. She lives in Seattle and travels to New Orleans a lot.

Follow her adventures at https://www.gothhouse.org/author/juliemcgalliard/

Photo by Andrew S. Williams

www.ingramcontent.com/pod-product-compliance
Lightning Source LLC
Chambersburg PA
CBHW030104260626
47156CB00008B/2515